The Greenest Branch

The Greenest Branch

A Novel of Germany's First Female Physician

BY

P.K. ADAMS

IRON KNIGHT PRESS

The Greenest Branch

ISBN 978-1-7323611-1-9 (paperback)
ISBN 978-1-7323611-0-2 (ebook)

Cover designed by Jennifer Quinlan

Iron Knight Press
25 W. Howard St
Quincy, MA 02169

www.pkadams-author.com
Twitter @pk_adams
Facebook P.K. Adams Author

Contents

# Glossary Of Terms

A S CLOCKS WERE not in use in the Middle Ages, the passage of time was typically measured by the eight daily services of the Divine Office. The exact timing of these services was dictated by the rising and setting of the sun and therefore varied depending on the season. Here's a rough approximation:

matins - in the middle of the night, any time between midnight and 2 a.m.
lauds - at dawn (around 3 a.m. in the summer)
prime - first office of the day, around 6 a.m.
terce - mid-morning office, around 9 a.m.
sext - mid-day office, around 12 noon
nones – mid-afternoon office, around 3 p.m.
vespers - the evening office, between 5 p.m. and 7 p.m.
compline - at nightfall, around 9 p.m.

Anchorite monasticism – an early form of monasticism particularly popular in the Middle Ages. It was characterized by complete isolation from the world for the purpose of practicing religious devotion. Most commonly, anchorite enclosures (cells or anchorholds) were attached to a church in the form of a wooden shack or a stone-walled annex. There were more women than men who practiced that form of monasticism, and they were referred to as anchoresses. Anchorite monasticism was in contrast to cenobitic (community-based) monasticism as exemplified by priories or abbeys, although sometimes, as in this story, the two could co-exist in the same place.

Rule of Saint Benedict (Lat. *Regula Benedicti*) – a set of rules governing the daily life in the Benedictine communities. It covers both religious practices and non-religious activities like work, study, recreation, and meals. It was written by Benedict of Nursia (Norcia) the founder of the order (c. 480-550). Note: Benedict was only canonized in the year 1220, much later than the events in this story.

Obedientiary – in the context of cenobitic monasticism a senior monk or nun who held an office within the community. In addition to the abbot/abbess and prior/prioress, they included such posts as cantor, kitchener, cellarer, porter, bursar, matricularius, novice master, infirmarian, etc.

Magistra – the Latin term for 'teacher', sometimes applied to leaders of female monastic communities who held a rank lower than abbess.

Investiture controversy – the power struggle between the papacy and the secular rulers of the Holy Roman Empire (encompassing roughly today's Germany, Northern Italy, and parts of western France) over who should have the right to appoint bishops by symbolically investing them with the insignia of their authority. It lasted some 75 years from the second half of the 11th to the early 12th century. It resulted in a state of civil war in most of the German territory as well as the appointments of several anti-popes by successive emperors in an effort to ensure a more pliable papacy that would allow them to preserve their investiture rights. The most acute phase of the conflict was ended by the Concordat of Worms in 1122, but attempts of kings to control ecclesiastical appointments continued intermittently for the rest of the 12th century and beyond.

1

Bermersheim, Rhineland
September 1115

THE NIGHT I learned that I would be leaving my family home, the sounds of talk and laughter took a long time to die down. Finally, a growing chorus of snores from the hall told me that the guests from Sponheim were asleep. But there was a murmur of voices close by, and a faint light was coming from behind the partition that separated my parents' bedchamber from ours. Despite the late hour and the warmth of the bed I shared with my two sisters and a brother, curiosity got the best of me and I slipped out of it, stepping silently across the rush-covered floor. I pulled my nightgown closer about me, for the autumn night was chilly, and put my eye to a chink through which the light was seeping.

On the other side, the hearth was burning low, the reflection of its flames dancing sluggishly on the walls. My parents, Mechtild and Hidelbert, sat facing each other across it. Their voices were low too, but they came clear and distinct through the crack in the wood.

"She is still a child, husband, only ten winters old." My mother's voice was sad.

"Almost eleven," my father countered.

With sharp strokes, my mother pulled a comb through the long strands of her graying hair. Normally, during her nightly combing ritual, those strokes were slow and deliberate.

After a lengthy silence, my father spoke again. "Oblates enter monasteries at all ages. Some spend years there before they are old enough to begin their novitiate."

"You know as well as I do that it is not a common practice."

"The count's offer to recommend Hildegard to his daughter's convent is not to be passed over lightly." Count Stephan von Sponheim and his wife, Sophia, in whose honor our feast had been held, were old family friends visiting Bermersheim on their way back from Speier, where the count had had a landholding dispute to settle. I had never met their daughter Jutta, but, like everybody in the Rhineland, I knew of the famous beauty whose abrupt decision to take monastic vows had dashed the hopes of eligible bachelors from Trier to Mainz.

Silence descended on the chamber, during which my mother gazed straight at her husband with her big blue eyes — like mine, everyone said. This often had an unnerving effect on him, and the clipped tone of his next words indicated that it was so this time too. "Hildegard was pledged to the Church on her birth."

"I know," she replied impatiently. As their tenth offspring, I belonged to the Church in accordance with a custom known as the tithe, a time-honored tradition that was a source of pride and prestige for families. So the question they disagreed on was not if I should enter the cloistered life but rather when. "The count's offer is generous indeed, and there is no doubt that Jutta von Sponheim would be a fitting teacher to Hildegard. But you heard what Countess Sophia said—their daughter founded the convent and took the veil when she was eighteen years old, a grown woman."

"That is because she had not shown signs of a deeper sensibility of spirit before then, but Hildegard—"

"Shouldn't she be allowed to reach womanhood and take this step with full awareness?" my mother interjected in a tone that showed she did not care to hear that argument again. "We have been preparing her for it since she was born; she knows her destiny and will follow that path like the dutiful daughter she is. But to cut short her carefree days seems so harsh."

My father ignored the interruption. "Hildegard has shown signs of a holy vocation since that day in the chapel—"

I knew the story well; in fact, I remembered it vividly, although it had happened when I was only three years old. One day I wandered into the family chapel out by the orchard and was dazed by the sunshine streaming through the narrow windows on both sides of the altar like two swords of light. It illuminated the wooden figures of the Apostles that my grandfather had ordered at Worms many years before in honor of Pope Gregorius's reforming efforts. The brightness of that light caused my head to ache, but it also made me feel weightless as if I were lifted off my feet like a feather in the wind. Apparently, I stayed there for hours as the entire household searched for me frantically. It was my father who finally found me, and it was to him that I described my strange sensations in my tremulous, childish voice.

But there was one thing my family did not know about—a remembrance of a command the meaning of which I did not understand at that time.

Such reveries happened to me on several occasions after that, especially when sunlight flooded the dim interior of the chapel during Mass, and always ended in strong headaches that would send me to bed for days.

"It's a manifestation of the touch of the Holy Spirit!" My father's voice rose enthusiastically, prompting my mother to bid him keep it down.

"They are just spells." She rolled her eyes wearily.

"It is a gift."

"Another two or three years would prepare her better for the rigors of the cloister."

"The best way to prepare for it is to leave this world behind and devote herself to the duties of the contemplative life." He added in a softer tone, perhaps sensing my mother's desire to hold on to her youngest child for as long as she could, "Hildegard will be happy, and the Abbey of St. Disibod is only a day's journey from here. She will be close, and we will feel it."

But my mother would have none of it. "You like the prospect of a smaller endowment," she said accusingly. "You think that Jutta's anchorite ways and the humbleness of her convent will allow you to pay less to secure Hildegard's entry."

"That is not the reason," he protested. "Our daughter has a gift that it is our duty to nurture." Then his tone became irritable. "But there is nothing wrong with economizing. You don't care for it because it is not your responsibility to ensure the wellbeing of this household. But you know as well as I do that salt prices have been falling for the past four years, and we are not earning as much from the Alzey mine as we used to. Meanwhile, the costs of educating Hugo at Mainz are higher than I expected, and the girls will reach marriageable age next year . . ."

The draft was making my feet cold, so I crept back to bed to take comfort from the warmth of my siblings' sleeping bodies. Roric turned over, and Clementia murmured softly in a dream; then all was silent again. After a while, the light in the bedchamber went out, and I lay in the dark listening to the screeching of mice in the rushes. Normally this familiar sound would have put me to sleep, but not now. My head was filled with too many thoughts.

Leaving the family home forever would be difficult. There was a chance, of course, that my mother would prevail and I would remain at Bermersheim a little longer, but it was not likely. I knew very well that when my father made up his mind, there was no changing it.

Listening to the steady breathing next to me, I was sure that I would miss Roric, although his chief entertainment those days consisted of chasing us with lizards and aiming them squarely down the collars of our frocks. I might even miss Clementia and Margaret, even though I found the pastimes that absorbed their entire attention boring. Unlike my sisters, I had no interest in sewing or embroidering amid giggly, half-whispered conversations about neighborhood weddings, and I was mystified as to how the ability to make one's chain stitch even and round would help attract a good husband. Instead — to their unending astonishment — I asked for reading lessons from our mother's Book of Hours or helped in the vegetable garden, planting and weeding alongside the kitchen servants, heedless of the warnings that I would end up tanned like a peasant.

What I would miss most was the forest surrounding Bermersheim — full of ancient oaks and chestnuts and quivering with the droning of bumblebees, the song of the thrush, and the cuckoo's calls on warm summer afternoons — and also the times when I would climb to our nurse's loft to watch her sort and mix bunches of dried herbs for use in drafts or ointments.

Uda was the niece of a healing woman who lived in the woods outside the village and from whom she had learned the best times to pick leaves and roots so they were swelled with juices at the height of their curative powers. Uda taught me to love and respect herbs, and it was in the heady atmosphere of her chamber, warm and rich scented, that I had first begun to marvel at the unseen power that seemed to connect all things in nature, nourishing and sustaining them. I called it *viriditas* after a word I had found in my mother's small gardening book. It means *weed* in Latin, but also *greenness, vitality,* and *freshness,* and it is the perfect way to describe the secret, life-giving force flowing through the world. The thought of leaving my beloved forest and Uda's loft behind filled me with deep sadness, and I felt two tears roll down my temples.

Yet the prospect was also exciting. For one thing, abbeys ran schools; my brother Hugo had gone to one at Lorsch before moving to Mainz to train for priesthood at the great cathedral there. I had always envied him and now I would study too! The thought gave me a shiver of anticipation. Also, the idea of traveling away from the village where I had been born—and which I had never left, save for one trip with my father to Bingen with a consignment of salt from Alzey— seemed appealing. The occasional visitors to Bermersheim had brought news of the latest developments in the emperor's long-standing quarrel with the pope about who should have the right to name bishops and of the emperor's expeditions to Italy while his dukes schemed against him at home.

These tidings filled my imagination with castles and knights like the raven-haired, dark-eyed Rudolf von Stade with a battle scar on his cheek, who was part of Count von Sponheim's retinue, or the heroes of Uda's bedtime stories, Siegfried and Roland, who wooed princesses and vanquished enemies.

The Abbey of St. Disibod would be no royal court, of course, but still I imagined it full of pilgrims and visitors, certainly busier than the sleepy valley of Bermersheim with its ancient house and a cluster of peasant cottages hugging the small parish church. When considered that way, the prospect of moving to St. Disibod was quite intriguing, in fact.

The crowing of the first rooster filled the air, and the eastern sky became a shade less dark through the shutters.

Before long, the guests would be rising to take their leave and continue on to Sponheim. With the arrival of dawn, I felt the turmoil in my head subside and the heaviness of sleep descend on me at long last.

2

November 1115

W E MOVED SLOWLY through the quiet countryside under an overcast early morning sky, my father riding
at the head on a bay mare. His easy posture in the saddle betrayed his past as a crusader in the Holy Land before he retired to tend to our ancestral land. Riding alongside him was
my eldest brother, Hugo, who had come down from Mainz
for the occasion of seeing me off to the Convent of St. Disibod.
My mother and I rode in a wagon pulled by two dappled gray
cobs and hemmed by several chests, including a carved cedar
box that my father had brought from the East and that contained my monastic dowry of one hundred golden bezants.

It was still ten days to the Feast of St. Andreas, but the
clean, sharp scent of winter already permeated the air. It had
snowed a little in the last few days, the grayish patches melting over the shriveled autumn leaves as the winds turned
milder again.

Wrapped in a cloak, I observed the countryside with interest, especially when the thick forest parted to reveal a farm or a village. Most of these were small and made up of ramshackle huts with thin wisps of black smoke rising from their chimneys. Among these abodes, skinny pigs and scrawny dogs mingled with children playing in the mud. The hamlets showed none of the prosperity that surrounded Bermersheim, with its whitewashed cottages covered in thatched roofs and abutted by vegetable plots. My father threw coins as we passed by, followed by watchful eyes staring from weather-beaten faces, dark with the perpetual tan of those exposed to the sun and wind all their lives.

In the early afternoon we stopped at an inn, a solid-looking timber structure with a tall column of smoke issuing from a single chimney in the middle of the roof. A small house, probably belonging to the innkeeper's family, was attached to the back. Beyond the buildings, a small area of the forest had been cleared for pasture. As it was November, the sounds of its seasonal occupants were now coming from the nearby cowshed, which also apparently served as a chicken coop and a pigsty. The property had a modest but well-kept look.

The innkeeper, a stocky, black-bearded man in his thirties, emerged to greet us and introduced himself as Burchard. He bowed as he invited us inside and shouted in the direction of the stables, from which a boy of about sixteen, also short and starting to sprout a similarly black beard, came out to take our horses.

The establishment was neatly furnished with rough-hewn tables and benches. There was a sizable barrel of beer in one corner while the center was occupied by a large hearth. A cheerful-looking matron, plump and brisk, came out from behind the counter and called the maid to set a table.

I took off my cloak and went to the fire to warm my hands. I wore a new frock of fine brown wool. A short veil covered my hair, recently cut in preparation for my new life. Instead of the thick braid that used to fall to my waist, ash blonde strands were poking from under the veil, curling slightly.

When the food was brought in, the matron was joined by a girl of about ten, whose gaze drifted toward me even as she helped carry the plates of boiled ham, pea soup, and bread.

"Are you taking the child to the Abbey of St. Disibod, my lord?" the innkeeper's wife asked as she set a jug of ale in front of my father.

"Indeed," he said, nodding proudly. "She was accepted as an oblate."

I noticed the young girl's eyes widen and her mouth open as if to ask a question, but her mother was already on the way back to the kitchen and beckoned her to follow.

We attacked the meal with great appetite, but when wine and fruit pies arrived, I slipped out of the inn. A pale sun had come out, and I stood in the yard enjoying its light on my face, if not its warmth. After a while, amid the intermittent bleating and squealing coming from the barn, I heard soft footsteps squelching in the mud and turned to find the innkeeper's daughter walking toward me with a bowl half full of grain.

She seemed shy for a moment, then mustered her courage. "I'm Griselda."

"My name is Hildegard." As she continued to regard me silently, I asked, pointing to the bowl, "Are you off to feed the chickens?" The coop was in the opposite direction.

"Yes." Griselda blushed as she realized that I had seen through her ruse. "I do that sometimes when Warin is busy." She pointed toward the barn, where a lanky, fair-haired boy, clearly a hired hand, was balancing a pitchfork heaped with hay.

I nodded. I had sometimes accompanied my father and his steward as they inspected Bermersheim's estates and had seen peasants at work in the fields and with livestock. It was hard work, but I envied them the chance to be outdoors and observe nature as it went through its endless cycle of birth, growth, and decline. I had once asked to be shown how to milk a cow, but my father had responded that ladies did not do that sort of work.

"What's an oblate?" Griselda asked. Curiosity shone in her green eyes, which were made even more striking by the whiteness of her skin and her dark hair. She was stocky like her father and had a heart-shaped face with a sharp chin that gave her a determined look.

"It means 'a gift to God'," I replied. "Someone who lives in a convent until she becomes old enough to enter the novitiate, which is when she learns to be a nun," I added with an air of authority.

Her eyes lit up. "My papa once took me to the market at Disibodenberg," she said. "It was a feast day, and there was a Mass in the abbey church that all the townspeople went to, and we went with them. I still remember the bells and the singing and the incense." She flushed at the memory. "It was beautiful!"

A shiver ran down my spine. Suddenly, I could not wait to be there.

"I wish I could become on oblate too," Griselda said wistfully.

"Then why don't you ask your father to take you there?"

She looked sideways at the inn. "Papa says girls must help their parents with their work and care for them in their old age."

I was mystified. I knew that parents cared for their children, but the other way around? I looked at Griselda, whose face darkened as she added, "He says my dowry will be barely enough to marry me off to the baker's son." She jerked her chin toward the forest, presumably in the direction of the baker's cottage, and set her jaw. "But I will never marry that oaf!"

I did not know what to respond to that, but Griselda's thoughts were already running along a new track. "It would be so nice to spend time with only girls!"

I felt a tinge of sympathy, realizing that the innkeeper's daughter must have had little female companionship apart from her mother. "There are monks at St. Disibod too," I said, as if that were a consolation.

Griselda shrugged her shoulders. "They have separate cloisters and do not mingle."

That authoritative-sounding statement made me frown. Nobody had explained to me what life would be like at the abbey, except that I would pray, work, and — this I had added myself, for it could not be otherwise — study with the other oblates and novices. The prospect of studying excited my imagination, conjuring an image of a vaulted schoolroom full of pupils.

I was about to share it with my new acquaintance when the sound of voices coming from the doors of the inn signaled that it was time to continue the journey. My mother waved, and I ran to her; together we climbed onto the wagon. As it wobbled back toward the road, I waved to Griselda, who was still standing where I had left her, a look of envy and admiration on her face. I turned again just before we entered the forest, but she was gone.

We travelled through the gray landscape, faintly illuminated by colorless sunshine, and the silence was broken only by the creaking of the wheels and the splash of the horses' hooves on the muddy ground. My father was dozing in the saddle, lulled by the gentle rocking movement and the ale with which he had washed down his meal. My mother gazed pensively ahead, and my thoughts kept returning to the girl from the inn and the unfamiliar world I had glimpsed through her.

"When peasants' children grow up, do they become peasants too, mother?" I asked.

"Yes." She lifted her eyebrows, surprised at the question. "Sons usually take over working their fathers' fields, although some become apprenticed to craftsmen to learn a trade."

"Can they enter monasteries?"

She thought for a moment. "They can become lay brothers, I suppose, but monks need to be able to read and write."

"What about girls?"

"They marry or remain with their parents to care for them."

"Why?"

"Because they do not have servants to do so, and besides—" she added, anticipating my next question, "they cannot afford an endowment."

"But what if that is what they want?" I felt myself flush. "It seems unfair!"

My mother smiled sadly. "Your indignation comes from the right place, daughter. The ability to answer God's calling should not depend on how rich one is. After all, Jesus asked the Apostles to give up their possessions to follow him . . ." her voice trailed off, and it was not until some years later that I understood her hesitation. There is a heated dispute within the Church on the issue of the poverty of Christ and whether monks and priests should imitate the simplicity of the first Christians or be free to enjoy worldly trappings, as many of them do. And because proponents of both approaches tend to accuse each other of heresy, my mother thought it prudent not to excite my young mind.

She had been fond of telling me that I was quick, inquisitive, and—even at that age—unwilling to accept answers as givens, and I could see that that gave her satisfaction. She liked to tell the story of how, when I was four, I had asked why God, if He was all-powerful, had not defeated Satan yet? And if He was the creator all things, as the Holy Bible said, then had he created Satan too? And if He loved all of his creation, did not that mean that he should love Satan equally?

My mother did not know how to answer those questions, but she was proud of me, even if that pride was bittersweet. When I had first asked for reading lessons, she was reluctant. "Reading only makes you desire to know more and see more, but women's lives are destined to be lived within the confines of our worlds, whether domestic or monastic," she had told me before relenting and teaching me to read anyway.

Now she put her arm around me, and I reciprocated the gesture. From the moment she had realized that she was with child again and that monastic life would be its destiny, she had prayed every day for me to be blessed with a vocation. She had heard of women — and men — cloistered against their heart's desire or their mind's inclination and felt the injustice of it. That was why, even though she was gifting me to the Church, she was determined to ensure that I would have the time to make the final decision on my own.

But she hoped the vocation would come. She later wrote to me that riding through those poor hamlets, she saw enough reasons why a cloistered life was a better option. The world was harsh and dangerous with the perpetual specter of famine and threat of violence, either from outlaws or from constant skirmishes among the empire's restless barons. And then there was Eve's lot: the brutal cycle that compelled a woman to give birth every year for as long as her body endured. She herself had brought ten children into the world at a great cost in bodily suffering — and anguish when four of them had died. Her only consolation on that journey was that I would be spared that fate and live out my life in relative security, protected from ignorance, privation, and violence by walls more respected than those of our house, even if it meant that we would never see each other again.

The trees were casting lengthening shadows onto the high road when we reached the final stretch leading to Disibodenberg's gate. Bare fields lay on both sides of the tract, bordered by the forest to the south and vineyards to the north. About a mile ahead, at the confluence of the Glan and the

Nahe, the abbey sat atop Mount St. Disibod, thickly forested and gently sloping toward the rivers. A small town walled by a wooden palisade hugged its western foothill.

A sleepy-looking watchman barely glanced at the abbot's letter before waving us through. We entered the main street lined with timber houses, with only a few — occupied by merchant families, as I learned later — a mix of timber and stone. The side streets were already dim, candlelight beginning to seep through the shuttered windows of their smaller, simpler abodes. Farther up was the market square, where sellers were taking down their stalls and shopkeepers boarding up their windows for the night. A few glanced curiously as we passed in front of the parish church and took the road that ascended toward the abbey.

At the gate, my father dismounted and knocked on the iron-bound doors. A moment later, the porter opened the small grille. When he learned our business, he began to manipulate the heavy latch, and the doors squeaked on their hinges and opened wide.

"The abbot is awaiting you, my lord." The monk bowed.

"Thank you, Brother."

As we passed under the stone arch, I noticed my father taking stock of it with his soldier's eye. The gate was new and solid, but the abbey wall was no more than a wooden palisade, much like the one surrounding the town. Despite the deepening dusk, it was obvious that it was in serious need of repair, with some of its logs rotten at the bottom and streaked with lichen, and weeds growing profusely in the cracks.

He clucked his tongue softly and made a motion with his head that I immediately recognized. I could almost hear him think, *The abbot must be a persuasive man to have enlisted the Count von Sponheim as a benefactor.*

Two months earlier at Bermersheim, the count had painted an intriguing picture of the Abbey of St. Disibod, where his daughter Jutta had founded her convent. Established more than four hundred years before by a saint from

Hibernia who had brought Christianity to the Rhineland, the abbey had once possessed an impressive library that attracted monks from as far as France eager to cultivate their minds.

But a series of plunders by the Normans and the Hungarians had caused its fortunes to decline, and by the time the fourth Emperor Heinrich ascended the throne, the community had been reduced to fewer than ten monks, and the buildings had fallen into such disrepair that the brothers considered abandoning the place altogether.

The abbey continued its unremarkable existence until Abbot Kuno's election five years before, after which he set out to increase the number of brothers in residence and undertake extensive repair works.

Although Count Stephan had at first thought of the abbey of St. Eucharius in Trier as the most suitable place for Jutta, he was sufficiently impressed with Kuno's efforts to support her wish. "I had no hesitation in giving my consent, and I am glad her endowment is contributing to the reestablishment of St. Disibod," he had told my father, before adding proudly, "In his letters, Abbot Kuno has praised her learning and piety."

The courtyard was dominated by a bulky church with small, square windows through which dim light filtered onto the courtyard, where traces of snow melted between the flagstones. A pair of grooms carrying torches appeared from the stables. A moment later, a portly, middle-aged monk came out from a building located along the northern wall. He made his way toward us at a surprisingly brisk pace, his black robes fluttering around the knotted belt girdling his prominent belly. He was followed by another monk, tall and thin, with a cowl pulled low over his face. The shorter one had graying hair around his tonsure and a jovial red face, which betrayed a weakness for food, and perhaps drink too.

As soon as he was within earshot, he exclaimed cordially, "Mein Herr Hidelbert, I am Abbot Kuno, and it is an honor to welcome you to St. Disibod." He pointed toward his companion, whose face emerged from under the hood to reveal a younger man with finely chiseled, aristocratic features frozen into a haughty and forbidding expression. "This is Prior Helenger. We trust you had a pleasant journey."

My father bowed slightly before addressing his hosts. "We set out early and rode most of the day, but God willed that we arrived safely and in good spirits, if a little tired."

"I am sure of that." The abbot nodded as if the exhaustion of long journeys was something of which he had extensive experience. "I had our guesthouse prepared and a meal laid out for you. After you fortify yourself, you are welcome to join us at vespers."

"Father Abbot, this is my daughter, Hildegard." My father turned to me. Thus prompted, I curtseyed, although under my cloak my heart was pounding against my ribs. But I lifted my chin, determined not to show the anxiety.

The abbot smiled and put his hand on my head. "God bless you, my child. We are happy that you are to join us on our spiritual journey, and we hope that it will be a fruitful one for you."

Emboldened, I returned his smile, but when I turned to Prior Helenger, I saw that his face had not lost its stony severity.

But I held his gaze.

3

Abbey of St. Disibod, November 1115

M UCH LATER, IN a letter she wrote me, my mother described those events I was not privy to on the following day. After breakfast, my parents and the abbot had a private meeting. Prior Helenger was also in attendance, standing behind Kuno's chair with his head bowed and arms folded inside the sleeves of his robe.

My mother complimented the abbot on the simple yet satisfying fare in the refectory.

"In recent years we have received generous gifts of legacy that include fertile lands along the rivers, and we were blessed with a good harvest this year," he informed them proudly.

"I am pleased to hear that." My father cleared his throat. Under pressure from my mother, he had come with a petition regarding the terms of my enclosure. It made him nervous, for he was instinctively deferential toward religious authority. Now he shifted from one leg to the other, struggling to find the right entry point to his business. "The abbey's reputation has grown greatly thanks to your wise management, and I am certain your successes will continue to attract generous benefactors."

The abbot inclined his head, visibly flattered. "And pious novices."

"Indeed." My father nodded. "The one I can vouch for—my own daughter—is endowed with exceptional gifts of spirit, and we are honored that she will be joining Sister Jutta and the other women who have elected to lead most holy lives as anchorites."

At Bemersheim, Count Stephan had spoken proudly of Jutta's ascetic inclinations, which seemed only to have deepened at St. Disibod. Anchorites were the most devout men and women of God, who chose to live in complete seclusion. They had food and water brought to them and refuse taken away, and that was usually the extent of their interaction with the world. My mother was not sure if I would find such a life to my liking. In the weeks since the count's visit, she had worked tirelessly to persuade her husband to negotiate a delayed novitiate for me, to which he had finally, if begrudgingly, consented.

Now, standing beside him, she despaired of his meandering.

"We are pleased also," the abbot assured him graciously.

"Father Abbot," my father resumed, prompted by a discreet nudge. "Hildegard is only eleven years old."

Kuno lifted his abundant eyebrows.

"We would ask that her novitiate be delayed until she is sixteen years of age, so she can take her vows at eighteen."

My mother thought she had heard a gasp from Prior Helenger, who raised his head for the first time.

"Our custom dictates that child oblates begin their novitiate at fourteen," the abbot protested.

"A custom is not an abiding rule." My father sounded almost apologetic. It had been my mother's idea to write to the learned monks at Lorsch to find out exactly what *Regula Benedicti* said about the maximum age and duration of a novitiate. It said nothing. "We request that an exception be made because of Hildegard's age. It would be of great benefit if she were given more time to prepare for the consecrated life, so her vows might be all the more pleasing to God."

"The Rule may not prescribe exactly when the novitiate should start"—the pleased look faded from Kuno's face— "but as abbot, I have discretion in the matter, and I see no reason to break with our tradition, especially as your daughter has already turned ten, the minimum age of acceptance into a monastic community set by the Tenth Council of Toledo."

The prior nodded in haughty approval, and my mother turned to my father expectantly. But his face only said, *I have tried. There is nothing more I can do.*

She made the decision in an instant. "With your permission, Father Abbot, as her parents, it is our wish that Hildegard should reach the age of reason before making such a commitment." Then she added, more forcefully, "We have come here on the recommendation of Count Stephan von Sponheim, who holds this abbey in high esteem. However, we can easily secure a place for our daughter at St. Eucharius, Hirschau, or the new Laach priory that is fast developing a great reputation."

The prior's expression froze in shocked disbelief, but the abbot's face betrayed a shadow of worry that was enough for my mother to realize he needed my dowry.

A moment of tense silence followed as Kuno struggled with the decision. Abbeys preferred short oblatures because during that time the candidate could still change his or her mind and withdraw, rare though it was, and take their dowry with them. Once the novitiate began, a departure meant forfeiting the dowry. "I will grant your request," he said finally.

"Father Abbot, are you sure?" the prior's voice was almost a hiss. "Hildegard belongs to the Church; why should she be given a choice? She is but a girl-child—"

"I made my decision, Brother Prior." He cut him off with a gesture.

Helenger's lips twisted as if he had swallowed something bitter, but he fell silent.

"Can this provision be added to the dedication letter?" my father asked.

The abbot motioned to a scribe who had been sitting by the window and instructed him to add the relevant clause. The monk returned to his desk, and soon the document was ready for the seal and signatures.

These steps completed, my father laid a heavy leather purse on the abbot's desk. Monastic endowments took various forms; lands, quarries, or mines were commonly deeded to the religious house by parents or guardians. Others chose to pay money. The golden bezants in my father's purse were his reward for service in the Holy Land, and he was proud of it, for he considered freeing Jerusalem from the Saracen to have been his duty as a Christian. And now this treasure would uphold his family's standing and support the monks' holy work.

"We are honored that you have chosen our house as your daughter's spiritual refuge, and we will do everything in our power to ensure that her service bears fruit." Abbot Kuno rolled up the parchment and handed it to Helenger, who shot my father a look of contempt for allowing his woman to have so much say in family matters.

My father bowed. "That is our sincere wish also."

The abbot rose as the bells rang out for terce. "I will send Brother Adam, our guest-master, to show you around the abbey," he said, bidding them wait in his parlor.

A moment later, my parents watched the two monks cross the courtyard toward the church, the prior talking animatedly and the abbot shaking his head. When they were out of earshot, my father turned to my mother. "Did you just give an ultimatum to the abbot of St. Disibod?" He tried to sound severe, but the brazenness of it was almost entertaining.

"It was not something I relished, husband, but I had to make sure Hildegard was not enclosed for life while being little more than a babe, and the way your petitioning was going—"

"But what if he said no?! You know very well we cannot afford any of the other places."

She impatiently swept her hand to encompass the abbey compound. "Just look at this place. It may have an ambitious abbot at its helm, but it still needs a lot of work, and that requires funds. You saw the state of the guesthouse." The walls of their quarters had not been whitewashed in a long time, and the door hinges squeaked atrociously. When the lights were out, she could swear she saw the sky through cracks in the roof beams.

"We are not offering a dowry that will make a significant difference." In addition to the golden bezants, my father was gifting a bale of white silk for altar cloth and a reliquary containing a finger bone of St. Simeon, an early Christian martyr, also from Jerusalem. "It is not as valuable as fertile land or a good acreage of forest with sturdy oaks."

"That may be, but the future of Church lands is uncertain." My mother dropped her voice as many people did when mentioning the imperial conflict with the pope. "Any income counts to abbots like Kuno. I am sure that is what he was just explaining to the prior."

My father narrowed his eyes; he had not thought of it like that.

"Besides," she added, "it did not hurt to remind him that we are on friendly terms with Count Stephan, who is quite possibly his largest benefactor."

He nodded admiringly. "If you were a man, you would make a fine diplomat," he said, just as the door opened and

Brother Adam, a pale-faced monk with a deferential manner, appeared and apologized for the wait.

Outside, the sky was overcast again, threatening rain. All around, there were signs of a community in transition: new buildings, ongoing construction, and structures that were old and would have to be replaced. The much-mended palisade wall looked ancient at a time when stone was increasingly the choice of builders. But the church was new, its gray stone silhouette looming over the courtyard. The monks' cloister was attached to it on one side. The bulk of the church was finished, though work was still being done on the roof; scaffolding surrounded the tower that crowned the structure at the point where the nave intersected the transept.

They stopped outside so as not to disturb the monks who were singing terce, the mid-morning office, and Brother Adam explained that the church had replaced a wooden chapel that had become too small to accommodate the growing community.

"How long has it been under construction, Brother?" my father asked.

The monk thought about it. "Must be nine years now. It was started by the previous abbot, but work proceeded slowly for lack of funds. It picked up after Abbot Kuno took over."

"Count Stephan von Sponheim speaks highly of his efforts."

"Our abbot knows many great lords in the Rhineland, and his dedication has inspired much generosity. In fact," Brother Adam added, "Sister Jutta's endowment contains a quarry downriver near Bingen, and the stone was used to finish the church."

My father shot my mother a glance that said, *This is what a large dowry can pay for.* Meanwhile, a thin drizzle began to fall and the guest-master led them toward the smaller, unpaved courtyard on the southern side of the church.

At one end stood a pair of thatch-roofed buildings, one of which faced a garden hemmed by shrubs that formed a natural hedge. Brother Adam said they were the infirmary and the medicine workshop, run by Brother Wigbert, the abbey physician.

At the other end, the women's convent was nestled in a corner of the abbey. Unlike the infirmary, it was surrounded by a fence of simple logs tied together, tall enough to obscure the view of the inside. Consisting of two plain buildings of roughly hewn planks with small, shuttered windows, it had a cheerless, makeshift look to it.

"This is where Sister Jutta and two others are living." Their guide lowered his eyes decorously. "They are the first women to have ever resided at St. Disibod."

The courtyard-facing house was the anchoresses' dorter, he added, while the other was the chapel. My mother felt a lump in her throat as she took in the poor space that was to become my new home, which looked even more miserable in the rain. Having exhausted the subject, the monk was already turning back.

Then he noticed my father examining the section of the abbey wall that ran from the convent to the kitchens behind the church. It was taller and thicker than elsewhere, and it had a disused-looking watchtower embedded in it. "You may be wondering why this wall is so fortified, my lord," the monk said politely.

"Indeed, I am." He peeked through the doorless opening into the watchtower. Despite its bigger size, the wall was in even poorer shape. Some of its beams were broken at the top, giving it a forlorn appearance.

"When St. Disibod, our holy founder, arrived here centuries ago to baptize the local Franks, he camped on this mountain with his followers. For years they were exposed to attacks from the pagan hordes that wanted to drive them away, so they built a wall around their abodes. What you are looking at is the oldest part of that wall; the rest was replaced in later times."

Then he added, "It is Abbot Kuno's plan to replace the entire wall"—he raised his eyes piously to the sky— "with God's help."

Behind his back, my mother rolled her eyes; the help the abbey needed was far more likely to come from novices' purses than any divine intervention.

In the guesthouse, my mother fastened my golden hair under the veil. "This is a special day for you, my dove," she said. "From now on your life will be spent in prayer and work. Do you understand that?"

"Yes, mother," I replied solemnly.

She walked around to face me and pulled a tiny wooden box from the pouch at her belt. "I want you to know that even though you have left your family home, you will never be far from our thoughts." Her face was serious, her eyes full of sadness.

"And you from mine!" I assured her eagerly, too excited to be sad just yet.

She smiled briefly, but the smile did not reach her eyes. "You are so young, and I fear that as time goes by you may start forgetting." She paused to control the tremble in her voice, then lifted the box. "That is why I am giving *this* to you to keep with you always." She opened the lid to reveal a small lump of salt, smooth and white, but of a whiteness that was almost translucent. It was shaped like a heart, though irregularly so, with one side slightly bigger than the other. "Your father brought this for me from Alzey the year you were born," she said. "I want you to have it to remind you of home."

I took the box and examined the gift. "I will always carry it with me," I said, clasping my fingers around it, then I looked up at my mother's face, "even when I go to the church."

She dropped her gaze. "Sweet child, you will not be going to the big church after today."

"Why not?"

"Because the anchoresses vowed to live in seclusion, and they do not leave the enclosure."

I frowned. "Does that mean I won't be able to go into the forest to pick flowers either?"

"I am afraid not. The beauty of the world is not for anchoresses to enjoy."

I was confused and thought my mother must have been mistaken. Nonetheless, my next words surprised me. "But I am not an anchoress yet; I am only an oblate, so I don't have to do everything the same way."

My mother opened her mouth, but no words came out. Afterward, I would sometimes wonder if she was loath to quash my hopes, or if the simple logic of what I had said prevented her from contradicting me. Or maybe it was something else entirely.

She proceeded to secure my veil, and as she did so she said softly, as if to herself, "Let God sort this out, as he ultimately does all things."

But I could feel her hands trembling.

The oblation ceremony took place during the evening office of vespers, by which time the rain was falling steadily, at times lashing horizontally in the chilly wind. The lay brothers had lit candles in the nave and around the altar, but shadows lingered in the corners and under the low-vaulted ceiling as the monks filed through the door from the cloister and took their seats in the stalls. From the front pew, my family and I listened to their voices soar to the rafters and echo off the walls.

Gloria Patri, et Filio, et Spiritui Sancto
Sicut erat in principio, et nunc et semper
Et in saecula saeculorum. Amen.

After the first reading, a succession of four psalms followed. The music was so sweet and the cadence of the Latin words so mesmerizing that my head began to swim. The blazing candles seemed haloed by scintillating stars that vanished and reappeared amidst the swirls of incense that rose heavily and dissipated into the corners of the church. It was exquisite but also painful, and I had to close my eyes against the brightness. The weightless sensation I had sometimes experienced at Bermersheim returned, and I felt as if I were floating, supported and surrounded by light.

"As Jesus went on from there, He saw a man named Matthew at the tax collector's booth . . . and He said to him, 'Follow me.' And he rose and followed," the abbot's voice reached me.

The monks intoned another psalm, and I approached the altar and knelt before the abbot, who laid both hands on my head. "We beseech you, Lord God, to look upon your servant Hildegard who embarks on her monastic journey with infinite love; we ask your Son to bestow His blessings, and the Holy Spirit to offer guidance as she labors on the path toward earthly perfection."

He turned to a novice who held a vessel of holy water and a lighted taper. He handed the candle to me and sprinkled the water on my head to the chant of *Magnificat anima mea Dominum.*

After the monks filed back to the cloister, the abbot led us to the women's convent. The rain had stopped, and the wind had died down. The convent's small windows, lighted by oil lamps, seemed almost welcoming.

The door opened and two anchoresses appeared on the threshold with folded arms. Sisters Adelheid and Juliana were no more than twenty years old and had the reticent air of those unaccustomed to seeing outsiders. Sister Jutta, in keeping with her adherence to the rule of seclusion, did not come out. I studied the women who were to become my companions, their heads covered by gray veils. They gazed back,

29

their expressions serious and steady, though not unfriendly. They wore gray robes of coarse wool without so much as a hemp cord around the waist, and they stood barefoot.

"Holy sisters," the abbot addressed the anchoresses, "I have brought Hildegard of Bermersheim to share your simple abode. I ask you to impart your wisdom on her and provide her with spiritual guidance as she prepares for the consecrated life."

The women bowed their heads, and Sister Adelheid extended her hand. I glanced at my parents, blinking away a sudden sting of tears. But I knew my duty and took the proffered hand, stepping into the dimness of the enclosure.

The door closed behind me, and everything was silent as night fell on the abbey.

This, too, my mother related to me later in her letter: early the next morning, they assembled outside the church under a gray sky. The gravestones in the monks' cemetery were still wet from the rain, but the air was dry, and a cold wind blew from the north. From time to time, my mother glanced toward the enclosure until my father noticed her brooding aspect.

"I am impressed by the work Abbot Kuno has done here." He tried to lift her spirits. "I reckon the abbey's best days are still ahead."

"It will take a long time." She did not even bother to hide the bitterness in her voice.

"Physical decay is not nearly as bad as a spiritual one." The previous night at supper, the abbot had complained about the lax rules, corruption, and lack of discipline found in so many monasteries that a group of French Benedictines decided to leave their house at Molesme and establish a new foundation at Cîteaux dedicated to serving God with simplicity, modesty, and rigor. "Thankfully, this abbey is guided with a firm hand," he opined as they rode out through the gate.

The image of the abbot's deputy, Prior Helenger, with his bloodless lips and eyebrows set in a permanent frown, stood before my mother's eyes, and she doubted that optimism. But she kept her misgivings to herself. "Let us hope, for Hildegard's sake, that his management of souls is at least as good as his management of the estate," she said instead.

"I have absolute faith in Abbot Kuno," my father assured her. "This place is going to thrive again, and our daughter will fulfill her vocation meaningfully."

My mother did not respond. In her mind's eye, she saw once again the cluster of plain buildings huddled in a corner of the abbey, and wondered if, even though they had done their duty by the Church, the same could be said of their duty by their child.

4

November 1115

W E STOOD IN semi-darkness, illuminated only by the taper in Sister Adelheid's hand and a shaft of light coming from a door across the small courtyard. The sisters motioned for me to follow, and we entered a rectangular chamber with a solitary window. On the far wall, a large cross hung above a wooden altar, bare save for a breviary in a gilded binding, the only expensive object in the otherwise austere space. The furnishings consisted of three rows of plain pine benches separated by a narrow aisle, and a corner table with a pair of prayer books on it. The chamber was lit by tallow candles in bronze holders in each corner. It was barely warmer than the outside.

I thought the chapel empty until I noticed a silhouette on the ground, barefoot and clad in a sackcloth robe, lying with outstretched arms at the foot of the altar. The two anchoresses stood in reverent silence until Jutta von Sponheim rose, bowed before the cross, and turned to us. She was older than her companions — perhaps twenty-three — and much thinner. In fact, her habit seemed too large for her bony frame and hung loosely from her slight shoulders. Her features were delicate; she had a shapely nose, large dark eyes, and a full mouth, and would have been beautiful but for the unhealthy pallor of her complexion and her sunken cheeks. But her eyes shone with an intensity that rivaled the light of the candles. I was mesmerized by this woman and her severe yet soulful aspect.

My fascination only increased when Jutta spoke in a voice that had an unexpectedly deep and rich quality, like a finely tuned musical instrument. "We have been waiting for you and prayed for your safe arrival."

With a surge of childish eagerness, I wanted to kiss the woman I had heard so much about, but Jutta made no move, and I remained in place. I recalled my mother's advice to observe and learn the customs of my new surroundings. "I look forward to joining your convent," I said. Then I looked around. "Where is your study?"

"This chapel serves as a place for prayer, contemplation, and learning. We do not need much room."

This was not what I had expected, but my pulse quickened nevertheless. "And what do you learn about?" I thought back on the oblation ceremony, the chants that had stirred me, and how much more thrilling it would have been had I been able to understand more of the Latin.

"We read Scriptures and copy passages to ponder them more deeply. The sisters also take turns playing the psaltery and singing holy songs for our souls' fortification."

"My mother has a psaltery that used to belong to my grandmother, and she plays it for us sometimes." I felt a sudden pang of homesickness, realizing that I would never hear that music again. "Can I learn to play too?"

A faint shadow of a smile crossed Jutta's face, but it failed to dispel its suffering aspect. "You will when the time comes, but now let us give thanks to God for your arrival among us." She motioned to the altar, and all of us knelt, Jutta in the front and I behind her, with Adelheid and Juliana on either side. Although I had heard that both women were nobly born—Juliana came from a Thuringian family at least as old and distinguished as the House of Sponheim—I sensed the deference they accorded Jutta as their *magistra*, and I imitated them. I folded my hands and bowed my head, and for a few moments I prayed fervently, excited by the novelty and the possibilities that lay ahead.

But it was not long before my knees started to hurt, and I felt the chill of the beaten-earth floor creeping up my thighs. At Bermersheim we had *prie-dieux*, but here there were none. I held the position for as long as I could, then my bottom sank slowly until I was sitting on my heels, hoping the folds of my robe would hide the offense. Relieved of the discomfort, I looked right and left out of the corners of my eyes, but the two sisters were so engrossed in their prayers that they were quite oblivious to the world. Jutta was in a similar state, judging by the low but constant murmur that caused her back to tremble slightly.

This went on for some time, and my gaze began to wander again. How different this chapel was from the one at Bermersheim. The stone building erected by my great-grandfather boasted pews lined with soft cushions, and wood-carved statues of saints he had commissioned—according to family lore—as a gesture of support for Pope Gregorius during his struggle against the old emperor and the wealthy bishops who had stood in the way of *Libertas ecclesiae*. I did not know what exactly the term meant, but I liked the clean, elegant sound of it.

Just when my legs were getting stiff again, Jutta rose and the two sisters followed nimbly. I, though much younger, found out just how difficult it was to quickly stretch limbs unaccustomed to such lengthy devotions, and fell back to the floor with a cry of pain.

Adelheid helped me to my feet. "Are you unwell?"

"I am fine, Sister." But the strain of the long day was beginning to take its toll, and I swayed on my feet.

"You should rest now, child," Jutta said. "The sisters will take you to the dorter."

"Are you not coming with us?" I asked from the threshold.

"I will stay a little longer to finish my prayers," Jutta replied, turning to the altar once more.

The dorter occupied the only other building within the convent. It was also a single chamber, with a row of straw pallets placed directly on the floor, under the windows that looked onto the smaller of the abbey's two courtyards. A table and a chest stood against the opposite wall. The only decoration was a simple cross above the door.

I was unsure which pallet to take because there were only three.

"Sister Juliana and I use the two closest to the door," Adelheid explained, seeing my confusion. She had a rosy face, smiling eyes, and a liveliness about her movements that Juliana, quiet and grave, seemed to lack. She was also clearly in awe of the *magistra*, for she added, with a mix of admiration and regret, "Sister Jutta prefers to sleep directly on the ground."

I eyed the uninviting hardness of the dirt floor. "Does it not hurt her back?"

Adelheid's face grew serious. "This is what all of us aspire to because true piety is the ability to suffer pain and discomfort like our Lord did."

What a strange idea, I thought, to try to please God by making oneself cold and miserable. I wanted to ask about it, but Adelheid was already pointing to a new-looking pallet at the far end of the room. "Father Abbot sent this one for you, if you wish to use it."

If I wished to use it? A wave of weariness swept over me. Sleep, ideally on something other than a hard floor, was all I wanted right then. I took off my robe, and in my linen shift, slipped under the thin blanket. Nestling there, I asked sleepily, "So why do *you* use a pallet, Sister?"

"I truly wanted to follow her example when I first joined, and I did sleep on the floor for a few days, but then I caught a terrible chill of the chest." Adelheid sighed. "I spent weeks in the infirmary, and Brother Wigbert warned me that my constitution was too weak for it." Her voice was tinged with regret again.

I stifled a yawn. "I am sorry."

"I have refused to use a blanket, however, even in winter," Adelheid added proudly. "God had a reason in making me unable to sleep on the floor, though I can always . . ."

But I was already drifting off to sleep, the candlelight-illuminated swirls of incense I had seen in the church dancing and then extinguishing themselves under my eyelids.

I was awakened by a shake of the arm and opened my eyes to find Adelheid's face hovering over me. It was still dark, the only light coming from the candle she was holding. For a few moments, I struggled to remember where I was.

"Wake up. The matins bell has sounded."

"What?" The haze of sleep was slow to dissolve, but I was beginning to recall the events of the previous day. I had arrived at the enclosure after the oblation ceremony, and after praying in the chapel, fell soundly asleep only to be roused in what seemed like the middle of the night.

"Matins. The midnight office," Adelheid explained. "Put on your robe and follow us." She held out the folded garment.

I slipped the robe on, and the three of us walked to the chapel, dimmer now in the light of only the altar candles.

Jutta was there already—or perhaps still—praying as she waited for us. Adelheid took the breviaries from the table, handed one to Juliana, and made a motion to share the other with me. Blinking, I focused on its cover until I made out the title: *Officium Divinum*. I had never prayed from a real breviary before—my family possessed only a small Book of Hours—and was unsure how to proceed.

Just then, a faint sound of chanting from the church floated in through the window. Adelheid opened the book on a page with the heading *Matins*, and they intoned *Venite exultemus Domino*, the invitatory psalm, in unison with the monks across the courtyard. For a while, I did my best to follow the hymns, lessons, and responses of the lengthy office, but the flickering lights and the monotonous cadence of the recitation made me drowsy. I kept drifting off to sleep, but for no more than a few moments at a time because the discomfort of kneeling made my legs ache and kept jolting me back into consciousness.

When the office ended, we silently filed back to the dorter, and I promptly went back to sleep again. The same process was repeated just before dawn with the service of lauds, and after daybreak with prime. And although I enjoyed the beautiful canticles, I was exhausted from the interrupted sleep by the time the sun rose over the abbey wall.

Days followed one another, turning into weeks, then months. On some mornings, as I struggled to clear my head from the vapors of sleep, I thought about my mother and how she would let us stay in bed until the sun was high above the forest. I felt such longing for home then that I would imagine myself running out of the enclosure, through the abbey gate, and down to the town to find someone travelling in the direction of Bermersheim to take me there.

My new life was not what I had thought it would be. The gray earth of the tiny courtyard, the dull wood of the buildings, and the many hours of silence made me long for the colors of the world, even the wintry ones, and its vivid sounds. Amid the unnerving stillness of my existence, I even missed the games my sisters had sometimes persuaded me to play with them.

The study of the Scriptures and the Latin lessons with Jutta were the few bright spots in my days. They commenced when it became apparent that my reading skills, while sufficient for my mother's gardening book, were inadequate for a deeper understanding of biblical passages. Twice a week after the midmorning service of terce, the usual monastic study time, Jutta sat with me at the table with a copy of *Regula Benedicti* to improve my Latin and enlighten me on the formal aspects of life in the Benedictine order.

"All of our daily activities are prescribed by The Rule," she explained on the first day of the instruction, "written by our order's founder, the Blessed Benedict of Norcia, in the year 530."

I made a calculation in my head—that was nearly six centuries ago! At first I found it hard to fathom that life had existed at such a distant time, its reality clouded by the darkness of the ages. Yet out of those shadows, my imagination soon picked out familiar images; the world could not have been that different back then—the hilltops must have been just as green, the ribbons of the Nahe and the Glan equally sparkling under the sun. "He wrote it especially for our monastery all those years ago?" I asked wonderingly.

A shadow of a smile crossed Jutta's lips but faded before it could blossom. "Our monastery did not exist at that time. The holy monk Disibod arrived between these rivers a hundred years later. Benedict had written for the existing communities as well as those that were yet to be founded."

"Did monasteries in Benedict's time have big churches and walls around them?" My mind was teeming with images of the bygone world.

"I suppose it depends on where they were located," Jutta said. "Benedict's abbey at Montecassino was known for its impressive size. It is still said to be the most beautiful abbey in all of the Italian peninsula. But there were also many small and poor foundations, just as there are today. The most important thing is," she steered the conversation back to the text, "that The Rule has survived unchanged all this time, and it requires Benedictines to spend their lives in prayer, work, and fasting, and to hold themselves aloof from the worldly ways. It also bans unnecessary speech and laughter, and enjoins us to practice chastity, humility, and obedience to our superiors."

I stared at my teacher, unsure of the meaning of 'worldly ways' and 'chastity.' Whatever these prescriptions referred to, they sounded harsh. I had already noticed that Jutta applied herself to fasting much more diligently than the others. Our typical fare, sent from the abbey kitchen once a day, consisted of black bread, boiled vegetables, water, and wine diluted according to the monastic custom. But Jutta ate hardly anything at all, taking only a piece of bread with a pinch of salt. "Does fasting make God happier with us?" I asked, unable to keep myself from glancing at her thin frame.

"God wants us to repent for the sins of the world, and the best way to do it is by denying ourselves those things that we find most pleasurable," the *magistra* replied.

"Is it better than praying, going to Mass, and doing good deeds, then?"

"They are all necessary for the redemption of sins."

"So God will not forgive us if we do good deeds and pray but don't fast all the time?"

Jutta hesitated. "The sins of the world are too great to be redeemed by prayer and good works alone." There was a hardness in her voice.

I was not satisfied. Why should one person, or even a group of anchoresses such as ourselves, take on the work of repenting for everyone else's sins? Surely that was not a feasible task; there were many people in the world who did bad things. How could the four of us ever accomplish that goal?

Then something occurred to me. "But Sister, did not Jesus die for our sins so we would be saved?"

Jutta blinked, but before she could answer, the church bells rang out to summon the community to another service. She rose hastily. As I followed her to the chapel, I reflected that there had to be better ways to serve God than what she was asking of me.

My only other diversion was music. I soon memorized all the chants of the Divine Office, but my favorite time was the hour before vespers, when the sisters sung and played the psaltery. Save for the gilded breviary, the instrument, delicately carved from young oak, was the only valuable object in the convent. As they plucked the strings, the pure, deep tones filled the pre-dusk hour with stirring solemnity, and no one brought them out better than Sister Juliana.

She had been educated in the art of musical notation at home. In a rare moment of confidence, she told me how she had used to listen to the *minnesingers* who stopped at her family's estate on their way to the imperial court. In exchange for food, they entertained their hosts with merry melodies about hunting, or with sentimental tunes about unrequited love. Sometimes the lyrics would take a ribald turn, and her mother would send young Juliana to bed, but she would sneak back, hide in the shadows of the hall door, and listen to the performances well into the night. In turn, I confided that I had used to eavesdrop on my father discussing business and politics with his guests at Bermersheim. Juliana was the sister with whom I formed the closest bond.

She became my music instructor. Using a wax tablet and a stylus, she wrote out a stanza of a chant, and drew straight lines in sets of four between the lines of the text. Then she covered the rows with little square marks.

"Are these the letters of music?"

Juliana nodded. "You could call them that."

"They are so different from the alphabet." I studied the marks. Some stood separately while others were grouped in clusters or connected to their neighbors with a line, either ascending or descending. "They look simpler than letters, but I cannot read them."

"They are called *neumes*. Few people know how to use them."

"Who invented them?"

"I don't know, but they are very useful. Writing a melody using this system can help preserve it more accurately than if it is learned by heart and sung or played from memory."

I pointed to the sets of four lines. "What are these for?"

"They allow you to specify the pitch of the sound, so that when you write a *neume* between the bottom third and fourth lines, like this" — Juliana drew a square in the place indicated — "it denotes a low-pitched sound. When you write it at the top, it indicates a higher one." By way of illustration, she sang the notes out in her well-trained voice.

"How clever!"

"It ensures that singers know how to perform without needing the composer's explanation."

"Who taught you these?" I asked.

"My governess, who was from Milan." A hint of nostalgia crept into her voice, and I felt a clutch at my heart as I thought of Uda who had taught me about herbs and their healing properties. But unlike Juliana, I was unable to practice my knowledge in the convent.

As I became more proficient, I tried my hand at composing a song about airy woods and gardens rich with the fragrance of summer roses. But when I played it, Jutta declared that songs extolling the world had no place in an anchorite convent and had me kneel before the altar for the rest of the day.

Increasingly, I was unhappy. I felt isolated and confined, like a caged bird allowed only a narrow glimpse of the world from which it had come. The lingering ache of separation from my family only compounded this feeling. Contemplating the sparse vine that grew out of the gray earth and clung feebly to the enclosure's wall, I felt a sense of kinship with the plant—neither dry nor green, neither dying nor living, its *viriditas*, like mine, seemingly in abeyance. I longed to see beauty and feel serenity but found only dullness and melancholy around me.

Yet I had a duty to fulfill as my parents' gift to the Church and wanted to do everything in my power to see it through. On occasions, these conflicting feelings flared into bouts of anxiety that gave me headaches, during which light and sound seemed to pierce my body with shafts of pain. I became wan and restless, and I knew the old illness was coming back.

But this time, Uda would not be there to take care of me.

5

May 1116

I HAVE A distinct early memory related to my recurring illness. I was six and the headache had lingered for days, forcing me to stay in a darkened room until Uda persuaded my parents to send for Herrad, her kinswoman and a healer known throughout the countryside.

Herrad took my pulse, listened to my breath, and brought a candle up to my eyes, making them hurt at the brightness. She declared that she was familiar with the symptoms, although they rarely affected children of such tender age. "These spells will likely become more burdensome as she grows," she opined.

"Is there no hope, then?" My mother was crestfallen.

"I can lessen her discomfort, but there is no permanent cure that I know of."

She left and returned some time later with a linen bundle and a container of greenish paste, which was a mix of mint, rosemary, and lavender. She scooped a bit of the paste and rubbed it gently on my temples, filling the room with the heady scent of a summer meadow.

"If it pleases God, she will be improving soon." Herrad took the silver coin my mother offered her and left the bundle. It contained crushed leaves of sweet coltsfoot from which Uda would make drafts to ease my pain.

Now I had to do without them.

The days grew warmer again. The trees in the infirmary garden I could see through the chapel window burst into clouds of white and pink, but the scents of flowering blossoms that wafted in after the rain seemed only to mock my senses.

One afternoon, I felt suddenly out of breath. The glare of the slanting sunlight was too bright, and the pitch of the chant bore painfully into my head until my ears started to ring. I tried to take a deep breath, but my vision darkened and then exploded into a spray of yellow sparks. Before I knew what had happened, the chamber went upside down, and I felt the rushes of the floor under my cheek. For a moment longer, voices came through the din in my ears, then my consciousness slipped away.

I opened my eyes to a gentle splash of water that grew more distinct at the same time as the pale wood of the dorter ceiling came into a sharper focus. I turned my head to find Sister Juliana wringing a linen cloth over a basin.

"God be praised! We have been worried about you!" She placed it on my forehead, where it was pleasantly cool.

I closed my eyes, wishing it was Uda or my mother bathing my forehead in fragrant rosewater. "It happens to me sometimes," I whispered, feeling guilty for my weakness.

"Don't worry. Brother Wigbert has sent a medicine for you." Juliana reached for a small stoppered flask from which she poured a measure into a cup. "Drink. It will make you better."

I swallowed the liquid, cringing at its bitter taste. "What is it?" I gasped.

"Wine mixed with the oil of valerian," Juliana replied as if she had just administered a miracle cure for every ailment in the world. "It is Brother Wigbert's favorite; he makes it for us whenever we feel melancholy."

But it only made me sleepy. When I was awake, it dulled my headaches, but it also made me sluggish and disinterested. I spent much of my time in bed.

"Do you like embroidery?" Sister Adelheid asked one day in her usual bright manner when she noticed that my eyes were open. There was a sizable piece of silk in her lap, and she was working on a pattern of golden lilies surrounded by green leaves.

"No." I sat up. "My sisters love it, but I'd rather do almost any other kind of work."

She looked disappointed; perhaps she had hoped it would cheer me up. "I am decorating a new altar cloth for the church," she explained. "We are expecting Bishop Otto of Bamberg for the feast of St. Disibod next month. He will be coming in place of the Archbishop of Mainz." She put the bundle on the table and picked up a bowl of fish stew, a rarity to which only convalescents were entitled.

I swallowed a spoonful. "Your flowers remind me of sunshine and spring." I pointed at the cloth with my chin. Indeed, the lilies were more artful and delicate than anything my sisters could ever do. "You have a talent."

Adelheid blushed. "I volunteer whenever the church needs new vestments or when linen needs to be replaced in the guesthouse. Sister Jutta does not approve of decorations, but we are the only women here, so who else will do it? Prior Helenger?" She chuckled.

The image of the haughty-faced prior stiffly working a piece of cloth with needle and thread was so funny that I could not help smiling myself. But there was something I was curious about. "Why is the archbishop not coming for the fair?"

"He has been imprisoned by the emperor."

An archbishop in prison? That dark, dank place where thieves, brigands, and other enemies of peace languished? "Why?" I asked, aghast.

Adelheid looked uncomfortable. "Archbishop Adalbert opposed the emperor's seizure of certain castles and supported the excommunication that had been pronounced against him a few years ago." She sighed as she pushed the needle through the silk. "We are living in disorderly times."

I was aware of the dispute between the imperial faction and those loyal to the pope in Rome over the control of Church lands and appointments of bishops, a process called *investiture*. I had heard it discussed at Bermersheim often enough. Now for the first time, I realized that even such a distant-seeming conflict could have an effect where I lived.

Adelheid must have sensed the direction of my thoughts, for she pointed to the embroidery again. "This is a great way to spend time, especially if you are sad or bored. If you keep your hands occupied, your mind will not wander."

"I'd rather spend my time reading," I grumbled. *Or making medicines.* Despite my dislike for the valerian concoction, I liked the idea of having a medicine workshop nearby. If only there was a way for Brother Wigbert to show me around! But, of course, that would never happen. There was nothing to look forward to but a stretch of dreary days, each exactly the same as the one before it and the one that would follow.

"I think I will sleep some more." I pushed the bowl away, still almost full, and turned to the wall.

The summer was pale, hot, and still. At least that is how it felt inside the enclosure, for the heat came without the relief of the breezes one can find only in an open field. I began to wonder if there was a way for me to fulfill my duty some other way.

In early July, the day before my first feast of St. Disibod, I was alone in the dorter when I heard footsteps outside. I was holding the lump of salt my mother had given me, its cool, pearly smoothness solid and comforting. I had just enough time to put it back in the box before Jutta came in with the unpleasant-tasting medicine.

"Why are we forbidden from going outside?" I asked, turning my head away from the flask.

The strange light in Jutta's eyes intensified. "It is no use pining for the world, child. There is nothing in it but obstacles to the salvation of your soul."

"Would going to the church threaten my salvation? Or if I worked in the infirmary garden?"

"Christ despised ornamented temples, and he did not pass his time tending to flowers. As His Brides, we must strive to attain Christ-like perfection by imitating his simple ways."

"Our priest at Bermersheim says that the beauty of the world is the reflection of the divine," I said.

"The world may be beautiful, but it is still full of temptation."

My eyes filled with tears as I remembered the sunny afternoons picnicking with Uda and my siblings. Homesickness swept over me in a numbing wave.

"Idle activities foster idle thoughts and bring about idle laughter, making us forget the evil that has taken hold of God's people," Jutta droned on. "As anchoresses, it is our duty to bemoan their plight and constantly pray for their deliverance."

There were many things I wanted to say in response— that I had never been closer to God than when I was running through the Bermersheim forest or sitting by the village stream listening to its silvery whisper. Or that I never felt more camaraderie with my companions at St. Disibod than when we were making music together. But when I looked into Jutta's eyes, I knew that her beliefs were unshakeable, and that I would have to find a way to live with them without letting them displace what I held so dear.

On the feast of St. Disibod, I asked to be excused from the Divine Office. The anchoresses showed no vexation at being excluded from the festivities, but my heart was heavy. I would have loved to attend Mass in the big church, which I imagined decorated with all kinds of flowers for the occasion, their sweet fragrance mixing with the more pungent scent of incense.

Toward noon, the buzz of activity grew markedly louder. The shutters of our dorter windows normally stayed closed during the day, but I opened one just enough to allow me to observe the proceedings in the main courtyard, my chin resting on my palms. Bishop Otto's cortege had just entered through the abbey gate, where Abbot Kuno was waiting to receive him.

I immediately identified the bishop by the dazzlingly white tunic and purple cassock adorning his large figure, a splash of luxuriant color among the simple black habits of the monks. After nearly a year surrounded by enforced poverty, my eyes widened at the sight of the large gem-studded cross hanging on a golden chain from his neck, the stones sparkling brightly in the sun. An attendant handed him his staff, and as he grasped it, I saw a glint of his great ring. The bishop had ridden in on a mule, after the fashion of churchmen, but it was a fine beast, muscular and shiny-coated, that would hold its own against any palfrey.

Preceded by the abbot, Otto of Bamberg entered the church, followed by his entourage and the monks. After that, the lay people crowded at the entrance, and I imagined them spilling into the cool interior of the church, filling every corner. Most were peasants, judging by their drab outfits and deferential air, but there were also pilgrims with walking sticks and provisions packed in bundles on their backs. The rest were townsfolk, including several merchants, similar in their dress and confident bearing to the salt traders whom I had seen at Alzey.

During the Mass there was a lengthy sermon delivered in a loud, commanding voice, which I guessed was the bishop's. If I had been born a boy, I mused, I would be able to participate in such ceremonies instead of having to grasp at distant echoes. Feeling dejected, I went back to bed and, lulled by Otto of Bamberg's peroration, dozed off.

I was awakened by the vesper bell. The festivities were over, but shortly after the sound of the bell had died down, I heard two voices in the small courtyard, just outside the convent. The speakers must have chosen the hour when the monks would be in the church and the anchoresses in their chapel to have a private conference.

"The emperor's defeat at the hands of Lothair von Supplinburg at Welfesholtz strengthens the Church's prospects," one of the men said.

On the other side of the dorter wall, I was all ears.

"May this bring peace and relief upon our people who have suffered greatly from these constant uprisings." I recognized the other voice as belonging to Abbot Kuno.

"Yes, of course," his companion hastily affirmed, "but what this means for *us* is that we will be in a better position to preserve our lands. The emperor has long wanted to trade his investiture rights for control over ecclesiastical estates."

The speaker, commanding and confident, could only have been the bishop.

"That is certainly welcome news," Kuno said, "although ours is a poor abbey with only a few vineyards, an orchard, and a mill. Hardly the kind of property the crown would be interested in."

I was ready to turn away and return to bed, satisfied the events had little to do with us, when Otto spoke again. "Perhaps not, but there is another way you can benefit." His voice took on a conspiratorial tone. "Now the emperor is weakened, I hear the barons will oppose new taxes, perhaps even demand lowering the current ones, which will leave more gold in their purses."

"And how does that favor us?" The abbot's voice was uncertain.

"It favors you *because*," the bishop was beginning to sound impatient, "they will have more money to support holy places like this one." I imagined him making a sweeping gesture with a bejeweled hand.

"But will they?" Kuno sounded skeptical.

"Father Abbot, what I am saying is that you should ensure that each novice brings in as large an endowment as his family can be expected to pay under these new circumstances." There was a moment of silence, and then the bishop added, as if in response to some grimace on Kuno's part, "Abbeys like St. Disibod need to use this opportunity to stop pinching every penny. Poverty limits our holy ministries."

"But how am I to judge who can afford what, Your Excellency?"

"I have thought of that." The bishop assured him smoothly. "My clerks are drawing up a list of noble families throughout the region who have sons or daughters destined for the consecrated life. We have sources that can help us estimate their wealth and therefore what they can be expected to pay in ecclesiastical dowries. I will send this information to every abbey under our jurisdiction."

As I tried to make sense of this, I remembered the girl Griselda whose family could not afford for her to take the veil. It angered me that only wealthy applicants were being accepted as if buying their way into the Church. With sudden clarity, I saw a difference between what Christ had preached and what the Church was practicing, and it was a lesson that would stay with me for the rest of my life. Many years later, standing at the pulpit of the great cathedral in Cologne, I would still remember every word of that exchange.

"We must ensure that as God's Church, we remain on the winning side," the bishop went on in the meantime, his tone now admonishing.

"The side of the nobles of the realm like Count Stephan von Sponheim, our largest benefactor, who has been recruiting supporters to the anti-imperial cause for years." Kuno seemed eager to show that he was not oblivious to high politics.

"That's right. But there is one noble *in particular* that we should back — Lothair von Supplinburg."

"Ah, of course. He led the alliance at Welfesholz."

"Not only that, but the Council of Bishops believes that Lothair will be the strongest contender for the throne. When it pleases God to call Emperor Heinrich, of course," the bishop added, perhaps realizing that he had sounded a bit too eager.

"Unless there is a legitimate heir."

"Rumor has it that the emperor is incapable of producing one." Otto dropped his voice confidentially. "He has been married to Empress Matilda for more than two years, but there is still no sign of a child in her womb . . ." The voices became unintelligible as they walked back toward the church, where the vesper chants had just died down.

Despite my dismay at the idea of selling novitiates at the highest prices, I was riveted by the conflicts playing out in the world from which I had been excluded. The struggles, the intrigue, the imperial couple's need to produce an heir who would stand in the way of Lothair's ambition brought the boredom of my existence into sharp relief once again. I craved knowledge and wanted to be part of what was happening rather than being so isolated.

Before I fell asleep that night, I knew I would have to get out of the enclosure, or I would die.

I awoke to a sensation that something was not right. The day had been calm, but now the wind had picked up, gusts howling in the eaves and corners of the abbey. I peered through the darkness illuminated by faint moonlight and made out the heads of Juliana and Adelheid. I remembered returning from matins with all three of them, but the floor where Jutta normally slept was empty. I strained my eyes again, but there was nobody there.

My apprehension deepened. According to the predictable rhythm of the conventual life, we were all supposed to be sleeping until lauds, which seemed to be some hours away. I rose noiselessly and walked to the door, hearing nothing except the regular breathing of the two sisters. As quietly as possible, I slid the wooden bolt and gently pushed the door open. It squeaked in its hinges, and I froze as one of the sleepers turned over, but soon everything was still again. I slipped out into the courtyard. The wind tugged at the sparse vine leaves on the wall, and a few stars shone behind the wispy clouds that flitted across the partial disk of the moon.

Everything was dark, and there was no sign of Jutta. At length I became conscious of a regular sound, sharp and short, accompanied by what sounded like muffled sobs. It came from the chapel, and I felt my anxiety welling up again as I walked toward it. I grasped the doorknob and slowly pulled it. At any moment, I expected the hinges to squeak and give me away, but they did not. When the door opened about an inch, I pressed my face to the crack.

At the foot of the altar, Jutta was on her knees, almost crouching on the floor, her back exposed down to the waist. My eyes widened as I saw her pale skin crisscrossed by crimson lines. I was still staring when Jutta's right hand rose rapidly, and a swishing sound pierced the air accompanied by long dark shadows momentarily cast over her flesh. I clamped my hand over my mouth as a tearing sob rang out, followed by a plangent plea. "Why have you forsaken me? Why are you so far from me and from the words of my groaning?" I recognized it as one of Jutta's favorite psalms.

There were new smudges on her back now, welling up with red ooze that slowly trickled down. Another lash. "I cry in the daytime, but you do not hear, and in the night, and I am not silent!"

Again. And again. "Be not far from me, for trouble is near, for there is none to help."

Each time the strips of leather crashed into Jutta's back, my body involuntarily jerked. I was mesmerized and horrified, and my head was spinning. *Why is she hurting herself? Should I call for someone? What if she dies?* I recalled our talk about repentance and sacrifice—was fasting and self-denial no longer enough? Did she have to suffer this terrifying punishment too?

A wave of nausea swept over me. Moving away from the door, I leaned against the wall of the chapel. When my back touched the planks, I felt a burning sensation, as if my own skin had been flayed. Fighting a growing light-headedness, I took a few steps toward the dorter, but the effort was too much. I lifted my eyes toward the stars, but their light had lost its sharpness, and then the world went dark.

September 1116

Brother Wigbert's assistant, a novice named Bertolf, conducted me to the cloister where he and Abbot Kuno waited. As we passed the scriptorium, Bertolf cast a longing gaze toward the desks full of scrolls, quills, and inkpots. At any other time, I would have done the same, but I was about to have a meeting that might change my life, and my mind was fixed on what lay ahead.

I had spent the past two months as an infirmary patient after the sisters had found me in the convent's courtyard. I was feverish, and they had trouble bringing me back to my senses. For nearly a fortnight, I lingered in that state before the fever broke. But my recovery had been slow; I had only taken a few steps around the infirmary until that day, and I still felt weak.

As we approached the inner courtyard of the cloister, I could hear steps echoing off the flagstones as the two monks paced the arcade, talking in low voices. The morning had been rainy, but now the sun came out, and droplets of water on the yellowing grass of the garth gleamed like jewels. Bertolf halted at the entrance, and we waited for them to make the final turn.

I had heard that Abbot Kuno and Brother Wigbert often took walks together to discuss points of theology or administrative matters. Today, however, they were to decide what to do with me. Already before my illness, the abbot had received reports that my residence at the convent was an uneasy one. Based on the monastic hierarchy, he should have consulted Prior Helenger. But when it came to such delicate matters, he preferred old Wigbert, a gentle and considerate soul benevolently disposed toward everyone. People trusted the infirmarian and felt comfortable around him, a rare gift even in a monastic setting. It was an especially fortunate trait in a physician. Kuno was also proud to have someone so educated among his brethren, for Wigbert had attended the famous medical school in Salerno, where young men from all over Europe went to study ancient texts.

When they came up to us, the abbot considered me for some moments, his face inscrutable. He seemed to tower over me — a squat and round type of tower, not a narrow and lofty one. But as nervous as I was, I was not afraid, for his eyes rested on me with kindness. "How are you feeling, child?"

"Much better. Thank you, Father," I replied with a small curtsy.

"She has been taking a few steps daily, and it will be a while before she can resume her duties at the enclosure," Brother Wigbert said. "But I am confident she will recover fully." He was ten years older than the abbot and similar in stature and roundness of figure, but the curly gray hair around his tonsure was already thin.

"Praise God." The abbot patted my shoulder. "Your parents entrusted you to us to keep you safe." Then he turned to the infirmarian. "Do you know what brought this crisis about?"

I tensed. Wigbert had asked me that question, and although I told him I had walked out of the dorter in the middle of the night and felt ill, I had not revealed my discovery of Jutta's nocturnal activities. I did not understand what it was that I had witnessed, and, truth be told, I wanted to forget about it.

"I do not." He raised his shoulders in a puzzled gesture. "The sisters say she had fainted once before, in the chapel during a service."

"Could it be the falling sickness?"

"I have not seen any evidence of that." The infirmarian shook his head. "She has not suffered convulsions, although I must observe her longer to be certain—sometimes they come months apart." Then he praised, "Hildegard has a serious disposition for a twelve-year-old and takes a keen interest in my workshop. Asks a lot of questions about herbs and medicine."

"Hmm." The abbot studied me again, and my cheeks grew warmer.

"She is eager to regain her strength so she can go outside and see my garden," the infirmarian added. Over the past few weeks, we had grown fond of each other. I liked his warmth and kindness, and I think my curiosity had injected a certain spark into his monotonous routine.

"Is she equally eager to return to the convent?" the abbot asked, addressing him but looking at me.

My breath caught in my throat. I knew what the right answer was, and I knew what the truth was. They were not the same, and I was happy to let Brother Wigbert answer. I had already told *him*.

"No." He looked at his superior honestly. "In fact, she doesn't want to go back at all."

Kuno's eyebrows went up. "You really are a most peculiar child." He spoke to me directly this time. "Your parents claimed you were docile, but from what I hear, you have a mind of your own."

This left me puzzled, for I did not know that having 'a mind of my own' — which I took to mean that I knew what I wanted and what I did not want — was a wrong thing.

"With your permission, Father," Brother Wigbert came to my rescue, "the rigors of an anchorite life are great and can be especially burdensome for one Hildegard's age. Even before her illness, they had often made her melancholy."

"But what are we to do, Brother?" The abbot frowned. "She was destined for the cloister at birth and never defied her parents' wish." He held my gaze, as if demanding a confirmation.

"No, Father," I whispered, dropping my gaze to the ground, then raising it to Brother Wigbert with an unspoken plea.

"We could find another arrangement, something less onerous," he suggested cautiously. "At least for now. She could help me with patients for a few hours each day." The infirmarian glanced at Bertolf, who had been standing silently behind me. I knew that both of them would be satisfied with that solution.

The abbot grunted — this was clearly not a complication he cared for — but his frown relaxed. "I would have to ask her father before I can make any changes," he said finally, and there was a note of hope in his voice. Hope that my father would say no, most likely.

"An excellent idea," Brother Wigbert agreed. "I will keep her in the infirmary until the matter is settled."

The abbot hesitated, then nodded. "So be it. I will write tonight and send a messenger first thing tomorrow."

The sun was already well on its downward course, the top of the cloister wall reflecting its fiery glow. The bell started issuing summons for vespers. The two monks proceeded to the church, and Bertolf took me back to the infirmary. I had earned more time.

The next day, I assisted at my first medical case. Brother Wigbert called me to the consultation room after breakfast, where a patient was waiting, an alehouse owner from Disibodenberg named Arnwald. The left sleeve of his shirt was rolled up, exposing a lacerated arm.

As Bertolf washed off the blood, Arnwald explained that he had been taking a barrel of beer down from a shelf when the accident happened. "I lost my grip, and the blasted thing—I beg your pardon, Brother," he added apologetically, "tumbled down and took the skin off my arm."

Brother Wigbert must have been used to salacious language from his suffering patients. Unperturbed, he examined the wound, which was not deep but stretched from the shoulder to the elbow.

"But at least it fell next to my foot, not on it." Arwald went on. "God watched over me today, Brother, for it would be the death of my family if this work tool"—he tapped his left foot—"came to harm."

"You are lucky, my good man, that all you have are badly bruised muscles, and you will be sore for a few days." The infirmarian went to his workshop and returned with a plate filled with a moist substance that had a pungent smell and the consistency of thick porridge. From the corner where I sat, I craned my neck to follow the procedure as he spread the poultice onto a piece of linen with a wooden spatula and applied it to the wound. Then he wrapped another cloth around it and told the man to return the next day for a change of dressing.

When Arnwald had gone, I asked Brother Wigbert what was in the poultice.

"Mainly bran, softened and warmed."

"But it smelled." I wrinkled my nose.

"That is because I added goat dung to it," he explained. "It draws out the pus."

I was puzzled. "What for?"

Wigbert puffed his chest authoritatively. "Greek medical texts recommend it. A wound will heal properly when it oozes pus with which the evil humor comes out."

I thought it wise to say no more. Uda had made poultices that included various grains, and ointments of lovage, betony, sanicle, or mugwort, but I could not recall her ever adding dung to them. I wondered if it would really speed up the healing and decided that I would soon find out.

When a kitchen servant brought supper for the patients, I took a few bites of the bread and cheese and climbed into bed. I was tired and my head hurt, but my mind kept circling around Arnwald's case. By all accounts, Wigbert was a caring physician. He devotedly nursed Brother Maurice, who was weak in the mind due to old age and spent his time slumbering on a nearby cot. I had also seen him deftly set a leg of one of the monastery grooms and expertly lance several neck boils. But there was something odd about the dung treatment, and I racked my brain until I succumbed to sleep without putting my finger on it.

Within four days, Abbot Kuno had a response from my parents. They consented to the new arrangement whereby I would be allowed to spend time outside the convent and be employed in a manner that was acceptable to the monks of St. Disibod. The letter concluded with this assurance:

> *It is our belief that if our daughter has more freedom within the monastery, she will come to better appreciate the consecrated life, and when the time comes, she will profess her vows with deeper conviction and purer faith, for we know that her dedication is unaltered.*

Brother Wigbert repeated those words to me, and they brought tears to my eyes. They were tears of longing, for I knew that, although written by my father's hand, the message had come from my mother. But they were also tears of relief that I would not be confined to the enclosure anymore.

Brother Wigbert told me that the abbot had summoned Prior Helenger to show him the letter. Upon reading it, Helenger had snorted. "Surely, Father, you are not going to indulge this kind of behavior? For all we know, it may be a ruse."

"Nobody who has dealt with her over the last year has any reason to doubt that her ailments are real," Kuno had said.

Brother Wigbert, who had also been present, nodded in affirmation.

"This has already caused a lot of distraction," the prior insisted, "and it is going to lead to even more confusion if you let her outside the convent. Inside is where she belongs."

"Why would it cause a distraction? She has been in the infirmary for the last two months, and there have been no problems. I am sure we can find an arrangement that will satisfy everyone."

"Such as keeping her permanently as a patient or a companion to Brother Wigbert?" Helenger sneered.

"Do not exaggerate, Brother Prior." Abbot Kuno's normally mild eyes had flickered with impatience. "The infirmary is busy enough; we will find a useful occupation for her."

"It is against our rules to have women around."

"She is a child, and she has struggled with the rigors of the enclosure," Brother Wigbert interjected. "We must be compassionate, Brother, for ours is a hard life, and we need not add burdens to it beyond what one can bear. Our faith has produced a great many hermits and anchorites, but I have never seen, nor heard of, a child of twelve among them. She is at a tender yet lively age, and it is unnatural to keep her so confined. We want to make sure we help Hildegard along in her vocation, rather than making it more difficult for her."

In response, Helenger only gave him a cold look. Then he turned to the abbot. "Her father would never have taken that position but would task us with putting the girl in her place. In this letter" — he jabbed a long finger at the parchment — "I see the hand of that wife of his."

"Brother Prior," Kuno sighed wearily, "if you cannot see any other benefit, think of her dowry. As you well know, there is much rebuilding work still to be done, and we cannot afford to lose any income."

Helenger rose. "I will pray that God does not punish us for making such compromises in the name of a few pieces of gold." His fine features froze into such an expression of offended virtue that it made him look even more like a statue than usual. As Brother Wigbert left the parlor in Helenger's wake, he saw the abbot sit back and cover his eyes with the tips of his fingers.

Arnwald's laceration was producing pus, all right. Each time he returned for a new dressing, the injured arm was hotter and more painful. On the third day, Wigbert took off the bandages and gazed at the wound for a long time, shaking his head. Peering from my bed, I caught a glimpse of the inflamed flesh, red and swollen. Arnwald declined any more poultice, and Brother Wigbert dabbed some oil on the arm and wrapped it in fresh linen. Then he gave Arnwald a cup of wine with a few drops of poppy juice for easier sleep and kept him in the infirmary for the night.

The next morning, Arnwald had a fever. He was given more wine, but although he drank it greedily, it was not much help. I offered to bathe his forehead in cool rosewater. Bertolf readily consented, for the day was getting busy. I sat with the bowl in my lap, dipped the towel, and touched it to Arnwald's face. The empty wine cup still stood near the bed, and my nagging thoughts returned. Wine was not an effective remedy against a fever, and yet somehow it was not entirely out of place. Why was that?

All at once, it struck me. I finished my task, hands shaking with excitement, then ran to the workshop. "I know what can help Arnwald!" I exclaimed, pushing the door open and startling Brother Wigbert.

"What?"

"Wine!" I was still breathless. Then something else lit up in my head. "Or vinegar!"

I had finally remembered! When Uda had tended to our cuts and bruises, she often said that it was important to bathe them in warm wine or vinegar to prevent them from corrupting. On larger ones, she would also apply honey, whose viscous sweetness was said to protect injured flesh from bad influence.

"Wherever did you get *that* idea from?"

"My nurse used to use it." I hesitated. "She knew about it from a wise woman."

The monk shook his head, half-disapprovingly, half-indulgently. "One should not listen to wise women, child. There is no telling what effect their remedies may have because they employ pagan incantations. Greek texts are the only appropriate source of medical knowledge."

I stared at him. Herrad was respected throughout our countryside for her healing skills, and many people owed her their lives or limbs. "Please, Brother, let's at least try," I implored.

"I am not going to put vinegar on his wound." Wigbert shook his head firmly. "Vinegar is harsh and will cause him more pain than he is in already."

"What about wine?"

He rolled his eyes. "Wine is meant to be imbibed, not poured on festering wounds."

Puffing with effort, he climbed onto a stool to hang up bunches of fennel and thyme from the beams. For a moment, Uda's loft stood before my eyes, warm and fragrant on September days, drying herbs rustling in the breeze that wafted through the window. Fighting another wave of homesickness, I returned to the infirmary and threw myself on my cot. I was convinced that one of those remedies would help. The abbey had both in abundance, and it was unfair not to even try them as the patient was getting worse.

Then my gaze fell to the floor where, on a tray by the door and among other dishes, there stood a cup of Brother Maurice's wine from breakfast. It was full since he had been sleeping all day.

Swiftly, I hid it under my bed. Then I looked out the window; it was midday and the bells would be ringing for nones soon which meant that Brother Wigbert and Bertolf would be going to the church. All I had to do was wait.

When the crunch of their footsteps had died down, I retrieved the cup and ran to the workshop. Thankfully, Wigbert had left the stove burning low. I found a small pot, poured the wine into it, and put it on the fire. Within moments its aroma filled the room, and I thought how lucky it was that patients were given undiluted wine. I poured the warm liquid into a wooden bowl and grabbed a jar of honey on my way out.

I found Arnwald awake from his fitful slumber, glassy-eyed from the fever. My heart was thumping—whether from excitement or fear, I could not tell. I put the bowl next to the bed. "I think I know how to induce your wound to heal," I said.

The man stared at me.

"I have some warm wine with which I'd like to wash your wound. Will you let me?"

Arnwald nodded slightly and closed his eyes. He remained motionless as I gingerly unwrapped his dressing, although he groaned when I pulled a piece of cloth that had stuck to the flesh. I caught my breath at the sight of the wound and had to steady myself. It was not until I dipped a cup and poured the wine over the arm that my self-control returned. I could hardly recognize myself; my motions were spare and precise, assured yet gentle, so that Arnwald had no cause for complaint. He winced at the first sting of the spirit, then smiled weakly. Perhaps the last of the wine, which was getting cooler, provided some relief from the fever that was gripping his body.

"The wound is no longer fresh, so it may take a bit," I said, scooping up some honey and dabbing it onto the flesh. Then I wrapped the arm so it looked exactly as before, and rolled up the wine-soaked linen. "Perhaps we should not mention this to Brother Wigbert for now," I added, clearing my throat. "It is a folk remedy, and he does not approve of such methods."

Arnwald smiled and winked. He was of a peasant stock, after all.

"I will save more wine tomorrow," I promised.

I returned the cup to the tray and was about to go back to the workshop with the honey and the dishes when Arnwald's voice sounded hoarsely behind me. "Thank you, young lady. You have a talent."

I turned and gave him a conspiratorial smile. I had begun to suspect as much.

Again through Brother Wigbert, I learned the details of Abbot Kuno's consultation with Sister Jutta regarding my new arrangements. He had gone to the enclosure armed with my father's response. The messages between him and the *magistra* were carried by Sister Juliana, for Jutta never came out to speak with outsiders.

"We hope it pleases God to restore Hildegard to health and return her to us swiftly," Juliana told him through the small opening for provisions in the door, the usual way the sisters communicated with the world.

"She is recovering well," the abbot informed her. "However, together with her parents, we have decided that she should not return to the convent permanently. At least for a while."

Juliana gazed at him apprehensively. "What are you saying, Father?"

"It appears that Hildegard's health is being affected by the rigors of your chosen life."

She lowered her eyes and remained silent.

"It may be that she is too young," the abbot resumed. "Whatever it is, things have to change if you are to be able to conduct your holy mission without further disruption."

"Am I to tell Sister Jutta that Hildegard is leaving us?"

"No. Her parents have not asked for it. But we must find a different arrangement, and I want to ask Sister Jutta's leave to make new dispositions."

"Let me confer with her, Father, if it pleases you to wait."

Kuno folded his arms into the sleeves of his robe and assumed a posture of patient expectation. After a while, Juliana returned. "Sister Jutta is greatly saddened by your news." Her tone was more official. "She is, as we all are, praying for Hildegard's deliverance both from bodily suffering and from the spiritual weakness that has caused her to reject our sacrificial way of life."

The abbot stirred uneasily. *It would greatly complicate matters if the* magistra *were to cast me out and declare me unworthy.*

"But we are ready to accept her back with compassion, even if she only spends part of her time with us," Juliana added. "And we will continue to pray for her to be delivered from this turmoil."

Kuno tried to hide his relief. "I applaud you for this most Christian attitude, Sister. I am hopeful we can find a solution that will allow Hildegard to pursue her calling with a serene heart."

When he returned to his lodgings, the abbot sent for Brother Wigbert to present him with his plan: *I was to be-*

come the infirmarian's helper and work from midday until vespers every day but Sunday.

After five days of the wine-and-honey cure, Arnwald's injured flesh began to lose its crimson flush. We both heaved a great sigh of relief, though for different reasons, for I had begun to have doubts about my memory of these remedies. But the deterioration had stopped. The wound was still tender, but the pus was gone and the fever had gone down. When I took the bandages off, it was no longer soft, and the first scabs had started to form. Arnwald said it was itchy, and we looked at each other hopefully; itchiness meant it was healing.

Brother Wigbert examined the arm and announced that it was finally on the mend and that Arnwald could return home. I handed Brother Wigbert clean pieces of linen as he bandaged it for the road. "A week ago, the wound was festering and you were consumed by fever, but today you are on your way to health," he said, shaking his head. "No earthly force has brought this about. God willed it, and it happened. Praised be his name!"

"Amen." Arnwald winked at me over the monk's tonsure. "It will be good to be back home, Brother. The first thing I will ask my good wife to do is warm up some wine."

I turned my head away to hide a smile.

Moments later, I watched Arnwald walk toward the abbey gate with more spring in his step than he'd had in days. I was about to close the infirmary door as the gate swung open to let him out, when I saw a boy. He had evidently just come up from the town. He approached the porter with what seemed like palms joined in supplication. But he was no beggar—his clothes were plain but neat, and he looked well-fed—and there was something familiar about him. I stood gazing a moment longer but could not think of where I might have seen him before. After all, the only boys I had ever known were my own brothers.

Then I closed the door and ran back to Brother Wigbert, for I was eager for my new life to begin.

7

March 1117

THE ACCESS TO Brother Wigbert's workshop, his inner sanctum, was from the herb garden. In the early days of March, the withered growth of the last season was poking desolately through the melting snow. Even so, the air of the workshop had that peculiar scent of dry herbs mixed with old timber that reminded me of Uda's loft. A counter stacked with mortars and pestles, clay bowls and glass vials, chopping knifes, spoons, and cups lined one wall, below a long double shelf. Two barrels of wine and several jars of honey were stored under the counter, and a sizable stove occupied the far corner, next to a basin filled with fresh water brought daily from the abbey well.

When Brother Wigbert had first showed me his medicines, which were all arranged along the bottom shelf, he had done so with considerable pride. They included cork-stoppered bottles of thick brown oil of valerian, vials of rose essence, lavender oil the color of a pale peach, and a flask of poppy juice of milky consistency. Next to them, an earthen jar contained gnarled sticks of ginger, which I had never seen before. It was to be used sparingly, for it came from the East and cost half a silver mark each. There were also several wooden boxes with dried leaves and flowers of rose hips, mint, thyme, marjoram, rosemary, fennel, and basil.

On the table by the window, two large glass jars kept attracting my attention. One housed a colony of leeches covered with a strip of gauze, and the other was filled with what looked like stiff black disks with whitish streaks on them. "What are these?" I asked.

"Dried goat dung," he explained matter-of-factly.

But, on the whole, the inventory was respectable, although I quickly realized that I would probably not learn any more about herbs than what I already knew. In fact, I noticed that there was no powdered willow bark, which Uda had used to make tea for us when we had a fever. Nor did the infirmarian have a stock of yarrow flowers that could be boiled in water to bathe the foreheads of those suffering from seasonal chills. Still, when the garden would yield its first herbs in the spring, there might be opportunities for me to try new combinations for various ailments. The prospect of experimenting and learning filled me with a thrill of anticipation.

By late winter, I was Brother Wigbert's assistant in all but name and had taken over many of Bertolf's duties. Not only did the poor novice not have the stomach for medicine, he regularly broke the infirmarian's precious glass. He now spent most of his time in the scriptorium, where he was happier, as were we in the infirmary.

That March afternoon, my task was to wash some dusty glass. As I was reaching for it, my gaze lingered, as it often did, on the three volumes standing on the shelf next to these lesser-used vessels. I had been intensely curious about them, though I dared not touch them.

"These are a few of my medical texts from Salerno," Brother Wigbert said, noticing my fascination. "I keep them here for reference."

"May I read them?" My Latin had greatly improved under Jutta's tutelage.

"You would not understand anything, child. It takes men years to master this knowledge. Besides" — he pointed at the water basin — "there is a lot of work to be done. When you have washed these, there are also clay pots that need to be scrubbed."

"Yes, Brother."

These dispositions given, he set out to prepare a strengthening posset for Brother Maurice. For a while we worked in silence, then I asked, for my mind was still on the books, "Can women study to be physicians, Brother?"

"Usually, no."

"Why?"

"It is the natural order of things," he replied, "that women should rear children since they are the gentler and more nurturing of the sexes. Who would guard the family hearth if they were to go to schools?"

I pondered this, frowning. "But if women are better at caring for others, they should make better doctors too, shouldn't they?"

Wigbert looked momentarily surprised, then chuckled. "You make clever arguments, Hildegard, but studying requires well-developed reasoning faculties, which women do not possess, being more impulsive and less logical then men."

I considered pointing out the contradiction, but decided not to. "You said that women do not *usually* become physicians, Brother — does that mean that sometimes they do?" I asked instead.

He nodded. "There have been instances of high-born ladies who read ancient texts and claimed to have mastered the medical arts. It is said, for example, that the daughter of the emperor of Byzantium is a physician. There is also a female scholar at Salerno named Trota who lectures and writes on the diseases of women."

"Is she a princess too, this Trota?"

"No."

My heart leaped. "So it *is* possible!"

"Hers is not an easy life." Brother Wigbert raised his considerable eyebrows as if in warning. "For there are many who claim that she is breaking God's law by doing so."

"And is she?"

"I am not a theologian, but St. Paul does admonish against women teachers."

Having no argument against that, I went back to rinsing the glass as he finished the posset and poured it into a cup. "It is getting warmer, and the garden will need weeding and planting soon," he said, wincing as he stretched his fingers. "My joints are aching again."

I held my breath.

"Would you like to help me with it, or should I employ one of the novices?"

Did he even have to ask?

As soon as the snow was gone, I set out to work. In my mind I already imagined the garden full of color and fragrance, filled with birdsong and the drone of bees from the hives Brother Wigbert kept behind the fruit trees near the abbey wall.

The wall offered natural protection from the wind, and a boxwood hedge separated the garden from the rest of the abbey, giving it a secluded feel, but besides that there was little structure to it. A few rosebushes were planted against the convent's chapel—I remembered their sweet scent wafting through the small window the previous spring. Next to them was a patch of poppies and, for some reason, strawberries. On the opposite side of the plot, there was a cluster of elderberry and apple trees. In between this jumble, herb beds of different sizes were covered with remnants of the last season's growth.

For several days I pruned, dug, and weeded, and delineated the beds by marking clear paths between them. Little by little, I located the fennel bulbs, rosemary and lavender shrubs, valerian stems, and the tangled horizontal branches of mint. At the far end of the garden in the shade of the fruit trees, I found marjoram and basil. Before long, an outline began to emerge. I felt great satisfaction when I surveyed the final results even though important healing plants, like sage or oregano, were missing. But those could be planted over time. Wild herbs, on the other hand—those that grew by the roadside or in the forest—would not be available unless I found someone to procure them for me.

Gardens bloom quickly under the sun and showers of a Rhenish spring, and the first yield comes in May. I was putting fresh blankets on the cots in the infirmary one morning, when, looking through the window, I saw a boy walking from the direction of the workshop with a basket full of fresh leaves. It was the same boy I had seen arrive at the abbey the previous autumn. I gazed after him until he vanished around the church on his way to the kitchens. He was not an oblate or a novice—he wore lay clothes—and once again I had that vague feeling of familiarity.

When I had finished my work, I went to the workshop. I found Brother Wigbert standing on the threshold admiring the herbs. They were growing profusely in neat clusters without so much as one shoot of a weed anywhere. The buzzing bees and the bright butterflies that alighted on the blossoms only enhanced the garden's wholesome, cheerful aspect.

"You have a green thumb and you are diligent." He looked genuinely pleased. "Unlike most of the novices who have had a go at this before," he added sardonically.

"Thank you, Brother." I felt myself flushing with pleasure as I followed him inside. "Who was that boy I saw coming out of here not long ago?"

"A kitchen help came for some cooking herbs. Abbot Kuno likes his fish seasoned with marjoram and rosemary."

We were going to prepare the season's first batch of herbs for storage. I started cleaning the wood boxes while he cut the dried bunches down from the beams. As he did so, he asked me how the sisters were dealing with my new employment.

"They are used to it now." Upon my return to the convent, I had sensed a certain resentment, mainly on the part of Jutta. The *magistra* said that she would pray for me, then spoke not a word to me for days. But I tried to please her with my diligence, and I always stayed in the convent for the study hour.

Eventually I regained her favor, albeit by accident. After my months-long absence, I had found myself out of practice kneeling on the floor of the chapel and took to alternating between kneeling and lying on my stomach, imitating the anchoresses. The face-down position was hardly more comfortable, but at least it prevented my limbs from going numb. So I was surprised when Jutta broke her silence one evening and whispered to me as we were leaving the chapel, "I am glad that you are humbling yourself before God by flattening your body during prayer. None of us deserve to look at our Savior's face."

The next day, she selected a passage from The Book of Job in which Bildad gave this reply to Job: "How can man be righteous before God? How can he be pure who is born of a woman? If even the moon is not bright, and the stars are not pure in His sight, how much less man, who is a maggot, and a son of man, who is a worm!" I quickly understood that this was intended to reinforce her earlier admonition.

Still, there was one thing that bothered me. "I am so much more content now," I said to Brother Wigbert as I lined the boxes up on the counter, "but I fear it may be against The Rule."

"What may be against The Rule?" Brother Wigbert was puzzled.

"Being happy."

"And why would you think that?"

"Sister Jutta told me about all the things we must refrain from." I proceeded to enumerate on my fingers. "We must not provoke laughter, we must reject pride, practice fasting, love chastity . . . What's chastity, Brother?"

"Uh . . . hmm." The monk was suddenly very busy with the herbs strewn on the table. "It is when a man and his wife are . . . uh . . . faithful to each other." He bent over a stem, closely examining its flowers, though they looked fine to me.

"Like my father and my mother?"

"Yes." The bald tonsure nodded without looking up.

"But married people don't live in monasteries."

Brother Wigbert straightened up, sighing. "What you need to know"—he was choosing his words carefully—"is that The Rule is above all about prayer and labor, each in sufficient measure to elevate the spirit and subdue the body. It is there to guide us and keep us on our path, but it also aims to make the monastic life a fulfilling one despite the sacrifices we must make."

"But Sister Jutta—"

"She is a holy woman and an example to all of us in her capacity for spiritual elevation and self-denial." Despite the lofty words, Wigbert's tone was rather perfunctory. "But she lives by her own strict *codex* that you are not expected to follow unless you make a formal commitment in the future. Do you understand?"

Relief washed over me. "Does that mean I don't have to fast every day?"

"The Rule prescribes extreme fasting only as punishment, not as daily routine."

That was good news, but the worried look must have lingered on my face.

"What now?"

"There is one other thing." I hesitated. "Sister Jutta seems somehow . . . sadder than before I took ill."

"As I said, she is devoted to the ascetic life."

"And yet she allows herself things she did not use to." I frowned.

"Like what?"

"She asks for extra salt from the kitchen. Before, she would only take a pinch with her bread."

"Does she?" I thought I saw a look of concern cross Brother Wigbert's face and wanted to ask more, but Bertolf poked his head in and said that we were needed in the infirmary.

———◆●◆———

It was a tradition at St. Disibod that as winter approached, the infirmarian made large quantities of elderberry wine and rosehips tincture. The year 1117 was no different. As the northerly winds turned colder, patients with chills and coughs began to arrive. I wondered what the real reason for their visit was, for the wine was justifiably renowned throughout the countryside.

As far as actual treatment, Brother Wigbert's approach was the same in most cases. He would give each patient a cup of warm wine, then bathe their foreheads in rosewater to cleanse the skin of the bad vapors the body was expelling. For more stubborn cases, he made fennel drafts, which seemed to ease the discomforts better, but we only had a small quantity of the herb as most of the yield went to the kitchen.

At Bermersheim, Uda had always kept a stock of horehound lozenges to soothe our throats, and I had made certain provisions that autumn. I had befriended the servant who brought meals to the infirmary and asked him to pick some horehound for me in the forest where it grew abundantly. When he did, I hung it up to dry in the tool shed behind the workshop. It was almost ready, and I was excited to make a batch of lozenges to surprise Brother Wigbert.

But before that happened, I saw my first severe case of the seasonal ailment when a girl of about fourteen was brought to the infirmary, feverish and shaking with a violent cough. Brother Wigbert applied his standard cures, but the next morning her fever was higher and pulse more rapid. He boiled the remaining fennel and she drank the draft avidly, but to no avail—she remained flushed and restless, with glassy, bloodshot eyes.

It was then that he decided to examine her urine. When I brought the requisite fluid in a special bell-shaped glass, he walked to the window and studied it at length, swirling and tilting the glass, and smelling the contents. "The scant amount indicates that bad humors are drying her body," he explained as I hovered behind. "The color is too intensely yellow; normal urine is paler, similar to straw in hue."

"And you can tell from that what is wrong with Rumunda?" I asked, amazed. I had never thought of my own water as anything other than waste and a nuisance in the middle of a cold night.

The monk nodded solemnly. "Urine is the repository of all manner of information about one's health. Its analysis is the very basis of the art of medicine. This specimen, for example, shows no signs of blood or pus, and its odor is normal. But look." He brought the flask closer to my face. "It is almost as if someone dissolved a dye in it."

"What does it mean?"

"It means that she suffers from an excess of yellow bile, which is making her blood warm, causing the fever," he opined. "I will bleed her to rid her of this overabundance."

He produced a sizable bowl with stains of previous procedures on it, and I recalled the words of Herrad, the wise woman who had treated me for my headaches at Bermersheim. My father had asked her about bloodletting, and she shook her head. "I have never seen people who languish from an illness improve after it," she had said. "Many get even weaker." Now I held the bowl under Rumunda's elbow as Brother Wigbert expertly cut the vein, and a line of thick dark blood welled up, trickled down her forearm, and started dripping into the receptacle.

"You have gone a little pale." Wigbert said as he wiped the knife. "Never seen this much blood before, eh?"

If only that were true. In fact, the sight reminded me of Sister Jutta flogging herself on the night I had fallen ill, and my anxiety returned. But I shook my head so as not to appear weak. "It's nothing. I will be fine."

"The first time can make one queasy, but you will get used to it," he said.

Meanwhile, the patient sat with her eyes closed, and her chest heaved with labored breaths. When Brother Wigbert deemed that enough blood had been let, he bound her arm up tightly. Even before he finished, she was asleep. "It is normal too," he said. "Bleeding causes drowsiness, but that is when the body sorts out the imbalance."

Herrad's words came back to me again, and I frowned in puzzlement. Yet was Brother Wigbert not an educated man who had studied at Salerno and done this many times? Uncertain who to believe, I decided that the proof would be in the outcome.

In the wake of the bloodletting, Rumunda's fever had stopped rising, but she was weaker, so much so that even her cough turned into little more than a flutter in her neck. Brother Wigbert insisted that the cure needed time to settle in order to restore the balance of the humors as the amount of yellow bile subsided. He also forbade Rumunda from drinking more than strictly necessary so as not to jeopardize the balancing process. On the third day, he ordered an application of leeches, but when she woke up afterwards, her eyes shone with fever again. I gave her a cup of water when Wigbert was away, and her eyes became less cloudy and more focused.

But she never recovered. She was bled one more time, but it was as if her *viriditas* had left her body with it, and she languished a few more days until she died on the morning of All Saints Day. She was poor and we laid her to rest in the abbey cemetery. Buried along with her was my confidence in bloodletting and leech cures.

8

November 1117

O N THE FEAST of St. Martin's, just a few days after Rumunda's death, Brother Maurice succumbed to old age.

"As you helped to nurse him, the abbot has invited you to the funeral," Brother Wigbert told me the next morning before leaving to take his turn at the vigil.

I had the workshop to myself. I was looking forward to going to the big church for the first time since my oblate blessing ceremony, but I also had a cold. The rosehips tincture had only gone so far, and now I was beginning to have a sore throat. I went to the shed and returned with two bunches of dried horehound and proceeded to crush the fuzz-covered leaves with a pestle. In a clay pot, I mixed honey with water and added the herbs as I heated the viscous mixture until it started to give off a mild aroma. After it had boiled and thickened, I used a wooden spoon to scoop up small amounts onto a plate to form round shapes. When they cooled and hardened, I peeled one lozenge off and tried it for taste. It was quite agreeable, but it reminded me of home, and my eyes filled with tears as the sticky sweetness melted in my mouth.

By then it was midday, and I threw on my cloak as the resounding knell of the church bell broke the quiet of the abbey. Despite the solemn occasion, I ran down the gravel path before slowing to a more decorous pace when I reached the courtyard. In the back of the church there was a large group of lay people, for Brother Maurice had spent many decades at St. Disibod and was well loved in the area. But I was a member of the holy community and felt a surge of pride walking to the section reserved for oblates and novices.

My heart was beating fast as I took a seat in the third pew behind the oblate boys. I folded my hands and tried to concentrate on the prayers, but I was seized by an irresistible urge to look around and take in the sights of a real Mass, with the incense, the candlelight, and the chants whose notes quavered sublimely as they echoed off the stone walls.

As the proceedings went on, the oblates in the front pews began to fidget, nudging each other and whispering. I noticed that one of them, an antsy boy of about eleven, was particularly given to pranks, reaching over two or three of his neighbors to pull on the back of someone's cowl. But they all bent their heads in unison and assumed postures of utter devotion whenever the sharp gaze of Brother Philipp, the novice master, fell on them.

A few pairs of eyes swiveled in my direction from the chancel where the monks sat, mostly curious, except for Prior Helenger, whose disapproving look sent a chill down my spine with its almost physical coldness. My excitement vanished and my mind filled with doubt. What was I doing here? Among all these men and boys, I must be breaking who knows how many rules. But then I caught the gaze of Brother Wigbert, and he gave me a slight nod to signify that everything was fine.

After that, I kept my eyes judiciously fastened on Brother Maurice's shrouded body, lying on a bier at the foot of the altar with two large tapers burning on both sides. The service was just coming to an end when sounds of a commotion floated from the outside and grew louder as someone called for help. Disconcerted, Abbot Kuno gave a signal to pause and sent a couple of junior monks to investigate. They came back reporting that there had been an accident.

Brother Wigbert rushed outside, and I followed him. There, we found that one of the men working on the chapter house roof had fallen from the scaffolding as he rushed to finish the work before the first frost. He was sprawled on the ground, groaning as he clutched his legs. That he could move was already a good sign, I knew. His fellows explained that he had been on his way down and fell less than twenty feet. Brother Wigbert examined him and found that both of his legs were broken, and the workers improvised a stretcher from two planks to carry him to the infirmary.

By then, most of the mourners had come out of the church. As the monks looked on with quiet solemnity, the oblate boys resumed their horseplay, glad for a distraction from the tedious service. A few of them cast shy glances at me — they were not used to seeing girls around the abbey — but the one I had noticed before considered me with frank curiosity, then gave me a wide grin, his hazel eyes sparkling with amusement. I was a little abashed, though I had to admire the cheekiness of the youngster who stood at least a head shorter than me. No boy had ever smiled at me before except my brothers, and they did not count.

The funeral resumed with the procession heading for the cemetery while Wigbert and I returned to the infirmary. The bone setting must have been terribly painful, for the patient groaned and cried out and had to be held down by two men. But as the infirmarian wrapped his legs tightly with bandages, I knew that he would be fine. I had seen Brother Wigbert's surgical skills many times on broken ribs, legs, or arms. Few who came in with such injuries were ever left lame. My teacher may have been a reluctant herbalist, but he was a first-rate surgeon.

We returned to the workshop, and Wigbert poured wine for us while I added logs to the stove. Then he noticed the lozenges and stood over them with a puzzled expression. "What is that?"

I had forgotten all about them. "I—I made some horehound pills . . . for the throat."

"Is it one of those things you learned from your wise woman?" His brows furrowed.

"From my nurse, who learned it from a wise woman." I faltered. "I am sorry, Brother, I should have asked you, but—" I cast around for an excuse "—they work for me!"

Brother Wigbert still looked skeptical, but his face relaxed a little.

"Maybe we should try them on a few patients, and if they do not work, we throw them away?" I suggested.

He grunted. "We will see." He moved the tray aside. "But now we have more important things to do."

Like making valerian oil. I sighed but not too loudly, and we set out to work, assembling the alembic brought out from the shed. When it was ready, we poured water over the dried roots in the pot and covered it with a lid with a cap on top to collect the vapor as the liquid started to boil. A downward sloping tube was connected to the cap, through which the oil would drip into a receptacle. It was the kind of apparatus my Uda had always dreamed about.

As the November night fell and the wind started howling outside, I watched the thick brown liquid collect and thought about Salerno, where Brother Wigbert had learned the principles of medical analysis. I was fascinated by that faraway land of plentiful sunshine, countless churches, and men from all over the world who studied theology, law, and medicine. And I asked him, once again, to describe for me the students' robes, their books, the university quarters, even the taverns where they gathered to drink and take their meals. Like each time before, I listened raptly, my cheeks flushed.

When he finished and rose to pour the oil into smaller flasks, I asked, my heart beating fast against my ribs, "Brother Wigbert, will you teach me about medicine?"

He raised his eyebrows. "What for, child?"

"So I can be a better assistant to you."

He considered this for a while, and I could see that the idea had some appeal to him. "But you have already learned a lot at the infirmary. You are helping me more than Bertolf ever did."

"I want to learn about anatomy and about the humors," I interjected before he could say no. "I want to know how their imbalance affects the body, and how doctors diagnose diseases. Everything." I added breathlessly.

Brother Wigbert chuckled. "I studied for four years to become a physician, so I will not be able to convey it all to you in one evening. But I can give you an overview after we are done with the lavender."

I jumped from my seat to fetch a sack of lavender buds as he emptied the pot of the valerian dregs and rinsed it. Then he filled it with the lavender, poured fresh water over it, and set it back on the stove. We used large quantities of that fresh-smelling oil to scent infirmary linen.

He sat down across the table from me and cleared his throat. "You have already witnessed urine examination," he began solemnly, and I imagined myself a pupil in a vaulted classroom, like I had once thought I would be. "Urine, being expelled from the body most regularly, carries with it the picture of internal health. Normal urine is pale yellow and clear, but disease can turn it red, which indicates the presence of blood. Various hues of brown signify gallbladder disease. If it is too yellow, it means there is an excess of bile, while a strong, unpleasant odor is a sign of the presence of an evil humor in the body. Those who suffer from too much sugar will pass water that is sweet and thick, but if it is cloudy the patient is likely afflicted with a case of . . . uh . . . burning . . . of the nether regions." Brother Wigbert looked uncomfortable. "Of course, you would not expect anyone from this holy community to come down with it," he hastened to add.

I tried to memorize everything he said. "And the humors?" I asked. "What are they exactly?"

"They are the very essence of health and disease." He poured more wine from the flagon and began to expound — with growing enthusiasm, for he had likely never encountered anyone at the abbey interested in medical theory — on the four bodily fluids and their counterparts in the physical world, the four elements. He explained how they influenced each other, the essence of health being the right proportion among them. When they were out of balance, disease ensued.

Blood was the equivalent of Air, a hot and wet humor, which gave the person endowed with it to excess a sanguine temperament. Black bile, being cold and dry, had Earth for its analog, with superfluous bile bringing on sadness, anxiety, and lack of sleep. Then there was the yellow bile, a hot and dry humor similar to Fire, that caused one to become flushed and feverish, like Rumunda had been. Lastly, phlegm, akin to Water in that it was cold and wet, brought on apathy.

"This theory," he added by way of a conclusion, "was first put forward by Greek physicians Hippocrates and Galen and gave rise to several therapies that aim to restore the imbalance between the humors and return the patient to health. Bloodletting is the most widely used method, a wonderful cure that purifies the body by draining the excess and resetting the equilibrium," he said without even blinking. "But there are other useful treatments such as purging, special foods, and drafts made from plants long established as having curative effects."

"Do you mean herbs?" I asked hopefully.

He gave me a significant look. "I mean *certain* herbs, ones that have been domesticated and are grown and picked" —

he pointed toward the garden — "where they cannot become subject to spells and other manipulations."

I hesitated. I was beginning to understand his views on non-monastics who dabbled in healing, but I wanted to defend them. "The drafts and ointments that Herrad makes from wild herbs restore many people to health. Many who come to her for help find relief, and she taught my nurse who never used spells when she made medicines for us."

"The Church is concerned with superstitions that call for such herbs to be gathered at different times of night, often by the light of full moon, which simple folk believe enhances their potency."

That, I must admit, was true. I had heard Herrad say as much to Uda.

"It is then, when there is nobody abroad," he continued, "that they pronounce incantations to summon spirits to their assistance. It is a practice that is perilous to the Christian soul."

I had no idea if that was the case or not, and I felt my shoulders slump. I had plans to expand the use of herbs at the infirmary to show how well they worked, but it seemed that nothing would come of it after all; we would go on giving patients warm wine, rosewater baths, and leeches for everything. "I know that many God-fearing women make potions," Wigbert added with a note of indulgence, perhaps sensing my disappointment, "but all the same, the Church frowns upon it."

I took a deep breath. Brother Wigbert, unlike Prior Helenger, was a person with whom one could at least try to reason. "I really hoped that I would be able to — that is, that you and I — would make medicines using the herbs from the garden, but also the abundance that grows in the forest." Then I added quickly, before courage deserted me, "All plants, even the most paltry of weeds, are God's creation, are they not? So if God gave them to us, why not use them to our benefit? We cannot know if they have healing properties if we never try. If wise women use sorcery to make herbs work, then they won't work for us. But what if they really *do* have curative powers? Imagine what we could do with them!" My voice rose pleadingly.

Brother Wigbert's face was serious but not severe. "You have a good bedside manner and a knack for healing for one so young. You also know how to argue your point even though you are a girl. But I do not want my workshop to become a playground for dangerous ideas."

Did he really believe it, I wondered, or did he want to avoid trouble? With Prior Helenger on constant lookout for real or imaginary transgressions, it was reasonable to be cautious. I saw that there was no point in pressing it further; besides, spring was still months away. Perhaps I could take small steps, make use of the herbs we already had, and learn more.

My gaze wandered again to the three books on the shelf. "What about those medical writings?"

"Ah." Wigbert rose from the table with surprising agility, glad of the change of topic. "These are basic texts that come very handy." He took them down and selected a small volume whose pages were bound in hard leather. "This is *De Urinis*, a translation of the work of Theophilus, a Greek physician who compiled existing information on urine analysis from a variety of sources. It serves as the definitive textbook on this matter for students and practitioners alike."

The second book was bigger and its cover was of better quality. It was an excerpt from *Medicinale Anglicum*, another definitive source. I examined each book reverently, but it was the last and largest volume that made me gasp. It was a translation of Galen's treatises on diseases, symptoms, and pharmacology, a term that Brother Wigbert explained referred to medications.

The subject matter may have been dense, but the presentation filled me with delight, for the book contained exquisite images. I gingerly turned the soft vellum pages and ran my fingers over the decorative first letters of each chapter, which showed philosophers and physicians at work examining samples in glass vials, or poring over medical texts. Each miniature was superbly detailed down to the last leaf on a tree bough, the smallest star in the sky, or the lightest crease in the robe, all painted in vivid greens, scarlets, yellows, and blues, edged in gold leaf. In addition to being breathtakingly beautiful, the book had to be very expensive.

"This is my most precious possession," Brother Wigbert said fondly, as if reading my thoughts. He went to the alembic to check on the lavender oil that was dripping slowly. "It was a gift from one of my teachers at Salerno. Abbot Kuno is good enough to let me keep it here since it serves me as a useful reference, but it should be in the library."

"There is a real library here?" I was stunned, although it made sense on reflection. Monks copied manuscripts in the scriptorium — right next to the oblates' schoolroom, a place I could rarely think about without bitterness — and those copies had to be stored somewhere.

"Yes. There is a small door in the back of the scriptorium that leads to it." He returned to the table and gathered his books. "Access is strictly controlled."

"Why?"

"Monasteries are repositories of knowledge through their collections of books, some of which may be unsuitable to uninitiated minds." Seeing my puzzled look, he explained, "We have monastic rules, the Lives of saints, and writings of Church Fathers, but we also have a good number of Greek translations, including most of Galen's works and some of Hippocrates, both of whom were pagans. It is their paganism that renders these writings potentially dangerous."

From that day onward, my thoughts became filled with images of the place — so close and yet out of reach — where the monks copied ancient texts and created a growing store they could peruse whenever they wanted. I had dreams in which I descended a staircase leading deep into the belly of the earth under the cloister to a large chamber with shelves piled high with volumes and scrolls. But when I opened them, the pages were always blank. Sometimes I saw Brother Bertolf in those dreams, seated at a desk covered with inkpots, bottles of dyes, goose quills, and brushes, a blank volume in front of him, and I would awake just as he dipped his quill and was about to put his hand to the parchment. Often, I would have trouble returning to sleep.

One night on my way back from the infirmary, I halted before entering the enclosure. I had to do something, or I might not get a good night's sleep again. I turned and ran to the workshop, fresh snow crunching under my feet. I opened the gate and paused momentarily, struck by the beauty of the winter landscape before me. The light that shone through the workshop window cast an orange glow on the pristine whiteness of the herb beds, and large snowflakes were falling slowly through the air, spreading a veil of calm over the world. The quietude was so profound that I felt a jolt of energy opening my mind to a greater insight. I was happy! I enjoyed Brother Wigbert's favor, I had this plot of fertile Rhenish land sleeping under the snow until warmer days, and I was determined to make the most of it.

Frost biting at my toes spurred me on, and I pushed the door open, inhaling the aroma of the sweet posset Wigbert made at Christmastime, a delicious mix of ale, eggs, milk, and spices. He turned from the stove, surprised to see me at that hour, but before he could say anything, the question tumbled from my mouth. "Brother Wigbert, will you ask Father Abbot to let me use the library?"

9

January 1118

B ROTHER WIGBERT AND Abbot Kuno had a private supper each month, and I was so anxious on the night of
their first such meeting in the year 1118 that I knew I would
not be able to sleep. It was already dark when we left the
workshop, the infirmarian heading to the abbot's house and
I returning to the convent. The January sky was clear and
speckled with sharp winter stars, bright and cold, and for a
moment I considered following behind to see if I could listen
at the door. Then I chastised myself for such thoughts and
headed for the enclosure, Brother Wigbert's promise to relate
the conversation to me serving as my consolation. A promise, I need not add, that he kept faithfully.

Brother Wigbert always looked forward to those meetings, especially on long winter evenings when the abbot's

large hearth burned brightly, and the food, prepared separately from the refectory fare, was of the highest quality.

That night was no different. The joint of beef was succulent and seasoned to perfection, and the spiced wine undiluted. At first the conversation revolved around the renovations of the abbey treasury which were to commence in the spring, then the infirmarian wiped his mouth and sat back. "There is something I need to tell you, Father." After Kuno motioned him to continue, he told him of my work in the infirmary and my interest in healing, although he omitted the part about the wise woman and my considerable knowledge of herbs. "She has a natural talent and learns quickly," he added. "I think perhaps we should find a way to foster this gift, especially since I am getting older and nobody has shown an interest in replacing me."

"But what are you saying, Brother?" The abbot looked surprised. "That we should train her as a physician?"

"No, but she could learn basic theories from the books we have in the library, and I could give her further practical instruction. That would ensure continuity when I am gone until the abbey secures a new physician."

"I have never heard of a woman practicing medicine." Kuno shook his head.

"What I am talking about," the infirmarian clarified, "are practical skills fortified with some of the theory found in Galen and Hippocrates."

"But can she read?"

"She knows basic Latin and reads the Bible with the anchoresses." In fact, I had been working my way through *de Urinis* since November and was more than half way through it. "Perhaps she could join the monastery school—"

"The school?" The abbot's eyebrows arched in astonishment. "But it is for boys!"

"I don't see why we could not make an exception; it would only be for a little while until she hones her skills."

But Kuno shook his head vigorously. "We cannot do that. Educating girls is unnecessary, and it is not what we do. Imagine the archbishop's reaction if he found out."

"The archbishop has just been freed from prison," Wigbert pointed out. "I think he has more important matters to attend to."

"That may be, but the Mainz canons are a meddlesome bunch, and they would not fail to lodge a complaint."

The infirmarian knew it was true; the episcopal bureaucracy was notorious for being a nuisance, and it was best not to attract their attention. "I suppose I could give her additional instruction in Latin," he offered. "Would you then allow her access to the library?"

The abbot shook his head again, and this time it was clear that it was not just the canons he was concerned about but his fellow monks who might be scandalized. Wigbert could easily imagine Prior Helenger haranguing against it in Chapter.

"You know as well as I do that it will not work." Kuno considered his friend through narrowed eyelids. "You seem to have a high opinion of Hildegard's intellect, but even if her Latin improves, what makes you think she can understand medical theories?"

Brother Wigbert knew that I could. "I have spent a great deal of time with her; she is bright and methodical, and grasps connections between facts faster than most people. I do not have to explain anything twice. That is why I have no doubt that under proper guidance, she can benefit from these texts." Then he added, musingly, "She tends not to accept answers as givens but wants to try for herself how things work. It is most unusual."

"So you are saying she is a skeptic?" The abbot picked up on it immediately. "What if she comes to question Church doctrines one day?"

"I have not seen anything that would suggest that," the infirmarian hastened to reassure him.

"She questions scientific facts but never our faith?"

Wigbert thought a while before speaking. This was as good a time as any to share with the abbot something else that was on his mind. "From some of the things Hildegard has told me about Sister Jutta, it seems that the rumors of bodily mortification are true. This may well be the reason why she does not want to stay permanently at the convent." He paused, and a heavy silence ensued. "I explained to her the concept of asceticism, but I think she is still grappling with it."

Abbot Kuno nodded sympathetically, but the look of discomfort did not vanish from his face. "She is still a child, but if she has such an inquiring mind, we should keep an eye on her."

"That is why I thought that proper monastic educa-tion — and not just Jutta's instruction — would be good for her."

Kuno sighed like a man out of options. "You may very well be right, but it would be problematic."

The infirmarian spread his arms in a gesture of defeat. But then the abbot added, dropping his voice although they were alone in the house, "I think, *however*, that *you* could bor-row books to refresh your memory of natural philosophy." He raised his eyebrows meaningfully. "As well as of Church Fathers."

Brother Wigbert understood immediately. As they part-ed a short time later, Kuno felt it necessary to add, "We must ensure that Hildegard's questioning does not lead her off the path charted by the Church. I leave it to you to oversee that, Brother."

That was how I laid my hands on my first library book, a translation of Lucretius' *De rerum natura*, in which he wrote that in order to discover truth, one had only to look at the natural world. I chuckled when Brother Wigbert told me how he had interrupted the nap Brother Fulbert was taking at his librarian's post, for the scriptorium at St. Disibod was a small and quiet place where only two manuscripts were being copied at any one time. Fulbert was therefore quite surprised to see the infirmarian appear before him, and more astonished still to learn that he had decided to reread major Christian texts. But he was also grateful for a relief from the tedium of his function, and he trotted off eagerly to fetch volumes of Ambrosius and Origen. Wigbert had asked for the Lucretius as if it were an afterthought, saying he needed to consult it on a medical matter.

By the end of the winter, I had worked my way through Lucretius, and in the spring, I did away with the strawberry patch to plant more fennel. Brother Wigbert had consented, although we would still be sending a portion of our yield to the kitchen.

Thanks to that arrangement, the mystery of the kitchen boy was finally solved. It happened when Brother Wigbert went to the town to buy ginger and cloves from the spice merchant. He was on his way out when he stopped at the gate. "I forgot to tell you."

I looked up from the herb bed I was weeding.

"The cook is sending someone to pick up fresh herbs. They ran out of the dry stock and there have been grumblings in the refectory." Without even realizing it, he patted his prominent stomach. "Would you prepare a few bunches of thyme, rosemary, and marjoram?"

I nodded obediently, although the new crop had only just come up. I was of the opinion that the kitchen should grow its own herbs in the sizable vegetable garden across the abbey. But I picked a few sprigs and took them to the workshop to rinse and tie up.

I was still at work when I heard a knock on the door. Without looking up from the basin, I bid the visitor come in.

"Good day," I said as the hinges squeaked behind me. "Please, make yourself comfortable. I am almost done."

"It is good to finally meet you, Sister."

I was shaking the water off the herbs and paused mid-movement as I realized I had heard that voice before. But I could not place it, so I laid the plants out on the counter and laughed. "I have not taken my vows yet, so you can call me Hildegard." The words were barely out of my mouth when it hit me like a bolt of lightning. I whirled around so fast I almost lost my balance.

The boy sprang up from the bench, a mix of fear and relief painted all over his face. We gazed at each other for a few heartbeats, then I managed, "It is *you*! The innkeeper's daughter!"

She joined her hands together. "Oh, please Sister . . . ah . . . Hildegard, please don't give me away!" She was taller now, but the deep green eyes were unmistakable. "They all think I'm a boy."

I could see how — her stocky silhouette and the cropped hair over the heart-shaped face gave her a rather boyish appearance. "But what are you doing here?" I was still incredulous, even though I knew that she was the boy I'd seen enter the abbey on the day Arnwald had been released. "And why are you in disguise?"

"I have always wanted to enter a convent." There was a pleading note in her voice. "But we are too poor."

I nodded. I remembered our meeting well.

Griselda continued, "After your visit, I could not think of anything else, so one day when my parents were away, I took my brother's old clothes, cut my hair, and left."

"Your parents don't know where you are?!"

Tears welled in her eyes and slowly rolled down her cheeks. She shook her head.

I patted her hand, too small for a boy, that rested on the rough wood of the table. "It will be fine." But in truth, I had no idea how this could ever end well; it was only a matter of time before she was discovered. My first shock over, I felt a surge of compassion for this child who had a dream but no way of realizing it.

"I really didn't mean to go away like that." Griselda wiped her eyes with the cuffs of her shirt. "But I want to be an anchoress, and I couldn't bear the talk of marrying me off to the baker's son."

I rubbed my forehead. "How long can you pretend to be someone you are not? And how is this going to help you accomplish your goal?"

"I don't know," she replied miserably. "I thought I would be able to earn enough for my dowry, but I am paid two silver pfennigs a week. I mainly just wanted to come here, and I knew they would not admit me if I showed up as a girl."

That was true enough. But this situation was bound to cause a scandal sooner or later, and then what would happen to her?

"Please don't give me away," Griselda repeated her plea. "I am happy here. The church is so beautiful, and Abbot Kuno gives such stirring sermons." Her face brightened as if a cloud had lifted.

The sense of kinship I had already felt during our first encounter more than two years before came back to me. I understood Griselda. "Of course not," I said softly, my hand still on hers, when the door opened and the frame filled almost completely with Brother Wigbert.

On impulse, we jumped apart.

"Welcome." He did not seem to have noticed anything out of the ordinary. "I see you are getting acquainted. What is your name, son? I think you told me when you were here last, but I am getting old and things escape me."

That was a good question.

"Christian, Brother," came the ready reply, and I had to stifle a smile. The girl was certainly resourceful; too bad she had not thought the plan through. I gathered the herbs and handed them to her.

"Give our best wishes to the brother kitchener. We hope he will find these to his liking."

Griselda smiled. "Thank you." She bowed to Brother Wigbert.

"God be with you, my son."

When her steps died down on the gravel outside, the infirmarian frowned. "What an unusual boy. Quiet. So unlike those urchins who work around the stables. Sometimes we can hear them in the church, and those walls are thick."

"He seems nice."

"He does." Wigbert replied, giving me a curious look.

I made another friend that spring. It happened when the season had reached that stage just before summer when nature was brimming with its most lively *viriditas*, pleasing the senses with the yellows, reds, and violets of late-blooming flowers and their heady scents.

There were still times when I felt sad about not being able to study in the monastery school, but the sight of the anchoress's chapel, its faded wood rising above the pink flowers of the rose bushes that separated it from the herb garden, was a constant reminder that I had avoided a worse fate. So I spent every moment I was not tending to patients in the garden, always thinking of better ways to organize it so as to maximize the yields.

I was working in the corner near the beehives when I made a curious discovery. It was the hottest hour of the day, the kind that intensifies the droning of the bees as they search for the last of the golden powder inside the fading blossoms. These hardworking creatures had always fascinated me, and I stopped my work to observe them as they came in and out of the beehives. I noticed two in particular that were climbing up one side of the hive, now turning toward each other and agitating their little wings, now moving apart, but always trudging in the same direction, which gave them the appearance of two quarreling friends. Then one of them took off and its companion, momentarily motionless as if stunned by this sudden departure, followed suit and both flew in their peculiar undulating fashion toward the abbey wall.

I followed them with my gaze and paused as I noticed something odd just opposite of where I stood: the wood of a section of the wall about three feet tall was darker and strangely shimmering, and the overhanging vines swayed gently even though the day was windless. I stepped closer and pushed the green tendrils aside, and saw that the bottom part of two beams had rotted through and crumbled to the ground while two others were in the process of doing so. That was what gave them a blackened appearance and caused moss to grow on them, resulting in a glossy veneer that glimmered when the occasional shaft of sunlight struck through the leaves. The hole that had formed allowed a draft that explained the swaying and rustling of the vines. As I contemplated my discovery, the nones bell rang out and I returned to the workshop, but, insignificant though the finding seemed, it tumbled about it my head for the next few days.

Until I understood why.

I chose the day carefully. The monks were spending the morning in Chapter to debate the progress of the renovation works, and Brother Wigbert would be away until after sext, which gave me ample time. I had told Jutta I was needed in the infirmary in his absence, and after checking on a few cases — and hoping there would not be any more for a while — I ran to the breach, lifted the vines, and examined the two rotten beams that still stood. They were too sturdy to push out by hand, so I fetched the garden hoe to break them, which allowed me to slip through.

A wave of exhilaration swept over me as if I had broken out of a cage. I twirled and threw my hands up in the air until I felt dizzy and had to stop. It had been so long!

I looked around. The breach gave onto a narrow path that ran alongside the outer abbey wall. It must have been well maintained once, but now it was overgrown with weeds. A few paces from the wall, the forest began and almost immediately sloped gently down toward the Glan. To the west

I could see the rooftops of Disibodenberg below. I knew the abbey vineyards were on the other side, sloping toward the Nahe, although I could not see them from there.

I pondered the implications of my discovery; now that I could come out, I should explore the woods to see which herbs grew in them. But, of course, I had to avoid being seen. With the forest on three sides, it would be easy enough to avoid the monks who went to the abbey mill to check on the work or to the riverside to collect fish for supper, for they never strayed from the direct path through the town. But my gray oblate robe would doubtless be familiar to any lay people who might be encountered in the forest.

I waited for Griselda's weekly visit and told her my secret. We were excited to share it, and she offered to procure a pair of trousers, a linen shirt, and a leather tunic for me. There were several servant boys around the abbey, and putting together an outfit should not be a problem. Indeed, I was in possession of a disguise of my own two days later.

I wore it under my robe and, once on the other side, hid the outer garment in the bushes. My first excursion took me away from the town and down toward the Glan, but I did not dare go as far as the riverbank. Instead, I ran and walked through the woods, rediscovering the delightful juiciness of a mouthful of fresh blackberries and the earthy taste of walnuts that satisfied a half-forgotten craving. Every now and then, I would stop to put my face to the rough bark of a tree and breathe its warm scent. I made careful note of the herbs I found, which were similar to those around Bermersheim. I spotted foxglove, angelica, wormwood, chamomile, yarrow, and many others, and was happy to find an abundance of horehound.

When I returned to the edge of the forest, I became aware of the sound of steps nearby. Light but deliberate, it was a person, not a beast. I stopped with bated breath, but the noise continued; in fact, it was growing closer. Small stones sprayed and dry twigs cracked under those unseen feet, and before I had time to lunge behind a nearby trunk, a boy emerged onto the path in front of me.

He looked to be about twelve and was a head shorter than I. He did not wear a robe, either, but I knew immediately that he was the one I had seen outside the church on the day of Brother Maurice's funeral. But this time he had a small bow slung across his chest, a few makeshift arrows stuck in his belt, and he carried a dead rabbit in his hand.

After a momentary look of surprise, he broke into a grin. He bowed and made an elaborate gesture with his free hand as if I were a high-born lady. But even as he leaned forward, his hazel eyes, flecked with green spots and shining with mischief, never left my face.

So much for the disguise. I was momentarily annoyed at what seemed like a mockery on his part, but his face, under a ruffle of brown hair, looked so friendly and his grin was so good-natured that I could not help but laugh.

"I am Volmar," he said gaily, straightening up. "And what do they call *you*?"

I hesitated. "Hildegard." The less said, the better.

He frowned, then recognition dawned on his face. "I knew you looked familiar! You are the oblate girl who helps Brother Wigbert in the infirmary."

I was mortified. No doubt he would tell the abbot, and I would be sent back to the convent.

"I am an oblate too," he announced matter-of-factly. "I saw you in the church. I remember because we never see girls there" — that impish smile again — "except for a few from the town on feast days."

The words came out of my mouth before I could check myself. "So what are you doing *here*?"

We gazed at each other for a few moments, then burst out laughing.

"Same thing as you, by the look of it!" Volmar appraised me from head to foot. "Though my disguise is not nearly as clever."

"I found a gap in the wall," I explained, feeling a surge of trust in my new acquaintance. "I missed the forest. It is the only place where one can find such perfect, pure green." I ran my fingers over the leaves of a nearby ash. "Besides, there are many more herbs growing here than in our garden."

He nodded. "We both have our reasons, then." He lifted the rabbit up for me to admire. "I used to hunt with my father before I came here."

"How long have you been sneaking out?" It was probably a while, I guessed, given his tanned, freckled face and obvious familiarity with the forest.

"Since Easter." Volmar waved toward the abbey. "The breach I come out through is near the kitchen. I discovered it not long after I arrived here, a year ago this summer." He paused as if marveling at that fact, but the smile soon returned to his face, where it seemed to be a frequent and natural guest.

It was getting late, and I took a step toward where my robe was hidden. I had to pass by him, and he moved aside. "Say," he called after me. "Maybe we could go together sometimes?"

I turned, surprised. I enjoyed these solitary excursions, but I realized it would be good to have company. "I would like that." I said, suddenly feeling shy.

He laughed again, then disappeared down the path.

10

August 1118

"I THINK I prefer this to the Bible," I said out loud before I had a chance to stop myself, so impressed was I by an erudite passage in a translation of Galen. Having finished Lucretius, I had turned to the famous Greek's anatomical drawings, the humoral theory, and the ways of reestablishing bodily equilibrium.

"You shouldn't say that," Brother Wigbert admonished me dutifully. "It is a sacred text from which all human wisdom proceeds, and it takes precedence over anything written by physicians and philosophers." But while his words were meant to refocus me on the proper hierarchy of knowledge, his tone was indulgent, and I thought I even heard a smile in his voice.

"Of course, Brother." I corrected myself. "I did not mean to suggest that human knowledge is above the word of God, only that the way this is written speaks to me so . . . *clearly*."

"And why is that?"

I thought about it. "Maybe because it is not composed of stories that must be explained by a priest." I paused, searching for the right words. "Galen writes about what causes disease, which we always ask ourselves when we become sick but often cannot answer. For example, he explains that pestilence is spread by corrupt air, and I understand that because I once travelled with my father to Bingen to sell the salt from our mine, and we passed by a large swamp that smelled so foul we had to change our route to avoid taking ill from the vapors."

"Miasmas are one of the six factors that tip the balance of humors toward disease." Brother Wigbert took the opportunity to move the lesson along. "The other ones are inappropriate nourishment, excessive rest, lack of sleep, retention, and passions of the soul."

"Only six?" I was surprised.

"Yes. Why?"

"Because the Bible mentions other causes too. It says that disease is God's punishment for sin and only those who obey Him will be spared." I searched my memory for the exact phrasing of one of Sister Jutta's favorite psalms. "'Whoever dwells in the shelter of the Most High will rest in the shadow of the Almighty. He will save you from the fowler's snare and from the deadly pestilence. You will not fear the terror of night, nor the arrow that flies by day, nor the pestilence that stalks in the darkness, nor the plague that destroys at midday. A thousand may fall at your side, ten thousand at your right hand, but it will not come near you. You will only observe with your eyes and see the punishment of the wicked . . .'" I stopped for a breath. "If that is the case, why did Galen not include God's punishment among the causes?"

The monk scratched his tonsure. "The Bible's wisdom is immutable and thus not subject to scientific study. Galen based his writings and his practice on the works of Hippocrates, another Greek who had investigated natural phenomena, to draw his conclusions."

"Of course!" I struck my forehead. "They were pagans, and therefore the word of God was not known to them." Then I frowned. "So who do we believe?"

"The Greeks were keen observers of nature and wrote of causes that we have come to accept as self-evident. But as Christians, we see them as the tools with which God chastises his people." It was an issue, I realized later, that he and his fellow students at Salerno must have pondered many times. And the answer he gave me must have been their way of reconciling their sources.

There was another contradiction that bothered me. "If God punishes the wicked with sickness, why do so many babes die still in their mothers' arms when they have not yet committed a sin?"

"That, my child, is a great mystery of our faith," Brother Wigbert replied in the same tone Jutta employed when I persisted in my inquiries, and I knew there was no point in arguing. Besides, my thoughts were already wandering. I had not been outside in days and wanted to go down to the riverbank.

As soon as the bell rang and the infirmarian left for the church, I changed into the shirt and trousers and went to the back of the garden, wondering if I would meet Volmar.

He had joined me on one outing three weeks earlier. I had just left my robe in the shrubbery when I saw him sitting under a nearby oak, chewing a blade of grass. He had extended a palm full of hulled walnuts and flashed his customary grin. "Finally! I have come here three days in a row and was beginning to think you'd given up."

"Of course not!" I took a few nuts and we walked down the slope away from the abbey. "I have been busy, and I don't have a set time for this anyway. I come out whenever I can."

"You are lucky. Our days are so planned out that I can only do it during the hour of rest."

I could not help but smile. Under my special arrangement, I had almost forgotten how structured the Benedictine life was. The Rule clearly laid out the eight daily services of the Divine Office; the remaining time was devoted to study and work, and the hour before vespers was dedicated to rest. It had once been my daily life, and it would be again, one day.

"You'd better not go too far, then," I cautioned, noting the deepening shadows under the green canopy of the trees. "I have work to finish for Brother Wigbert, but I have enough time before nightfall for a walk."

"Are you skipping the services now too?" Volmar's voice assumed a tone of mock severity.

I flushed, but seeing his amusement, I laughed. "Sometimes," I admitted. "The sisters think I am too busy in the infirmary and don't ask questions." I felt a little guilty, so I added, "God can hear me anywhere."

"You are right," he said in the same matter-of-fact tone I already knew and liked. "Unfortunately, Brother Philipp would not fail to notice my absence, and I would be in trouble."

I had enjoyed that first walk together and found myself hoping it would become our regular habit, disciplinary risks notwithstanding. Now I scrambled through the breach, looked around, and sure enough, there he was. But instead of the bow and arrows, he carried a wax tablet and stylus. "I will show you the new Latin words we learned at school today," he announced as we started down toward the river.

We sat on the grassy bank in the shade of a white poplar. He wrote out the words, then handed the tablet to me. I took it eagerly, for I wanted to show off too. I wrote the first line of a new chant: *O frondens virga, in tua nobilitate stans sicut aurora procedit.* Then I sang it out.

"I like it." He looked up into the branches swaying above our heads, the shimmering sunlight streaming between the silver-bottomed leaves and dappling the ground with ever-shifting patches of light. "O leafy branch, standing in your nobility as the dawn breaks forth," he translated. He closed his eyes, savoring the words. "Did you compose it yourself?"

"Yes."

"How does the rest go?"

Suddenly, I felt shy. I had been working on it in secret because Jutta disapproved of music that was not about God or the Holy Virgin. I was also not sure about my Latin. "Maybe next time." I put the tablet aside and leaned back against the trunk. "Tell me about your family."

Volmar was the middle of three sons, but his little brother had succumbed to whooping cough before his first birthday, and his mother had died shortly thereafter. The family had extensive lands north of Mainz, and it had been a tradition for generations for the eldest son to inherit the estate, and for the younger ones to enter the Church. As a result, Volmar's relatives numbered among the most illustrious ecclesiastics in the Rhineland. They included a dozen abbots and bishops as well as Siegfried, the long-time archbishop of Mainz during the previous century who had sided with Pope Gregorius against the old emperor. The inheritance system ensured that the family's wealth had remained intact, and to Volmar, that arrangement was completely natural. He had been prepared for the monastic life ever since he could remember, just like I had been.

He did, however, miss hunting with his father, riding ponies, and swimming in the ponds that dotted the estate, so he had embraced the unexpected opportunity for outdoor excursions with enthusiasm and fashioned a bow from the wood of a young yew tree. With a knife pilfered from the kitchen, he had made arrows to hunt rabbits that he then stealthily dropped off among the game and poultry waiting to be cooked for supper. Sometimes he amused himself by fishing, though he had not been able to procure enough rope to make a net and had to do it with his bare hands.

"Really?" I lifted a skeptical eyebrow. "Aren't they too slippery for that?"

"I'll show you." He jumped up. The river was shallow where we were, and he waded up to his thighs, standing firm on the rocky bottom with the familiarity born of experience. For some moments all was still, and I held my breath as he scanned the current, the silence broken only by the waves lapping against the bank. He spotted something and bent slowly, arching his back, then thrust both arms into the river as swiftly as a heron going for a tadpole. There was a bit of commotion, and the water whirled and foamed. Volmar straightened up, water dripping from his arms and from the frantic creature he was gripping with such force that his knuckles had gone white. He had one hand just above the fish's tail and the other between the head and the stomach, under the gills. That gave him enough control, for after a few more moments of thrashing, the fish started to exhaust itself. Soon it was quite still but for occasional spasms, like a final silent protest. When it ceased all movement, Volmar relaxed his grip and grinned triumphantly.

"The cook will find a random carp among the venison for tonight."

"That was amazing!"

He waded back. "The carp are fat and slow this time of the year; that is why I could catch this one so easily."

"Still!" My admiration was genuine.

"Do you want me to show you how to do it?"

My attempt ended with a lot of laughter and splashing as two fish escaped from under our feet, startled by my unsteadiness on the uneven bottom.

With the carp swinging on a rope between us, I pointed out various herbs on the way back and explained their applications. Volmar declared himself impressed with my knowledge. In a fit of pride, I showed him the cuts on my fingers, already healed to fading pink lines, from my first attempt at pruning the fruit trees in the spring.

Our chatter was interrupted by the sound of footsteps from the direction of the abbey. We froze. Even the wind seemed to subside for a moment. All was silent, and the hot air was still. The footsteps grew louder, then Griselda emerged around the bend straight ahead of us.

I let out a breath of relief as Volmar looked from me to her, puzzled. I was surprised too, for although Griselda ran occasional errands to pick up fish from the fishermen who worked the stretch of the river belonging to the abbey, she usually took a path well west of there. Besides, she was not carrying a fish bucket — or anything else.

I was in a bind; I could hardly ask Griselda what she was doing without letting on that we knew each other. That Griselda was known as a boy made it trickier. I cast a quick glance at Volmar and saw the look of tense concentration on his face that comes just before recognition lights up the darkness of confusion. It made my decision easier.

"You have probably seen Christian before." I said. Volmar nodded. I added, "Her real name is Griselda. She is from a village across the Nahe."

Griselda's eyes widened in alarm, but I walked up to her and put a comforting arm around her shoulders. "Don't worry. Volmar is my friend, and he will keep your secret." I turned to him. "Won't you?"

He gazed at us steadily for an exaggerated moment, then the corners of his mouth lifted and broke into a broad grin. The boy recognized good mischief when he saw it. "You can count on it! It is too amusing to put an end to it," he added appreciatively.

We breathed a sigh of relief, although Griselda's was much louder. I felt she trusted my judgment.

"But I want to know why you are pretending to be a boy." Volmar's eyes sparkled with curiosity. "It looks like there is a lot going on around here that Father Abbot has no idea about, and I wonder if your reasons are as good as ours."

"They are," Griselda spoke for the first time, softly but firmly. "I am sure Hildegard will tell you all about it, but now I have to speak as to my reason for seeking her out." She turned to me. "Sister Jutta is fallen gravely ill, and Brother Wigbert is looking for you everywhere."

11

August 1118

THE INFIRMARIAN'S GRAVE countenance welcomed me at the door of the workshop. I had already decided to offer no explanation for my absence unless he asked, but he had other things on his mind.

"Sister Jutta is delirious with a fever but will not be brought to the infirmary," he spoke in a clipped tone of urgency. "The anchoresses are asking for a medicine to restore her." He held out a stoppered flask which I knew contained diluted oil of valerian, most likely not what she needed.

"I will go right away. I will need some wine," I added, for the convent did not keep a store of its own.

"I already sent a flagon."

I took the flask and hurried to the enclosure. I had been expecting this for a while, what with Jutta's sleepless nights, poor diet, and harrowing spiritual regimen. In fact, I was surprised that whatever it was—and it had to be serious for the sisters to seek outside help—had not happened years before.

I found her in the dorter, lying on Juliana's pallet. When I approached, Juliana, who had been bathing Jutta's forehead in cool water, rose silently and moved back. A layer of perspiration covered the *magistra*'s face, and her skin was flushed and warm to touch.

"What other symptoms does she have?" I asked.

"Nothing more than this sudden weakness and fever. She was with us in the chapel but faltered at the end of nones and never rose from her knees."

Hearing our voices, Jutta opened her eyes and a grimace of discomfort crossed her emaciated face. I leaned closer. "Sister, can you speak to me about what's ailing you?"

But there was no recognition in her eyes. They were glossed over with the unnatural shine of the fever. She closed them again, and her features relaxed in a sign that her senses had left her once more, taking the pain with them.

I rubbed my forehead. This was no ordinary fever. The season of chills had not arrived yet. Besides, they came with coughs and congestion. As I pondered this, I became aware of the stifling air inside the chamber. I moved to open the shutters. It was late August and still light out despite the evening hour. A fresh breeze wafted in, scented with the earthy aroma of the approaching autumn.

"You can go," I said to Juliana as the vesper bell rang out. "I will keep watch over her."

When she was gone, I pulled down Jutta's blanket to allow her feverish body to cool. It was then that the faintly sweet, unmistakable odor of a festering wound assailed my nostrils. I surveyed the sackcloth-clad figure and found nothing immediately amiss, but of course I knew what her back was regularly subjected to. It had to be the source of the infection. It would also account for the high fever, which could be deadly given her weakened condition.

After vespers I went back for a bot[]
gar and some leaves of betony, sorrel, and []
remedies—I had collected by the river an []
in a corner of the workshop.

When I returned, Juliana and Adel[]
a vigil together at the sickbed. They raise[] [].....g .y .. ..
me, and I wondered if they knew about our superior's nocturnal activities.

"The fever is likely from an infection of a cut . . . or cuts.
I have brought vinegar and fresh plasters to dress them."

Their faces expressed no great alarm or surprise, which
answered my silent question eloquently enough. I could
not help wondering if either of them, or both, also practiced
mortification of the flesh. But I dismissed the thought and
focused on the task at hand.

"We must turn her over and strip her back bare," I said.

They stood in silence, unsure how to proceed, so I slid
my palms under Jutta's left flank. It was so meager that I
could feel every rib as if the only thing that stood between
them and my fingers was the coarse fabric of her robe. "If
you take hold of her hip"—I motioned to Juliana "and you
her shoulder"—I turned to Adelheid—"we should be able to
turn her."

But as we moved to heave the left side of her body—
surprisingly light even for one as thin as Jutta—her eyes flew
open so suddenly that we gasped and let go. Juliana took a
step back and Adelheid clung to my side, and I realized that
in the last three years I had grown taller than the diminutive
anchoress.

Jutta stared at us. Although there was no telling if she
recognized us, she looked terrified.

"Sister," I ventured. "You are ill and you need medicine. We must take off your robe."

"No!" Jutta protested, firmly enough. "No!"

"It is necessary, otherwise you will not heal." I touched
her shoulders, hoping that there might be persuasion in action.

No!" she cried. Her voice, suffused with pain, stopped in my tracks.

Adelheid fell to her knees and started praying.

"You will die if you don't let me treat you."

But Jutta crossed her hands over her hips and thighs in a protective gesture that might have been virginal modesty had there not been something wild in her face. The alarm that had brought her out of her stupor was beginning to take its toll; her lips quivered and her eyes swelled with tears.

I felt a surge of pity. "As you wish, Sister." I reached for the blanket and covered her again, then brought a cup of wine to her lips. Jutta took a small sip and fell back, closing her eyes. "I think we should take turns watching over her." I turned to the anchoresses. "I will start while you get some rest."

We sat at Jutta's bedside during the night and the following day, trying in vain to persuade her to accept treatment. At most, she allowed her feet, hands, and forehead to be bathed with yarrow water to bring down the fever, which did not help much. Most of the time she seemed insensible, and it was only then that her features would smooth out and the traces of her former beauty emerge in the delicate oval of her face and the fine shape of her cheekbones.

But there were also periods when she was shaken by agitation and spoke unintelligibly, often ending with this warning: "God looks on our deeds, and His anger is great! If we don't undertake penance, our punishment will be a thousand-fold . . . Oh, it will never end!"

On the morning of the third day, I helped her to some wine and put a cloth soaked in yarrow water on her forehead.

"You are wasting your efforts. Better pray for my soul," Jutta said with surprising lucidity.

"I can pray for your soul *while* I bring you relief and offer a cure. Will you let me?"

She shook her head. "God sends suffering, and it is for us to bear it till it pleases Him to release us. Health, life, and death can only proceed from Him."

"But I may be the instrument through which He acts," I suggested.

"We have no right to reverse the course of God's plan. I am happy He has chosen to try me in this way, for it is by being steadfast and meek in the face of adversity that we can obtain forgiveness and hope for salvation."

I remained silent as I realized that for Jutta, this was yet another opportunity to repent for the sins of the world and make a sacrifice on the altar of its redemption. Indeed, what offense could *she* be guilty of?

"This body," she resumed after a while, laying her hand on her sunken belly, "is not mine to tend to as if it were a garden plant. The body is but a shell that carries our soul on this dreary journey. It will be discarded at the end as we ascend to the true life."

This was followed by several hours of fitful sleep, during which the fever rose once again, and the odor of the infection became more pronounced. Even the sisters, accustomed though they were to the smells of the enclosure, noticed it. I had to bring in freshly cut fir branches that Brother Wigbert used in such cases. Fortunately, the heat had finally broken. It started to rain, which helped the balsamic fragrance to spread more effectively and purify the air.

But time was running out for Jutta. As I contemplated this, I felt angry at what I believed to be a distortion of faith, perhaps a sin in itself.

Finally, a solution dawned on me. When Jutta opened her eyes and asked for a drink of water, I took advantage of the sisters' absence to reason with her one last time. "I have thought much about what you said, Sister, and it has stirred me so!" Something akin to contentment flickered in her eyes. It lasted only a moment, but her body relaxed a little. "Yet I fear that if you die, we who remain in this convent will lose the beacon that shines so brightly for us." I paused. "Please, Sister, stay with us for our sakes. Your mission is not yet complete!"

The plea made the desired impression, for Jutta's eyes focused more clearly and something — was it disbelief? — flashed across her face. She must have thought me beyond retrieve. "But if this is what God wills?" she asked with effort.

I grasped at it. "How can we know what God intends for us? We won't until we are no more. And it is a grave sin to bring about one's own demise." I was conscious of the risk of speaking thus to my superior and the possibility of losing any chance of convincing her to accept treatment.

Jutta closed her eyes, but her breathing showed that she was not asleep. After a while, she opened them again. "What medicines have you?" Her voice was resigned, and I was astonished at this unnatural inclination to see a cure as an unpleasant necessity rather than welcome relief. But there was no time to lose; I moved swiftly to the table where the vinegar, the jar of moist leaves, and a quantity of fresh linen had been laid out for four days.

"The vinegar will cleanse the wounds," I explained in the same tone I used with infirmary patients, "and the plasters will speed up the healing. When I change the dressing later, I will rub honey on the broken skin to protect it from malignant influences."

But when I made a move to help Jutta turn over, she raised her hand to check me. "I will do it myself."

"You cannot reach your own back." I shook my head as if I were taking to a child.

"Reaching the Kingdom of Heaven is difficult," Jutta replied in a tone that precluded further argument. "This is not."

"Let me do this for you to ensure that the entire area is treated," I persisted.

Jutta looked straight at me with the same desperate expression I had already seen before. "I will manage." After a pause for breath, she added, "Trust me!"

I was puzzled but also astonished at this plea. *Trust me!* They were the first words of such power and intimacy Jutta had ever spoken to me. I said no more and withdrew from the dorter, closing the door behind me.

There was nothing to do but wait, and the strain began to take a toll on Adelheid, who barely ate and often fell asleep during her vigils. Fearing oncoming exhaustion, I began to relieve her of the duty. I sat for hours by Jutta's bed, watching anxiously for signs of improvement or deterioration, spending more time inside the convent than I had done in more than two years.

But my mind was often on the questions that animated Jutta's unbending spirit and had taken her to the brink of self-destruction: the purpose of life, the meaning of suffering, and the route to salvation. They were terribly complicated, but I had already begun to understand that the way to make at least some sense of them was to pay attention to the signs through which God communicated His design.

Outside, the summer had turned into autumn, and my gaze often wandered to the window. On the far side of the herb garden, the trees stood in mature majesty, their tops already flaming with the gaudy splendor of the season. Even the birds nesting among the branches had lost their urgent chirruping notes, and their songs assumed mellower, reflective tones. As always, this contrast between the expansive life outside and the withdrawn, almost resentful existence of the convent oppressed me so much that sometimes, for a few heartbeats, I was unable to draw breath.

Once I gasped so loudly that Adelheid looked up from her breviary. I lowered my head apologetically, but my thoughts drifted back to my earlier preoccupations. The image of God as a severe judge who keeps a score of transgressions—prone to anger, hard to placate, and harsh in punishment—to which Jutta was so devoted did not satisfy me.

To me, God was inextricably linked to those warm afternoons bathed in the sunlight that streamed through the windows of my family's chapel. He was the source of the *viriditas* that breathed life into every creature from a blade of grass to man—a loving, benevolent force. God the Creator communicated with us through His work, and that work—all of nature—showed that He was generous and kind. All we needed to live a healthy, wholesome life was to accept that gift.

As if to prove it, Jutta opened her eyes that afternoon, and for the first time in many days, they did not shine with fever.

When I returned to the infirmary, it was beginning to fill with the first cases of seasonal chills and coughs. I warmed elderberry wine, boiled fennel in water, and made a mint-based ointment to be rubbed onto the chest, where the body's heat caused the pungent vapor to release and relieve congestion. I also made horehound lozenges, which the patients reported soothed their throats and made them cough less. Brother Wigbert left most of the herbal work to me and only cautioned me not to talk to the monks about it, so they were the only ones who did not experience the benefits of my remedies.

All through this I cared for Jutta, until one day I was able to report that she had risen from her bed to attend the service of prime.

"Father Abbot will be glad to hear that." The infirmarian regarded me with pride. "You have done a fine job, better than any of my previous apprentices would have."

Under any other circumstances, I would have basked in the compliment and in his reference to me as 'an apprentice' rather than a mere helper, but I had other things on my mind. "I have been asking myself these last few weeks whether Sister Jutta really does follow The Rule as it was laid out by our founder," I ventured.

"What do you mean?" He looked curious, but his curiosity was tinged with the concern I had already seen. "She may be an anchoress, but she is also a Benedictine nun."

"She is, without a doubt, but . . ." I searched for the right words. "She seems to have her own version of the monastic life. We live very differently from the monks, though we follow the same daily routine of services." I paused, unsure if I should go on, but since I had already started I might as well finish. "The life in the enclosure is based on The Rule only very generally; it is much stricter than the Blessed Benedict demanded." By then I had read and memorized the whole of the *Regula Benedicti*.

Brother Wigbert set the flask of poppy juice he had been mixing with wine aside and turned to me. "What you should understand," he said after a momentary hesitation, "is that the women of St. Disibod are strongly attached to the doctrine formulated by St. Augustine, one of the Church Fathers."

I had heard of that saint but did not know much about him, so he explained, "Augustine, who lived eight centuries ago, found God late in life and became converted to our Catholic faith after a dissolute youth. He believed that humanity inherited the sin of Adam, and a Christian life should be dedicated to atoning for that sin to achieve redemption. Augustine also taught that although body and soul are both essential elements that constitute a human being, they are in constant struggle with each other on account of the original sin, with the soul being morally superior to the weak and corruptible body."

That certainly sounded like Jutta. "Did he mean, then," I wondered, "that we are all born sinful, even before we have the mind to turn to vice?"

"Yes, in principle. And some of his followers have interpreted that as a suggestion that the only way to salvation is through perpetual penance and bodily mortification, so the soul can soar toward God pure and holy and untainted by passions."

"That is such a bleak view!" The image of the knotted whip streaking Jutta's back with blood at the darkest hour of the night flashed before my eyes.

Wigbert nodded like a schoolmaster acknowledging a student's challenge. "It would appear so, but St. Augustine left a gate of hope open. If we let divine grace enter our hearts, we can be saved."

"What can divine grace do?"

"Enlighten us so we can tell good from evil, strengthen us against temptation, and inspire us to do good works."

As I pondered this, he finished the poppy infusion and motioned for me to follow him to the infirmary. We passed the cot where a woman from across the Glan was recovering from a hernia, another occupied by a monk with jaundice, and approached a cobbler from Disibodenberg. He was the one in need of merciful sleep, for the once stoutly built man had been reduced to skin and bones by the wasting disease. He groaned when the infirmarian raised his head to help him drink.

As we watched the cobbler drift off, I asked, "How many Church Fathers are there?"

"Eight." Wigbert wiped sweat from the man's face with a towel soaked in rosewater from a bowl I held for him.

"So Augustine's teachings are not the only ones to follow?"

"No, although he is considered one of the Great Church Fathers, along with Ambrosius, Hieronymus, and Gregorius the Great, and his is an officially upheld doctrine."

"But not all Christians adhere to it as much as Sister Jutta," I protested, remembering Otto of Bamberg. "For example, the bishop who comes here for the feast of St. Disibod every year is fat and wears sparkling jewels like a king —"

"Keep your voice down!" Brother Wigbert hissed, casting a wary glance at the neighboring cot where the jaundiced monk was resting.

I obeyed. "What St. Augustine teaches seems so impractical," I whispered. "It does not help those who don't know about doctrines but want to live good lives."

The infirmarian sighed as he arranged the cobbler's blanket. "Let's go back to the workshop." As we walked past the peasant woman with the hernia, he winced and stretched his fingers. "My joints are beginning to ache again in this damp weather."

When we emerged into the chilly November evening, he turned to me, and his tone had something definitive about it. "We are talking about things that are not subject to debate, Hildegard. Church doctrines are not meant to be agreed or disagreed with—or critiqued, for that matter. They are to be accepted, and it is best that you remember that."

12

April 1119

T HE ABBOT WANTED an account of Jutta's health.
"Don't be nervous; Father Abbot is a kind man," Brother
Wigbert assured me. But it was not the idea of talking to Kuno
that I was worried about. It had been eight months since the
magistra had first taken ill, and the fever had returned twice.
She had not let me cleanse and dress her wounds, insisting
on doing it herself. Although she had recovered, I still did
not know how serious her injuries were or if the cycle of the
relapses could somehow be stopped.

I was also concerned that Prior Helenger—who har-
bored an inexplicable dislike for me, evident in the contemp-
tuous gaze of his cold gray eyes as if my mere presence was
an offense—would use my inability to help her against me,
and try to send me back to the convent.

But I did not want Brother Wigbert to guess my fears, so I lifted my chin and hoped that my smile was confident enough. "I am ready, Brother."

It was unusually hot for April and the sun was beating on our heads as we crossed the courtyard. Volmar and a young monk emerged from the cloister, each carrying a set of gardening tools. They were bound for the abbey orchards where Volmar was assigned to work that spring, and I had to fight the urge to run and join him. Instead, I inclined my head as they greeted us.

"God be with you, Brothers," the infirmarian called out cheerfully, "and may He send you a cool breeze to make your work lighter." Then he turned to me, wiping his brow. "On days like these I am truly grateful to be able to work in a shaded workshop."

The abbot's house had been rebuilt in stone, a fitting dwelling for the head of an abbey with a growing reputation in the Rhineland. The parlor was pleasantly cool, and seemed rather dim until our eyes adjusted from the glare outside. But soon the contours of a spacious, sparsely furnished chamber came into view. Arched windows gave onto the cemetery and the vineyards beyond, and a big desk carved of dark wood stood nearby to make optimal use of daylight. It was covered with a quantity of parchments and a tray with the abbey seal and a block of wax. A simple cross with an oil lamp at its foot hung on the wall, and the hearth, cold and empty now, was twice as big as its predecessor in the old house, or so Brother Wigbert later told me.

Abbot Kuno motioned us to sit across his desk. As the prior was nowhere in sight, I felt my nervousness ebb away.

"Father, we bring good tidings from the convent where Sister Jutta seems to be on the road to recovery again," Brother Wigbert announced.

"God be praised," the abbot replied, a little wearily, I thought. "She is a holy woman and a great treasure of this abbey."

"Indeed. And Hildegard deserves the credit, for she has spent these last few months treating Sister Jutta with remedies of her own making," the infirmarian added. "Her accomplishments in the art of healing rival those of students twice her age."

The abbot regarded me thoughtfully, and I blushed at this acknowledgment of my skill. I always found it hard to bask in compliments, which made me shy. I held his gaze nonetheless.

"And what sort of remedies are those?"

"Diluted vinegar to wash the cuts; plasters of betony, sorrel, and lovage to dress them; and a honey rub to soothe and protect the skin," I replied.

I waited with bated breath for him to object to the use of the 'wild' ingredients, but something else caught his attention. "So her fever resulted from cuts?" He frowned.

I shot a glance at Brother Wigbert who gave a slight nod. "Yes, Father. I believe so."

"And how did she come by them?" His frown deepened.

"I believe she had inflicted them upon herself"—I took a deep breath—"by means of a scourge."

The abbot's fallen face told me he had known, or at least suspected it, for some time. "What is the extent of these . . . injuries?"

"I cannot say because Sister Jutta will not let me dress them." I dropped my gaze, feeling inexplicably guilty. "She insists on applying the medicines herself."

The abbot looked puzzled. "Perhaps that is just her modesty," he said hopefully. "She follows strict rules that don't allow another person to see her body, even if it is a physician or"—he hesitated—"his assistant."

But I was not convinced. There was something about Jutta's demeanor that still bothered me, and it was not just the difficulty of self-treating one's back. It was also the length of time it had taken her to recover from what were unlikely

122

to have been deep lesions. Then there was the fever and the relapses. But, try as I might, I could not make any sense of it.

Abbot Kuno's voice broke through my musings. "What about Sister Adelheid? Are her indispositions also the effect of mortification of the flesh?"

"I doubt it," I said. "Sister Jutta's practices may be something Adelheid aspires to, but she does not seem capable of going that far. Most likely she is suffering from nerves. I make wine mixed with valerian oil for her, though it has yet to produce an improvement."

That was hardly good news, yet he looked relieved. "Mortification may be encouraged by some in our Church, but it is not a practice I want to see spreading about this abbey," he said as if it were my responsibility to enforce that rule. Then, before either of us could say anything, he changed the subject. "Come on Friday for our monthly supper, Brother," he addressed the infirmarian, "and we will discuss this year's fair. The archbishop will be joining us."

I gasped. "The Archbishop of Mainz?! But I thought he was in prison."

Brother Wigbert gave me a surprised look. "He was, but with God's help, he is free now."

I knew it was not my place to discuss politics, but I could not help myself. High matters of state held a great fascination for me. "The battle at Welfesholz must have really weakened the emperor if he released the archbishop. Does that mean the dispute over inve . . . *investiture* has been settled?"

The abbot stared at me; he knew nothing about my accidental eavesdropping on him and the Bishop of Bamberg three years before. "No." He raised an eyebrow. "The papal faction's victory caused significant losses for Emperor Heinrich, but it did not weaken him enough. He is now in Italy and no doubt plotting further mischief. But," he added pointedly, looking from me to the hapless Brother Wigbert, "you need not concern yourself with such things."

Taking this as a dismissal, the infirmarian rose with a reproachful look in my direction. He took his leave of the abbot, and I followed him outside. Many questions swirled in my head on the way back to the workshop, but I dared not ask them, knowing I had already tested his patience. But as we reached the garden, I saw that despite his effort to look stern, the eyes that met mine were affectionate. "I don't understand why the emperor wants to be able to name bishops." I risked one more question. "He is not a priest. Isn't that the Church's business?"

With a sigh, Brother Wigbert led me to the bench under the fruit trees. After some deliberation, he said, "I am, like Father Abbot, of the opinion that you should not spend your time contemplating worldly things. It is not for us monastics. But since I know you will keep asking until you get an answer" — he smiled half-ruefully, half-indulgently — "I will satisfy your curiosity. Better that than if you were to inquire of the archbishop directly when he is here."

And so, shielded from the sharp glow of the early afternoon sun by the young foliage, we sat side by side as he began to explain the origins of the long-running dispute, just as he had done with medical theories.

"This investiture conflict has been going on for years and has grown more complicated with time. It is not something that will be so easily solved as you might think. Do you know of the history?"

I shook my head.

"It started more than forty years ago, when Pope Gregorius, the seventh of that name, asserted his right to install bishops over Emperor Heinrich's father, who was then in power. The old Heinrich, being a proud and ambitious prince, was outraged and called on German bishops to sign a letter rejecting the papal claim. He sacked those who had refused, then he demanded that the pope resign."

"I'm sure that did not go over well with the Holy Father."

124

Brother Wigbert chuckled, then grew serious again. "It did not. Gregorius excommunicated the bishops who remained loyal to the crown, then excommunicated Heinrich himself and denied his sovereignty over the empire's lands."

"And there has been fighting ever since?" I asked breathlessly.

"Years of struggle. Some of the nobility, mainly the Saxons, rebelled and allied themselves with the papal forces to overthrow King Heinrich. They elected Rudolf, Duke of Swabia, as anti-king. But Rudolf was defeated, and Heinrich appointed the Archbishop of Ravenna as anti-pope. I still remember his consecration . . ."

Brother Wigbert gazed into the distance at the faded images from his youth. "It was in the year 1084. I was a student visiting Rome from Salerno, and the fighting between the forces supporting the rival popes was fierce. A few days after his installment, Clement, the anti-pope, crowned Heinrich Holy Roman Emperor at St. Peter's." A grimace of pain flashed across the old monk's face. "Soon afterwards the Holy City was sacked by the Normans and their Saracen allies amid a fury of plunder and rape."

I was horrified and mesmerized in equal measure. Until then, I'd had no idea how relentless and violent that conflict had been. The notion that kings would claim the right to control who occupies Church offices, and to interfere in its affairs in such a blatant way, angered me. "Did the old emperor ever reconcile with Pope Gregorius?"

Wigbert shook his head. "Not with Gregorius, nor with the three or four popes who succeeded him. Heinrich went to his grave at loggerheads with the Church's authorities, though he remained popular among lower clergy. And his son, our current emperor, had good relations with Rome at first but eventually followed in his father's footsteps. In fact, he has gone even farther, putting forth demands for Church lands to be turned over to the crown. The Archbishop of

Mainz is firmly opposed to this, and that is what had cost him his freedom."

"The emperors have been treating the Church as their plaything," I said hotly. "No wonder the archbishop preferred to go to prison in its defense like a true martyr!"

In the silence that followed, the chirping of the birds and the buzzing of the insects suddenly seemed more intense, as if they too were expressing their indignation.

Then Brother Wigbert spoke again in a measured tone. "The Church certainly has the right—nay, the duty—to preserve its spiritual domain and its property. But . . ." he paused, reflecting. "The fault lies on both sides, not only with the emperors. Beginning with Gregorius, popes have been trying to assert their authority beyond the godly realm to include worldly power as well. Many clerics agree with that line, but to me it has never been clear that it is in the Church's best interest to interfere in secular affairs."

I nodded, now understanding the complexity. This was my second lesson in Church politics, and it would one day pit me against its hierarchy. But only the top hierarchy, for common clergy, like Brother Wigbert, seemed to understand that simple truth.

13

July 1119

T HE MONTH OF July, when the feast of St. Disibod, the patron saint of the abbey, was celebrated, was always a merry time at Disibodenberg. Before High Mass, a procession of all able-bodied townspeople would follow the relics around the church, and afterwards the fair would officially open in the town square. The monks avoided the market, for it was hardly a holy event, full as it was of itinerant musicians, jugglers, soothsayers, pet monkeys, and hawkers of all manner of goods vying for customers' attention. Only Brother Wigbert took interest — and only professionally so — by preparing the infirmary for the inevitable bloodied noses, cut lips, and broken arms.

For me, the day could not come soon enough. I still remembered that first summer when I'd had to listen to the celebration from inside the convent. This time I would go to the church with everyone and see the notorious Archbishop of Mainz.

But there was another reason for my impatience. For weeks I had been planning my most daring escapade yet—a foray into the town, dressed in my boy's outfit and a hooded caftan procured by Griselda. It was a precaution I had to take because ever since Wigbert had started sending me on errands, I had become recognizable. I had even made friends with Renfred, the fruit and spice seller, who liked to regale me with tales of his adventures in the Holy Land when I stopped by for ginger root and cinnamon.

At Mass I had a clear if distant view of the archbishop from my perch in the novices' pew. Amid the chants, the incense, the murmur of prayers, and the sermon about Disibod's harrowing journey from Hibernia to the Rhineland, I was struck by how different he was from Bishop Otto of Bamberg. He was taller and carried none of the extra flesh that betrayed the other's weakness for food and leisure. In fact, Archbishop Adalbert's entire posture and spare movements exuded humility and modesty, which stood in stark contrast to Otto's imperial manner. It was yet more proof that the Church and its men were not as uniform as I had been accustomed to thinking.

The afternoon was conveniently visited by occasional showers, which made wearing the hood less suspicious. I slipped through the breach and was soon walking in the town square among the stalls loaded with bales of cloth, embossed leather, hot buns, and sweetmeats. I admired the wares sellers were hawking from their trays, which included wooden flutes, ribbons, copper bracelets, and amulets to ward off evil spirits. An old hag was selling love potions in the form of a brownish liquid in little stoppered bottles.

I was reflecting on the irony of such spells being offered under the monks' very noses when another hawker came within my earshot loudly extolling the benefits of pills that would "help a man last longer." This promise set my inner healer on high alert, and I turned curiously, wondering what exactly they were for. Did they boost stamina for long days of work in the fields? That would be most useful as the harvest was to start in a few weeks. Or maybe these remedies gave men stronger heads for evenings of drinking at the alehouse? After all, so many women who came to the infirmary complained about their husbands coming home drunk out of their senses and being useless the next day. And what were these pills made from? I was about to ask the small, shifty-looking man who was shaking a box full of them at the passersby, when straight ahead of me I saw none other than Prior Helenger.

I froze in place; he was the last person I had expected to find there. Even Abbot Kuno would have made for a less out-of-place presence at the fair. Was he there to keep an eye on other monks? None were to be seen, and the prior was standing by a stall, looking over a cutler's shiny tools with seeming interest.

However, as the pill seller came closer and raised his voice again in praise of his remedy, Helenger turned toward him slowly and purposefully, as if he had been waiting for this opportunity. An expression of contempt mixed with outrage colored his features.

I was still unable to move, and everything seemed to slow down around me. Even the crowd had become quieter as if its noise was coming through a closed door. At the same time, I was acutely aware that if the prior, now standing on the other side of the piller, shifted his gaze only slightly, he would see and, without a doubt, recognize me.

Fortunately, his entire attention was fixed on the hawker, and those precious moments allowed me to gather my wits. Careful to avoid any abrupt moves, I pulled the hood deeper over my face, turned, and walked away at a measured pace until there were enough people between me and the prior. Then I broke into a run.

Maybe this is a bad idea, I thought as I ran, a little panicky, weaving among the crowd until I realized I had veered into a side alley and become lost. I could have asked for directions, of course, but after the near-encounter with Helenger, I felt that all eyes were on me and dared not raise my hood. As long as it was still light, I would try to find the way on my own. To that end, I took the first turn to the left, hoping it might lead back to the square.

But it was just another alley, narrow and cluttered with barrels, wooden crates full of vegetable peelings, and other refuse that filled the air with an unwholesome smell. I made two more turns, always coming to an alley with a tavern, a cobbler's workshop, or a cheese shop, all empty now that everyone was at the market, but none of them looked familiar or took me any closer to the town gate. When I decided to retrace my steps, I swiftly realized that I had lost my way back even to that first alley, and tears of frustration welled in my eyes. I fought them and pushed the hood back because there was nobody around.

I took a few aimless steps and heard subdued voices from around the nearest corner. A burst of female laugher rose suddenly above these murmurings but was quickly hushed by another—lower, more masculine. Relieved, I ran up the street toward what I expected to be a group of tradesmen—and tradeswomen, clearly—discussing the day's business. I abruptly stopped at the sight of a young couple in tight embrace.

The woman stood with her back against the wall of a shack, her companion pressing his chest against hers. His hand had found its way under her skirts and was caressing her leg. The woman's demeanor belied what I imagined should have been a terrible discomfort or even peril of this arrangement because she was whispering in the man's ear in cooing tones. While she was trying to arrest the hand's progress up her thigh, her effort seemed rather half-hearted. This scene played out in front of me for only a few moments because the pair sensed my presence. They turned toward me without relaxing their embrace.

I stared at them, unable to produce a voice to ask for directions. The man must have seen my confusion, for he asked in a hoarse voice full of impatience and urgency, "What do you want here, boy?"

"I . . . I was looking for the town gate and became lost," I finally managed.

"Well, it's not this way. You have to go back." He pointed over my head with the hand he'd had to take off the girl's leg, which seemed only to increase his annoyance. "See the church spire? Walk down that alley" — he pointed to a narrow street nearby — "then turn left and follow it until you reach the market. You'll see the gate from there. Now run along," he growled.

The parish church spire! Of course. I turned and walked away with a sense of relief, but I could not get the picture of the couple out of my head. I had an idea, albeit a vague one, of what the two had been up to, but I was surprised at my own reaction. It was as if all my nerves, especially those around my throat and in my fingertips, had been plucked by an invisible hand and were vibrating like a string, exquisitely and painfully at the same time.

To make matters worse, I inexplicably thought about Volmar, and, for one mortifying moment, I imagined *him* pressing like that against *me*. I reached for the hood and pulled it over my eyes as if I could shield myself from those images that way.

Back in the square, I was about to cut diagonally across the market when I felt a tug at my sleeve. I turned, my eyes instinctively going to the sleeve first, then heat rose to my face as I lifted them to find Volmar. He was standing at the bowyer's stall, weighing up a fine-looking weapon, too large for him even though he was nearly as tall as I was.

"It *is* you!" he exclaimed with his usual roguish smile. "I thought I recognized you even with the hood up. Clever," he acknowledged respectfully. "But—What's wrong?" He frowned as he noticed my distress.

"I saw Prior Helenger and he may have recognized me . . . I don't know." I was close to tears now. "Then I got lost in the back alleys, and there was a man and a woman, and he was pushing her against the wall . . ." I hardly knew what I was saying anymore, and I covered my mouth with my hand before I blurted out more. "I just want to go back."

Volmar returned the bow, took me by the elbow, and guided me toward the gate. "I should have guessed you would find a way to come here." He laughed softly. "Let's sit down somewhere."

We went out through the gate, so thronged nobody paid any attention to us, and walked along the town wall toward the forest. We sat at the edge of the woods and watched people and carts going in and out of Disibodenberg.

"What were you doing at the fair?" I asked when I felt calmer again, though I still could not meet his eyes. "I thought the monks did not attend."

"They don't, but Brother Philipp allowed the oblate boys to go down for a little while. We cannot buy anything, of course."

My head was clearer now, and I concluded that there was little chance Helenger had noticed me. "Did the prior come with you to chaperone?"

"No." Volmar shook his head. "But I hear he likes to task himself with ensuring that nothing inappropriate is sold at the market."

I thought about the amulets against evil spirits, some of which contained wisps of dried herbs in little glass chambers melted into their centers. As if reading my thoughts, Volmar added, "People were saying that some of the herb sellers had been kicked out."

We sat in silence for a while as the late sun broke through the clouds. On the opposite side of the sky, the pale moon had already risen. It sent my thoughts down a different track. "Do you think that stars can influence people's health and the outcome of cures?"

Volmar frowned thoughtfully, and I was fascinated — not for the first time — by the change that seemed to come over him whenever his usual cheeriness was replaced by a more contemplative mood, and his face assumed a softness that was almost feminine. His ability to so seamlessly shift from the spirited to the sublime never ceased to amaze me. "I don't see how," he said at length. "People pray to saints for deliverance from illness, and sometimes their prayers are answered, but stars? I cannot see how they can help or hinder anything."

"Medical books say otherwise." I told him about the volume of excerpts from Avicenna's *Canon of Medicine* I had read the previous winter, which the monk-translator had prefaced with a commentary on the link between the configuration of stars at a person's birth and the therapies best suited for his illness. I had been struggling with it because I had no direct evidence — something I always preferred in the treatment of patients — for faraway bodies' ability to exert such powers. And yet to me, the world was a whole, where every element, no matter how distant, was connected to every other element, all of them infused with the same vital energy of the creation. And since God had designed it all, who knew what mysteries were hidden beneath the layers inaccessible to our minds?

"Does Brother Wigbert believe it?"

"Hard to say. When I asked, he said he had not received training in reading astrological charts, but that many physicians swear by them, and that celestial influence over human affairs is well known. For example, the appearance of comets in the sky portends catastrophes like floods, wars, or royal deaths."

"Does it?"

"That's what he said." I paused, thinking. I was often struck by the selectiveness of monastic medicine. Dioscorides dealt extensively with the healing properties of herbs, as did *Medicinale Anglicum*, suggesting that even in Christian England scholars used and studied them. And yet our infirmarian shied away from herbal cures, preferring surgery and bloodletting while others turned to the stars for help. It seemed that there was no unified approach to treatments; monastic physicians relied only on what they considered doctrinally safe and discarded what they deemed inconvenient or suspicious.

The blue of the sky had lost its clear summer quality and assumed a more somber color tinged with streaks of purple over the horizon. In the west, the crescent of the moon had grown whiter. "Have you ever wondered what the stars are made of?" Volmar asked.

I nodded.

"Brother Rudeger says they are made up of divine matter."

"What's it like?"

"Nobody has seen it since the heavens are unreachable." Volmar's parody of the pompous tone and self-importance of the schoolmaster made me burst out laughing. "But natural philosophers say it is more rarefied than terrestrial matter."

"I wonder why."

"Let's see . . ." He racked his brain for the half-forgotten lesson. "Because the celestial region is immutable, unlike things on earth which are subject to corruption. But the sun, the moon, and the stars are always the same; they don't change or age, and they move on the spheres with circular motion, which is perfect. It follows that they must consist of matter that is also perfect, and therefore divine."

I pondered this. Heavenly bodies did seem the same from day to day and year to year. "But why would God take the trouble to create a different substance for the heavens if He could use the same four elements He created for the earth?"

Volmar lifted his shoulders. "Brother Rudeger would say it is not for us to question God's design."

I pursed my lips. "But since nobody has seen this divine matter, there is no proof that it *is* different, is there? So it is at least possible that the moon is made of the same thing that is under our feet."

"It seems reasonable." Vomar said. "Though imagine what would happen if the prior heard you say that." He shot me that mischievous glance again.

I smiled and looked up at the sky again. My imagination had long been fired up by its mysteries. What was it really like up there? How was it all organized? If the natural order on earth, for all its fragility and — as Brother Rudeger had put it — corruption, possessed such great beauty and such extraordinary regenerative powers, who knew what marvels hid in the heavens?

I turned to Volmar. "You have access to the library through the school; did you see any drawings of the sky?"

He shook his head. "Only anatomical charts."

"I have those. Brother Wigbert brought them for me to study." I rose from the grass. It was getting late, although the activity on the high road continued unabated. "And yet the workings of the heavens are just as fascinating as those of the body."

14

September 1119

I HAD NOT been studying anatomy for long when I had to set the charts aside to attend to another illness. Adelheid's condition, which I had at first attributed to the strain of Jutta's bouts of fever, worsened in the autumn of 1119, leaving her alarmingly thin and with an ashen complexion. I replaced the valerian oil with infusions of fennel and lemon balm that I had witnessed restore strength to patients weakened by seasonal ailments. I also boiled nettle leaves and sweetened them with honey. But nothing worked. Her once vivacious spirit had faded into a ghost of itself.

I had begun to suspect the real cause of Adelheid's decline; I had seen it enough times in the infirmary. I was preparing myself for an honest talk with her when she called me to the dorter one day she was alone there. She stood facing away for a while, head bowed in prayer or meditation, then turned to me. "Sister — I can call you that, for soon you will be one of us," she said softly, "I believe God is going to take me soon."

Though I was prepared for this, I felt a lump rising in my throat. "Why do you think that?"

"I am in pain . . . have been for a while." She swallowed. "I have a growth on my breast, and I think it is consuming my vital humors."

"Can I see it?" I was cautious after my experience with Jutta, but without a word Adelheid slid the robe off her right shoulder to reveal a breast, still youthfully firm, with a protuberance under the nipple the size of a hen's egg.

I dropped my gaze so she would not read the dismay in my eyes. I had seen this before. Growths like this appeared in various places, most commonly on breasts and around the neck, but also on people's bottoms and other fleshy parts. While some had claimed to have had them for years, others wasted away and died soon after discovering these lumps. On rare occasions, if they were small enough, Brother Wigbert excised them with the knife he used for lancing boils, but there was nothing else — no powder, draft, or mixture — that would slow the disease down or reverse its course.

I touched the growth. It was more solid that the normal flesh. I gently lifted Adelheid's right arm and felt around the armpit, causing her to grimace with pain. More swellings there, also familiar. Yes, her presentiment was likely correct. My heart sank, for my attachment to her was deep. The vesper bell tore through the air with its metallic urgency, and it seemed particularly mournful just then.

Gingerly, I lifted the sleeve of Adelheid's robe to cover her and was struck by the serenity of her gaze when I finally met it. With a sense of relief, I realized that she was reconciled to her fate and accepted it. That was probably for the best. "I will make sure you are as comfortable as possible," I said in a low voice, still not trusting myself to be able to control it.

"Comfort is not in store for me." There was no fear in her voice, only a hint of resignation. "My mother died of the same disease when I was a little child. She suffered greatly."

"There are infusions I can make for you that will alleviate the pain and help you sleep." I tried to sound reassuring, but I was worried. The agony this disease often brought with it was fierce; if it lasted long enough, the poppy syrup, though effective at first in numbing the senses, would become increasingly useless in procuring relief.

I spent the next several days frantically reviewing each of Brother Wigbert's reference volumes, hoping to find a cure everyone else had missed. I consulted with him, and he brought Book XXVI of Pliny's *Naturalis Historia* from the library, which classifies remedies according to specific diseases. Wigbert dismissed the herbal treatments because of Pliny's suggestion that they should be applied while repeating invocations to Apollo, one of the ancients' heathen gods. We also reviewed the sections of Galen and Hippocrates about growths, which Hippocrates referred to as *carcinos*, after a mythical Greek creature. But few of the suggested treatments were feasible; given the size of Adelheid's lump, a surgery would kill her before the disease did. As for purgatives, which Galen strongly recommended, they seemed a bad idea for an already weak patient who was unable to swallow more than a few spoonfuls of broth.

In the end, the poppy extract was our only recourse, and perhaps the only blessing was that Adelheid's death, a month later, came in the depth of the dreamless sleep it induces.

Jutta spent the first day of mourning prostrated on the chapel's floor, but Juliana was unable to pray. She threw herself on the body of her companion, and after I managed to persuade her to let go, she lay on her pallet, turned to the wall, and remained that way for hours. She did not rise even when we washed the body and wrapped it in a shroud. But she did come to the chapel, drawn and hollow-eyed, during the overnight vigil and started to wail again, the tremulous circles of light from the candles by Adelheid's head giving the scene an almost demonic quality.

Juliana regained a measure of peace only after the body had been removed to the church on the night before the burial. After matins, Jutta announced that she would stay in the chapel for the rest of the night, and I tried not to think about how she was going to spend those solitary hours. Back in bed I was hoping for some sleep, for my exhaustion was great, when Juliana's voice reached me from the shadows barely scattered by the single candle. "She was a recluse like myself, but she had about her something of the world without." Juliana's voice was low, but it seemed to ring out in the darkness. Despite my weariness, I turned toward her.

"I left that world unwillingly," she went on, haltingly at first, then with increasing forcefulness. "I did not have a calling for the monastic life. Like most young girls, I expected to be married and looked forward to it. But my misfortune started when I fell in love with a man well below my station, the son of our groom, a handsome fellow with such gentle blue eyes . . . I believe he loved me, too, for although many women in our household talked about him—not just the serving girls, but even my sisters noticed how fair he was— he only had eyes for me, and I was quite lost!" There was a shudder of emotion in Juliana's voice, and she paused for a long moment.

"I would invite him to walk with me in the garden, and sometimes we kissed. But then my father accepted a marriage proposal from a neighbor, a childless widower over thirty years older than me with an estate adjoining our lands." She laughed bitterly. "With this dual obstacle between us, we did not stand a chance. When rumors began to spread of our affection, my parents moved quickly to try to conclude the marriage, but I found out their plans and swore I would rather become an anchoress than spend my life with an old man I did not love. Oh, the cries that followed, the threats, the implorations!"

She laughed again, but this time there was a note of vengefulness in it that chilled me. "But I never relented, no! I asked to be taken to the convent of St. Disibod because Sister Jutta's reputation was already spreading. At first, I enjoyed the isolation—it soothed my pain—and before I understood the true burden of the anchorite life, I had taken my vows." In the silence that followed, her mystifying demeanor—the lack of the zeal that characterized the other anchoresses and aversion to the extremes of austerity—finally made sense to me. "But at least I had Adelheid," she resumed before her voice faltered again. She broke into a lament, "Now she is gone and I am left alone, sealed alive in this tomb!" Her chest heaved with a series of desperate sobs.

My heart ached for her, and I could find no words to comfort her in such depths of sorrow. "I am also here," I said gently. "If you ever need to ease your mind, don't hesitate to come to me."

Juliana did not respond, but I felt her calming down. Soon she was quiet and her breathing became more regular. She had succumbed to her exhaustion.

I lay awake for a long while, pondering the irony and the injustice of Adelheid's early demise; she had had such a desire to serve God through the rigors and privations of the anchorite existence. And I regretted even more the loss of the only vocation in that convent that had joy—not sorrow or duty—at its core.

Apart from Abbot Kuno and the lay brothers who lowered the body, I was the only mourner at the funeral. Anchorites were obliterated from the world in life as everyone was in death, so it was fitting that Adelheid should embark on eternity in that way. Yet it made me sad, for she had made great sacrifices, and even if her life had been spent in seclusion it was surely worth more than a pauper's burial.

The freshly dug earth fell onto the shroud from the lay brothers' shovels, the dull thuds providing a melancholy counterpoint to the abbot's recitation of the Office for the Dead. "I am the resurrection and the life; he who believes in me, even if he die, shall live; and whoever lives and believes in me shall never die."

I repeated the lines mechanically, then watched him sprinkle holy water on the grave. After he left, I reflected on the situation in the convent; it had a *magistra* who was all but unable to lead the community in mourning, and the other sister was in such a fragile state that she could not be relied on for much of anything. It was a ship without a captain sailing through turbulent waters, and there would come a time, sooner or later, when that responsibility would fall on me, even though I was the most junior of the crew.

The thought scared me. It would be tough under any circumstances, but it would be a particularly lonely task at St. Disibod. And yet this was my home now, and I would do anything to save it from perishing. If called upon, I would accept the burden, then steer the ship toward calmer waters where the warmth of the sun would give us hope not just for clinging on, but for happiness along the journey.

That promise should have been a consolation to me during that woeful season of illness and death, yet I was uneasy. Beyond the low wall of the graveyard, the green of the leaves had already faded, their edges crisping with gold. Down the slope toward the Nahe, the vineyards were bare of grapes, the joys of making new wine a memory. But it would happen again next year and the year after that, and that was reassuring. So what was that doubt that was lurking in my mind?

In that moment I became aware that even as my thoughts were on the convent, my eyes kept wandering toward the monks' cloister, to the row of windows in the western wing. I caught myself wondering if it was the refectory or the dorter, and was jolted by the realization that the only reason I wanted to know was because Volmar lived there.

Confused, my stomach twisted into a knot, I looked down at my hands and saw that my knuckles had turned white from clutching the small wooden cross he had whittled for me after Adelheid's death. I kneeled at the edge of the grave and dropped the cross into it.

As I walked away, the ache that had been lurking in the innermost part of my head all day began creeping out and spreading its crushing fingers around it.

15

September 1120

THE YEAR I turned sixteen, we built a new infirmary at St. Disibod. It had been paid for by a gift from a wealthy merchant who had been robbed and left for dead in the near-by woods. After he had recovered under Brother Wigbert's and my ministrations, he left a purse of gold, and we had spent months pleading our case for the expansion against Prior Helenger's argument that there were more pressing expenses. We prevailed in the end, for the abbot was a rea-sonable man who understood the benefits of a large infir-mary, where, in addition to dispensing Benedictine charity, we could treat patients of means from Worms, Ingelheim, or even as far as Mainz.

By the end of the summer, we were getting ready to re-open our doors. As I carried bottles of medicines from the workshop to stack in the spacious new cupboards, I paused to admire the building for what seemed like the tenth time that day. The freshness of the new timber, the clean lines of the walls, and the solidity of the tile-covered roof gave it a welcoming aspect the old infirmary had lacked. Once flowering shrubs were planted and vines covered the walls, it would become an even more wholesome place. But that would have to wait until next year, as I was reminded by the cool eastern breeze; soon leaves would turn russet and gold, days would grow shorter, and all gardening work would stop.

Brother Wigbert was in the main ward, arranging piles of fresh linen on the shelves. He had aged lately; his hair, already thin when I had first seen him, was reduced to a few gray wisps about his skull. His fingers were more swollen at the joints, and he found it increasingly difficult to handle implements like knives or shears, so I had to relieve him of any work that involved those tools. He had also grown thinner in the way old people do; he had lost fat from under his skin, so it had become saggy and gave the impression of less bulk. But he had remained quite round overall and showed few signs of slowing down. "These will be kept in the surgery." He motioned with his head toward a separate chamber opposite the front door where sounds of something heavy being moved across the floor could be heard. I guessed that was Thietmar, a strong, large-boned novice who had been helping us arrange the furniture.

I deposited the bottles in a large cupboard behind Brother Wigbert's new desk and returned to the ward, still fragrant with the aroma of fresh wood before odors of disease would overpower it. It was nearly twice as large as the old one and had two sections — one for men and one for women — that could be further separated by a cloth partition. "I will talk to Father Abbot about sending us another assistant." Wigbert smoothed the linens, scented with lavender oil, and closed the cupboard. "Ideally someone with an interest in medicine."

"So not Brother Bertolf again," I joked. Then I added, tentatively, "What if we hired someone from the town . . . a woman?"

"Why?" The monk's still-abundant eyebrows went up in surprise. "There are enough people around the abbey, and some of them could do with a serious occupation."

"Yes, but . . ." I was not sure how to breach the subject that had been on my mind. "I think there is more that we could do here as far as . . . women's care."

"What sort of care?" The infirmarian turned to the nearest bed and pressed his palms to the new straw mattress in three different places to check its strength and thickness. The mattresses had been delivered that morning. After examining the first one, he moved on to the next. There were ten beds on one side of the ward and ten on the other.

"Childbirth." I followed him.

Brother Wigbert straightened up, looking genuinely perplexed. "Wherever did you get *that* idea from?" He went back to his work. "These are not matters for monks to concern themselves with."

"But labor is a complicated process, and so many women die that it seems to me that an infirmary would be a better place for it than a home, with medicines and skilled staff —"

"It is not monastic business to deliver babes." He was already at the fifth bed, and I saw him wince as he stretched his fingers. "The town has a midwife and many villages have their own. They have plied their trade for generations and certainly know more about it than I do."

"But so many women do not survive! I have heard about some of these midwives who bring about the deaths of mothers and infants by their carelessness." It was a common enough story among women, young and old, who came to the infirmary.

"Bring about their deaths how?" The infirmarian was growing impatient. "Women should always call on midwives they know and trust, and watch them at their work.

A good midwife will do no harm. And if the mother or child dies, that is God's will."

I sighed inwardly. There was no arguing once God's will had been brought up. But my instinct told me that the primary cause of childbed fever was of this world. I had befriended Bertrade, Disibodenberg's midwife, and from her I had learned how unpredictable births could be; some women delivered quickly and without complications, while others of similar age and health died, often along with their child. Most puzzlingly, there were women who succumbed to a fever as much as two weeks after a seemingly successful delivery. Blood loss was often implicated in the quick deaths; as to the fever, the midwife was at a loss for an explanation, saying only that it seemed to happen more often in the warmer months.

I had visited the little shack where she lived and cared for some of her patients and noticed immediately that Bertrade did not concern herself overmuch with cleanliness. Her black fingernails and the linens of questionable freshness she kept in the bag she carried on calls were proof enough of that. I cleansed all cuts and wounds in the infirmary with wine or vinegar, but Bertrade only rinsed her hands in lukewarm water while praying to St. Margaret, the patroness of childbirth, prior to handling a patient. I had no proof that that was why those fevers occurred, but if the town midwife was so careless, what about the ones serving villages who often worked in the fields or with livestock before delivering babies?

I watched Brother Wigbert as he finished with one row of beds and moved across the ward to the women's section, and I could see that I would not get anywhere. But I was also aware that it would be difficult to persuade the abbot to allow a lay woman around who was not a cook. I turned away, not wishing to fight a futile battle, but I vowed to come back to it again.

Outside, the first drops of rain were falling with a muffled sound on the dry earth beneath the wilting summer plants. I went back to the workshop to make a rubbing oil for Brother Wigbert's creaking joints. It was a new medicine I had learned about from a peasant woman who had brought me a basketful of aconite roots and flowers. It was the same patient who had stayed in the infirmary with a hernia the previous autumn and heard the infirmarian complain about his aches flaring up in chilly weather. Since then, she had been bringing me a supply regularly.

Aconite was an unusual plant. While it apparently grew in abundance across the Glan, I had never seen it on the abbey side of the river. In fact, I had never heard about it before. According to the woman, despite the herb's unassuming appearance — it had common-looking palmate leaves and purple flowers that resembled a monk's cowl — aconite was extremely dangerous if used improperly. She had warned that it could prove fatal if ingested. Even when rubbed on a painful area, it could cause more harm than good if too much was applied at once.

I set up the alembic. As soon as Brother Wigbert had felt the oil's effect, he offered the treatment to the abbot who suffered similarly. As a result, I was now free to make the medicine, although the abbot had been careful to impress on me the importance of keeping quiet about its provenance. "Praising the benefits of herbs will only stoke the peasants' superstitions. They already hang amulets everywhere instead of praying to God for health," he had told me.

I was still working when Brother Wigbert returned, his bald head glistening with the moisture of the now steadily falling rain, and announced that we had a patient.

"A case that requires an overnight stay?" I inquired practically. The new building was not officially open yet, though exceptions could be made if necessary.

"Yes. Young Volmar."

"Volmar!" An image of a terrible accident flashed through my mind, and I dropped the knife I was holding. It hit the edge of a mortar bowl with a clang. "Is he all right?"

"Just a cough and a bit of a fever." The infirmarian did not seem to notice my agitation. "The season is starting early this year."

I composed myself quickly. "And we are keeping him?" I asked to cover my embarrassment.

He nodded as he set out to warm some elderberry wine. "The cough seems benign enough, but I want to keep an eye on him for a few days to see if it is not a more serious affliction of the lungs." I shivered at the specter of consumption, even though Volmar had never shown any signs of it. "Besides, we might as well see how everything works before we open up."

"Good idea."

"When you are done, take this wine to him with one of your throat pills."

I smiled behind his back. Brother Wigbert still would not dispense them himself, but he was happy enough to see my medicines work.

It rained for the next three days. Grumblings began around the abbey that the grape harvest would be ruined, but I was content. Volmar was doing well, and with nobody else for me to take care of—and Brother Wigbert either in the workshop or in church—we spent hours together. I showed him the lump of salt from Alzey that I always carried in its little box in the pocket of my robe so I could look at it whenever I missed my mother. In the five years it had been in my possession, it had not changed in any way I could discern; it was still hard and smooth, and white as a freshly fallen snow. Volmar told me about the Church Fathers they had been reading in the school, and we practiced Latin conjugations, at which he was considerably better than I.

On the fourth day the rain ceased, and I came in at midday with a message from Brother Wigbert. "You have been coughing up no blood, so you will be released today."

Volmar leaped from his bed; three days of enforced rest was probably as much as any fourteen-year-old could take.

"Here." I opened a medicine box Brother Wigbert had ordered for me from a carpenter in town and produced a cloth-wrapped bundle. "A few more horehound pills. I added a little lemon juice to them. My nurse used to say that the juice of lemons is good for colds, although the fruit is expensive and hard to come by." Indeed, at a silver mark a pound, Brother Wigbert would only let me buy one at a time from Renfred.

Volmar took the pills. For a moment it seemed as though he would give me a hug, but then he stepped back and pressed the bundle to his chest in a gesture of gratitude. To my annoyance, I blushed fiercely.

"Come, I want to show you something before you leave." I turned around, calling over my shoulder more brusquely than I had intended. I wished the ground would open and swallow me whole.

I led him down the narrow corridor between the ward and the surgery to the door that gave on to the backyard. I opened it, welcoming the cooling effect of the damp breeze on my face, and felt myself regaining my composure. The day was warming up quickly—it was still September—and we stepped out onto the drying gravel. "This is a retreat I am working on."

I had already planted box hedges along one side of the yard, all the way to the abbey wall, forming an isolated, rectangular space for ambulant patients to take the air. And benches had been placed against the infirmary wall and under the fruit trees that separated us from the herb garden.

"It is lovely out here," Volmar said, "and will be even better when the trees are in blossom."

We sat on the closest bench. "I believe that fresh air speeds up recovery. That is contrary to what many physicians recommend, but I simply don't agree with those who want the sick to stay indoors away from the sun and the greenness. It is what restores vitality."

"I was brought up to believe that the air had an ill effect on a weakened constitution," Volmar admitted.

I sighed. There were so many misconceptions regarding nature and its purported evil influences on the health of the body and the soul; my experience had been quite the opposite. "I have noticed that patients who languish in bed take longer to recuperate than those who begin to move around as soon as they are able to."

"I can see why. Three days in the infirmary and I was going mad."

I felt warmed on the inside by our shared appreciation for the world out-of-doors. There was no other person with whom I had that kind of understanding—save Brother Wigbert, perhaps, but the intensity of it did not come even close.

It also reminded me of something. "When I was looking for a cure for Sister Adelheid, I read the sections of *Naturalis Historia* that deal with remedies derived from plants." I lowered my voice, though we were alone. "It is fascinating, although—" I broke off.

"You are worried that it is a pagan work?" He put the question without disapproval. "Brother Rudeger says that is the reason we are not studying Pliny."

"Well, he does recommend praying to the ancients' gods, but . . ." I dropped my voice even lower. I had noticed that some monks who came to the infirmary gave me strange looks and watched me when I spoke with Brother Wigbert. The infirmarian himself had told me they were likely to report what they saw and heard to the prior, and that I should be careful. I was speaking in a near-whisper now, in case someone had wandered in looking for us. "He describes such a variety of remedies that I never knew existed that . . . I wonder if I should . . ." I hesitated again.

"Make them for your patients and try them without the pagan incantations?"

I nodded briskly. "There are so many useful applications. For example" — I started enumerating on my fingers — "wild mint juice can be used for jaundice and ear worms; rue taken with wine and mustard applied externally are both good for dropsy, as is the root of wild vine boiled in water and wine. Wormwood mixed with honey helps heal bruises, and mixed with raisin wine can cure defluxions of the eyes — "

"Ugh!"

"The point is," I checked myself, "that even though the Church is suspicious of folk remedies, ancient texts talk about them all the time!"

I had told Volmar of Brother Wigbert's distrust of herbal healing long ago, so he understood my dilemma. "I think whenever you have the ingredients, you should try them out," he said. "The worst thing that can happen is Brother Wigbert will tell you to stop, but he will never denounce you." Then he laughed. "They say that this infirmary" — he pointed with his thumb over his shoulder — "used to be a place people went to die. But now the monks are rubbing their hands at all the gifts that are going into their coffers. They probably no longer object to the use of wild herbs, though they won't admit it."

I smiled. He was likely right. "I started writing down recipes for herbal treatments and noting the results," I confessed, my voice back to a loud whisper.

"What for?"

I explained that it was my growing belief that the essence of effective healing lay in observing the outcomes, and that it was necessary to consider each patient as a unique case because not everyone responded in the same way to the same treatment. Medical texts were mainly theory, even Galen, who otherwise noted the importance of observation. I was especially mystified by his stubborn endorsement of the practice of bloodletting. I was also skeptical of the insistence on treating medical knowledge as given once and for all, which compelled physicians like Brother Wigbert to apply it without giving the results much heed.

"I daresay it should be a success!" Volmar exclaimed enthusiastically. "Maybe one day monks will study from your book, not from Galen's! What will you call it?"

I waved my hand. "It's just a reference for me. Women don't write books."

His face crumpled into an *I-hadn't-thought-of-that* look, but even as it did, a question pushed its way into my mind: why not? It was clear to me that despite what Prior Helenger—and even Brother Wigbert—would say, women possessed reasoning faculties just like men did. Besides, not everything men wrote was so great. There were many things with which I disagreed in St. Augustine, including his claim that unbaptized infants went to hell, even though they had not done anything to offend God. It struck me as unreasonable, therefore, that men could freely voice such views, but a woman was not allowed to write something that was useful.

A swell of enthusiasm filled me. The notion that I might write—*really* write, write for others to *read*—seemed daring, dangerous, and utterly thrilling. It would be a challenge unlike any other, but instead of terrifying me, it made me want to do it all the more.

16

December 1120

I BEGAN TO write differently: I was more thorough, checked everything twice, and made sure my Latin was as correct as it could be. Something that had been buried in the back of my mind since I was three and became lost in my family's chapel started resurfacing in my daily thoughts.

My recurring headaches had started on that distant afternoon, but now I began to suspect that it was no ordinary illness. For, as it weakened my body, it made my mind sharper and more receptive to understanding. I still did not know what it was that had happened to me all those years ago, but I felt that I was getting closer. So I kept writing in secret from everyone except Volmar.

Then the day of my novitiate vows came.

Under the terms of my enclosure, I could become a novice only after my sixteenth birthday, which fell in October.

Traditionally, the abbey held this ceremony the day after Christmas. Throughout the autumn, I had made an effort to immerse myself in the study of the Bible, but, outside of the hour I spent with Jutta each day, I had little time for it between working, attending services, and scribbling on parchment scraps whenever I thought no one saw me. So when I walked into the church on a snowy day of St. Stephanus, I was less clear on the finer points of the Holy Writ than on the best remedies for a tooth abscess or the ways to lance a boil while minimizing the pain.

Abbot Kuno, dressed in white priestly vestments woven through with golden thread, led the procession of the black-robed monks into the church. With the rest of the soon-to-be novices, I was seated in the front pew and could see melting snowflakes twinkle in the candlelight like tiny jewels on the brothers' cowls. Behind the abbot, Prior Helenger marched in a plain robe, the expression on his face the same glum primness from my oblate blessing five years before.

As always, the Mass thrilled me with every soaring note of chant and every swing of the censer that discharged bursts of aromatic incense. I wondered if Volmar felt the same way, but his face was solemn and inscrutable. Perhaps he was worried that the novitiate would put an end to his secret hunting pastimes, as it is the Church's view that no man can be holy who hunts. I was so engrossed in my own sensations and in thoughts of Volmar that I completely forgot about another friend, and only noticed her as I stepped down from the altar after receiving my blessing. Griselda stood in the shadows in the back of the church, observing me with admiration and a bit of envy, just as she had the day of our first encounter on the road to St. Disibod.

The snow had subsided by the time I returned to the workshop with Brother Wigbert, who was beaming with an almost paternal pride. He was pouring us wine when a servant arrived saying that Sister Jutta wanted to see me. I wrapped myself in my woolen cloak and stepped from the firelit warmth of the workshop, back into the swirls of snow the wind was still blowing from its piles.

As I walked, I was seized by a sudden fear that I might have to serve my novitiate inside the convent after all. It would be contrary to the agreement struck between the abbot and the *magistra*, but through Brother Wigbert I knew that the prior had been advocating my permanent enclosure. I was afraid he may have finally come up with some clever argument to achieve this, the more so since the abbot was known to give in to the prior if his own peace was at stake. Jutta could have changed her mind as well. As the founder of the convent and my superior, it was in her power to make the final decision.

As I knocked on the door, half-covered by snowdrifts, I thought I already felt a distant echo of a headache.

Sister Juliana let me in and motioned toward the chapel. Inside, it seemed to be lit by all the candles we had, and their glow made it feel cozier than usual.

I was surprised to find Jutta sitting in a pew instead of kneeling or lying on the floor. She gestured for me to sit by her side. "My heart is glad today," she said. "You have taken the first step on the road on which I embarked many years ago." My face must have registered some alarm, for she added, "I am aware that your vocation is of a different nature than mine, and that you will chart your own way."

I swallowed. "Yes, Sister."

Jutta spoke again in a tone that, for once, lacked the martyr-like quality. "I have been observing you since that night you stood before me for the first time, a mere child yet undaunted. You faced me and this life seemingly without fear. I may have wished for you to take a path similar to the other sisters, but I knew even then that it was not to be." She paused, gazing pensively at the oil lamp at the foot of the cross. Something akin to a smile fleeted across her lips. "God bestowed a gift on you in your talent for healing, and you have made a good use of it. For a long time, I found it difficult to accept," she added honestly, "but this abbey needs you, and it shall have you."

Relief washed over me, but I was careful not to show it. "All I want is to make you and this convent proud."

"You have been successful at healing broken bodies," Jutta resumed, "but I hope that as you continue to perfect that art, you will also learn how to heal broken souls."

I looked at her uncertainly. We had duties as women of the Church, but 'healing souls' sounded like something that priests and bishops were more suited to do.

"It is a task that has a greater value than medicine, for it restores us to everlasting life," she said. "It also requires much wisdom and strength."

"I don't feel that I possess either," I confessed.

"We are none of us born with these qualities. But you have an agile mind and an open heart; that is all you need."

I always felt ill at ease when others praised me, and this time was no different. "You think so highly of me, Sister, because I have learned to provide relief to the sick, but it is God who created the ingredients for these medicines. Besides, caring for the unfortunate is what The Rule requires us to do."

Jutta gazed at me with an expectation in her face that at first surprised me, and then I knew . . . The words tumbled out of me. "I have suffered from headaches for many years that leave my body weak and spent but my senses unusually acute, so that all light is brighter, all sound sharper, and I seem to float in the air like a feather." It was the first time I had shared this with anyone. "Once, when I was little, I heard a voice inside that light that spoke to me and said things I could not understand then, but now I am beginning to."

"It told me to speak and tell what is shown to me, for *He who rules every creature bestows enlightenment on those who serve Him, and eternal vision on those who act with justice.*" I closed my eyes as the words, hidden for so long in the depths of my mind, came back to me.

A long silence ensued. A pale wintry sun had come out and its tepid rays shone directly through the window, illuminating Jutta's face. "Is it possible that God spoke to me?" I asked.

"To you," she said softly, "and He is still speaking *through* you."

"Through me?"

"Yes."

"But who am I, Sister? Why hasn't God chosen you? With all the . . . sacrifices you are willing to endure, surely —"

Jutta shook her head, and it was obvious that it pained her. "Evidently He sees you as a better instrument in His hands. Do not fight it. It is a gift that you must accept and use wisely. Let Him speak so that others may know."

"But what if I speak and nobody listens? Or they think that my wits have left me?"

"Then write." Her gaze on me, despite her body's weakness, was powerful, magnetic. "As you have done already."

And with that, she rose and left the chapel, and I was speechless once again.

17

May 1122

I HAD NEVER been happier about the arrival of spring than in the year 1122. The melancholy that had descended on the convent after Adelheid's death seemed to have intensified that winter, leaving me with strong headaches and causing Juliana to become even more withdrawn, so that weeks had gone by without her talking to anyone. I infused hypericum in wine for both of us to stem the excess of black bile, and when the weather turned milder, I persuaded her to help me prune the vine that covered the wall. The fresh air helped me, but its effect on Juliana was more limited.

Perhaps that was because she really did have nothing left, whereas I had the infirmary, my books, and my writing. I had come to believe that writing was what I was meant to be doing—besides treating patients, of course. It had not yet crossed my mind that I could write about anything other than herbs; I was simply happy to have found a way to share my knowledge with others as the voice in the light had told me.

Abbot Kuno had finally agreed to the expansion of the kitchen garden, which meant that we had more space for healing plants. On a pleasant April afternoon, I was busy gardening when the gate squeaked and Griselda walked in, as she did sometimes at that hour before supper preparations started in the kitchen. She picked up a hoe that rested against the workshop wall and made her way toward me. She was sixteen, but with her cropped hair, pointy chin, and small breasts — which she flattened even more with cotton bandages — she could easily pass for a boy. Indeed, in some ways, she seemed more like a boy than a girl; when her monthly bleeding had started, she had come to the infirmary in tears, and it took me a while to convince her that she was not dying. She calmed down eventually and accepted practical suggestions for handling the flux, but the episode had left her shaken.

We began digging up old roots to make room for new plantings. Griselda was a competent gardener, and we worked in contented silence for some time, but at length she leaned on her hoe and sighed.

"Is something on your mind?" I had just started to demarcate the beds for rue, sage, and oregano, and was too absorbed to pause my work.

"No." She resumed digging but stopped again a few moments later. "Yes," she said shyly. "I am wondering if the convent is going to fill the vacancy?"

"The vacancy?"

"After Sister Adelheid's passing."

I was trying to estimate the yield from the new herbs and was momentarily confused. I put down the trowel, straightened up, and wiped my hands on my apron. "What about it?"

"Is Sister Jutta looking for a novice to fill her place?"

I scratched my temple. It had been more than two years, and although we had received many letters of inquiry, the abbot had been reluctant to give us permission to admit a new candidate. Lately, though, Brother Wigbert had mentioned a discussion in Chapter about the possibility of accepting a female novice, and the news had clearly spread. I considered Griselda, surprised to see her usually dreamy eyes fastened intently on my face. "I don't know of any immediate plans," I said truthfully. "But it will probably happen sooner or later."

I must have frowned as I said it, for she asked, "Does that worry you?"

"A little," I admitted. "Sister Jutta's reputation is strong in these parts and is likely to attract candidates who think bodily mortification is a virtue." Despite my best efforts to keep it quiet, somehow word had gotten out that Jutta lashed herself with a leather whip until she bled. It was being further reported that the practice regularly led her to the brink of death, from which God mercifully brought her back each time so she could continue to be an exemplar of piety and sacrifice. The details and the magnitude of what went on were often distorted, but the effect was powerful. We were seeing more and more pilgrims with purses full of gold and silver coins, and wealthy parents were offering their sons and daughters to St. Disibod like never before.

"Would Father Abbot want that?" Griselda asked.

I shook my head. "I don't think so." But I could hear the uncertainty in my voice. Kuno had been concerned about Jutta's practices before they had become common knowledge, but now that they were making the monks rich, I could no longer be sure.

"Do you think . . . that I could join the convent?" Griselda asked, her eyes boring into mine like two shining green gems. I was aware that for a few moments she was not breathing at all. "As a novice," she added in a whisper.

I cleared my throat and moved toward the bench under the fruit trees, their branches covered in swollen buds on the verge of bursting into a fragrant white cloud. "You know that I would like that, but it is not possible," I said as we sat down. How had I not seen this coming? "Not at the moment, anyway," I added, seeing her face fall. "Things may be different in the future."

"What do you mean?"

I thought carefully before answering. I did not have the heart to tell Griselda that any one of the women queuing up to become a novice could offer much more than she had saved from her kitchen wages. Instead, I tried a different tack. "You have been living here for four years as a boy; imagine the monks' reaction if they found out who you are."

"I suppose they would be very surprised."

"Yes." I nodded slowly. "And also angry." I paused to let it sink in. "I doubt they would let you join under such circumstances."

Tears rose to Griselda's eyes, though she fought them back. "So now I will never be able to become an anchoress?"

I felt a wave of frustration. What kind of a world was this where the monastic life was often imposed by threat or force on those who did not want it and denied to those who did?

"I did not say that," I said gently. "It may be possible, but you will have to go about it in a different way."

"But how?" There was a note of helplessness in her voice.

I did not have an answer then any more than when I had first learned of Griselda's disguise. "Perhaps by going away for a while," I suggested. "You could find better-paying work and save more . . ." I faltered, knowing the futility of such a plan.

"But I don't want to go away! There is nothing for me outside. My family has renounced me, or they think me dead. This is my home now."

I was casting around for an answer when the gate creaked again, and Brother Wigbert walked in. He halted when he saw us and pretended to survey the garden, but I saw him glancing sideways at us. He beckoned me to join him in the workshop, and I rose from the bench as Griselda went to pick up our tools to return them to the shed.

Brother Wigbert was stoking the fire in the stove, for the afternoon was getting chilly, and wine was already warming on the top. He seemed pensive as he poured me a cup, and I wrapped my fingers around it, letting the heat permeate them as I sat across from him. His face was kindly but also serious.

"I feel obliged to tell you that your association with young Christian has come to the attention of the abbey." He shifted on his bench.

"What association?" I was puzzled.

Wigbert cleared his throat. "You are spending a lot of time with this young man, and it may appear unseemly now that you two are no longer children." He looked uncomfortable now. "It is not easy for me to talk about such things; they don't often happen in a place like this."

"I don't understand," I said. "Gris—Christian is very useful in carrying messages, helping me in the garden, and—" I broke off as comprehension dawned on me, and I felt myself blushing at the implication.

"I know you have not done anything wrong," Wigbert hastened to assure me, "but it would be for the best if he did not come here anymore. It would save you suspicion from . . . some quarters."

"Some quarters!" I scoffed. "I know exactly what quarters this is coming from." I put my nose in my cup sullenly.

The monk reached across the table and patted my arm. "There, everything is fine." I noticed that he did not deny my suspicions. "I just don't want you to go down a troubled path. The boy is free to indulge in such fancies, but they are a distraction to a girl whose parents offered her to God." He rose as the bell sounded a call to vespers.

"I still need help in the garden," I said.

"I am sure I can get one of the novices to come. In fact" —
he paused on the threshold, struck with a thought—"I hear
that Volmar has done a fine job in the orchards; he might like
this kind of work!"

On an early summer morning, I went to the town on
errands, stopping first at Renfred's shop for ginger root. He
apologized for the stacks of crates piled along one wall—the
consignment expected the previous week had only arrived
the day before, after the unloading of the ship had been delayed at Cologne. It took him some time to locate and open
the right one, all the while telling me, with all the energy and
eloquence of his profession, of his recent visit to his cousin, a
fruit seller in Canterbury.

I listened avidly as he described recent improvements
to its famed cathedral, where the choir was bigger than the
entire church of St. Disibod, and which boasted new marble floors and stained glass windows that gave the interior
a multicolored glow like walking inside a rainbow. It was a
change from his usual tales of the crusade, in which he, like
my father, had participated more than twenty years before.
I loved those tales of Christian warriors defending cities of
the Holy Land from the Saracen, and Renfred was always
happy to have someone with whom to share them, for most
of his customers had no time or patience for anecdotes about
foreign lands.

I could have stayed and listened for hours, but I had another errand to do, so before he could launch into another re-
telling of the siege of Antioch, I bid him goodbye and moved
toward the potter's shop to order clay bowls.

An urgent thud of hoofs rose over the stirrings of a new day when I was halfway across the square, and I saw peasants scatter in all directions as they pulled carts piled with vegetables and chicken crates to safety. A pair of knights rode through the gate at full gallop, barely slowing to shout a few words to the watchman, and continued on their foaming coursers through the main street and up toward the abbey.

Disibodenberg was a quiet enough town for this to stir curiosity among the traders opening their shops. Renfred had also stepped out and followed the riders with his gaze, a deep frown creasing his forehead. "On my way back from England, I met a merchant from Mainz who told me there were rumors of the emperor's imminent return to Germany and a likelihood of a war with those loyal to the pope." He crossed himself. "May God help us."

My anxiety mounting, I looked around as if someone else could confirm or deny this. Just then, one of the vegetable-hauling peasants passed by, a thin, graying man with the bright eyes and alert face of a busybody, accompanied by a small, scared-looking woman. Seeing my monastic garb, he took off his hat. Perhaps in response to my questioning expression, he said in a half-whisper as if delivering a secret message, "There is a word of mercenary troops abroad, looting and burning."

The news sent a chill down my spine. I exchanged a glance with Renfred—he had told me enough stories about the terrible fate of cities under siege to leave me with no doubt about the danger facing us. And Disibodenberg was no Jerusalem; it had flimsy walls and a population wholly untrained for combat. Clay pots forgotten, I ran back to the abbey. Just as I passed through the gate, I saw Brother Wigbert disappearing inside the abbot's house.

I followed but stopped when I caught the sound of several voices inside. The knights were in conference with Abbot Kuno, who must have summoned the obedientiaries. This was serious. Just before I pushed the door open, it crossed my mind that this was not a place for a woman to be. But I was not going to miss anything that might affect the convent.

This is what a war council must look like, I thought. The abbot's face was drawn with worry; next to him, Prior Helenger wore his usual haughty expression, which, for once, failed to mask his anxiety. Across the abbot's desk, the two knights were about to start their debrief as several senior monks stood attentively on either side. In addition to Brother Wigbert, there was Brother Ignatius, a graying man of fifty, as tall as the prior but with a friendlier demeanor, who served as treasurer; Brother Odo, the small, lively bursar of about forty; and Brother Ordulf, the abbey's matricularius, fat and pale, and bald as an egg. The abbot raised his eyebrows as I entered and made a small obeisance, and the rest of the group turned in my direction.

"Who is that?" one of the knights asked. His tone was curious rather than hostile, and he looked vaguely familiar.

"Nobody." Prior Helenger's voice rang out, prompting Brother Wigbert to send him a sharp look. "Just a novice who should not be here," he added.

Abbot Kuno raised his hand, and Helenger fell silent but continued to glare at me from under his cowl. "Hildegard needs to hear the news, so she can keep Sister Jutta informed," the abbot told the knights. Then he turned to me. "These messengers have been sent by the Count von Sponheim."

I regarded the men who had come from Jutta's father. Then I remembered — the familiar-looking one was Rudolf von Stade, the black-eyed squire who had accompanied Count Stephan on his visit to Bermersheim seven years before. I noted that the fresh scar on his left cheek had healed and was now just a pale line from his jawline to the ear. He had matured from his lanky youth and settled into the broader frame of manhood, and his raven hair had begun to thin at the crown, but otherwise he looked much the same. I, on the other hand, must have changed substantially, having outgrown my chubbiness and acquired at least two feet of height. Most likely, he did not recall me at all.

At a gesture from the abbot, the knights spoke. Emperor Heinrich had returned from Italy and accused the nobles of fomenting chaos in his absence. The papal faction had rejected those allegations as a pretext for grabbing even more privileges for the crown, to which the emperor responded by challenging Archbishop Adalbert to battle. The emperor was marching on Mainz after calling on all loyal men to join him in standing up to those to whom he referred as "the enemies of the empire."

"It is a quest for revenge for his defeat at Welfesholz at the hands of the Duke of Saxony," Rudolf concluded. Most worryingly, mercenaries from Bavaria and Swabia had been streaming into the Rhineland to pillage villages and undefended towns around Mainz and Ingelheim for supplies and entertainment as they awaited the confrontation. "However," he added, "papal supporters now have information that some of these bands have been spotted farther south, and that Disibodenberg might be in their sights."

Tense silence descended on the parlor until it was broken by Prior Helenger's voice, imperious as usual but with a tremble that he was not quite able to hide. "Surely they would not dare raise their hand against a house of God!"

Rudolf inclined his head respectfully, but his tone left no doubt about the seriousness of the threat. "For the safety of everyone here, I would not make that assumption, Brother Prior. Mercenaries, far away from home and unencumbered by the laws and customs of their land, have been known to attack monasteries and slay holy men for profit."

Helenger opened his mouth to reply, but the abbot interjected before he could do so. "What options do we have?"

"You can evacuate the monks, the anchoresses" — Rudolf's dark eyes flicked toward me — "and the townspeople across the Nahe as there is no indication of marauders in those parts. Or you can stay and defend yourselves."

"Defend ourselves?" Kuno's eyes widened. "But we are not a burg. These walls offer little protection." I thought of all the breaches Volmar and I had crept through over the years and shuddered. They offered no protection *at all*. "Also, except for a few old crusaders," the abbot went on, "there is nobody here with any military experience. Can the count offer us assistance?"

Rudolf von Stade shook his head regrettably. "Count Stephan wishes to warn you of the danger so you can make preparations, but he is unable to provide reinforcements as a battle with the imperial army is expected."

This statement was followed by another interval of silence. I looked around the room and saw varying degrees of helplessness on the monks' faces.

"I will not abandon the abbey," Kuno said at length. His voice was quiet but firm. "It is my duty to stay here and share its fate, but I won't stop anyone from leaving or the town from evacuating."

It was courageous of him, but it hardly solved anything. My mind was working fast. "How large is the band heading our way?" I asked.

Rudolf blinked. "Not very large—eighty, maybe a hundred men, but they can wreak havoc in a small town like this."

"We should head across the river," Helenger announced as if it were his decision to make. "From there we can pray for deliverance, for our faith is the strongest armor."

The abbot stirred impatiently and turned to the obedientiaries who had remained silent thus far. "What do *you* think, Brothers?"

They looked at one another uncertainly. They, too, had a duty toward the abbey, but it was obvious they had no idea what to do if they stayed. "As Brother Prior has said," Brother Ordulf ventured weakly, "we must trust that Christ will shield us—"

But I was already shaking my head, barely able to contain my impatience. "The town can be defended if we reinforce it and mobilize the people." I was thinking clearly now; the threat came from only a handful of rogue men, not an army of forty thousand that had covered the fields outside of Antioch with canons, catapults, and other siege machines. Eighty men-at-arms were nothing to be complacent about, but it would be foolish to abandon the people's livelihoods and the abbey's treasury to them. "The town wall is shorter but more solid than the abbey wall," I went on, merely explaining my observations, "and we could dig a ditch to make it harder to scale it. The abbey wall has breaches in several places through which men could enter if they found them, but we could disguise them or patch them up."

The knights dipped their heads in agreement, but the monks visibly struggled to comprehend. I felt a wave of irritation. The plan was simple and logical, and they would not be so stunned if they had ever bothered to talk to ordinary people about life in the wider world, the threats they faced, and how they dealt with them. But the monks considered such fraternizing beneath them.

"I think it can be done if we start immediately," I urged.

"This is preposterous!" Helenger's nostrils flared with anger. "I suggest we evacuate immediately, there are—"

"Brother Prior, please." The abbot cut him off and gave me an intent look as if the defense instructions were written on my forehead. Taking advice from a woman was highly unusual, but he had enough sense to recognize a feasible plan, especially if it could save his monks from the disgrace of abandoning the abbey. "Now tell us," he asked a little acidly, but it was clear that he was eager for an answer, "how are we to accomplish this feat of fortification?"

I ignored the sarcasm. "We are on a hill, surrounded on three sides by the forest and the rivers, and that gives us natural protection." I took a deep breath. "So the main threat comes from the high road and the fields, which means that we must concentrate on strengthening the town's western wall.

"We could dig a ditch on both sides of the gate and use the earth to plug the holes in the abbey wall. I can show you one, and Vol—some novices know about others." I saw the corners of Rudolf von Stade's mouth lifting. The abbot raised his chin, and I continued, "As far as weapons, we may have more than we think. Many townsmen own bows, and they can shoot because they compete in the meadow by the Glan every summer. They can be posted along the wall, and we can gather stones and have those who don't shoot sling them at the attackers. People also have pickaxes, hammers, and other sharp tools"—I enumerated on my fingers—"that could be useful in a fight. The blacksmith probably has a few swords in store, although I don't know if anyone besides Renfred knows how to use them—"

"A few might," Kuno said, hope coloring his voice. "There are at least three other former crusaders living at Disibodenberg, and I believe the brewer had a stint in the archbishop's army. It is not much, but it is something."

"The monks could organize and supervise the preparations," I suggested.

The abbot thought for a moment, then turned to the brothers. "I call a grand meeting for this afternoon. See to it that the announcement is made in town."

18

July 1122

D ISIBODENBERG'S LEADING CITIZENS arrived at Abbot Kuno's conference. Renfred was there, as well as Johann the blacksmith, Gunther the stonemason, and several craftsmen and traders whose businesses provided services to the abbey. The town's parish priest, Father Diepold, came as well. They all vowed to stay and defend the town, and by the end of the day, vulnerable points were identified, plans drawn, and roles assigned for the work that was to begin the next morning. At nightfall, a rotating system of sentries was set up to supplement the watch at the gate, where the regular guard was known to take naps on duty.

After prime, the abbot and Brother Wigbert went down to the town square where all the able-bodied men over the age of fifteen had already assembled. Those who had been selected to dig the ditch had brought spades and went off to start immediately, working south and north of the high road all the way to the forest. Another group was dispatched to procure supplies of food and firewood, and the rest followed the monks to the abbey, where Volmar and I showed them the areas where rotten beams left the compound open to intrusion. Those gaps would be filled with the earth from the ditch and strengthened with the timbers from dismantled scaffoldings.

When we came to the hole at the back of the garden, I could not tell from Brother Wigbert's face if he suspected anything. Not that it mattered in that moment.

"Shouldn't we dig a ditch around the abbey too?" Kuno asked anxiously.

"The forest is too close," I repeated what I had said the day before. "It would be cumbersome to bring horses up the slope through the trees. If they approach here, it will be on foot."

"So despite the hill and the cover of the woods, this wall is still vulnerable?" The abbot looked at me as if I were some battle-tested general.

I spread my hands. "There is no guarantee, I suppose."

"Then we will have to use the old watchtower and have archers there as well," he decided, which impressed me, for he was clearly scared. As was I.

"Father, I am a good archer," Volmar offered, not without a boasting note in his voice. "I can supervise the defenses here."

The abbot looked surprised, but this was no time to ask questions. In a place of scant military expertise, any talent was welcome. "Very well. Now let's inspect the tower to ensure the steps are solid. If need be, we will have the master carpenter fix them."

As we crossed the courtyard, I felt cautiously optimistic that we might yet defend ourselves.

After four days of intense work, Disibodenberg was as prepared as it could be, but there was no sign of the mercenaries. The plan was that if the sentries spotted anything, women, children, and the infirm would be moved into the abbey precincts, and everyone else would take their pre-assigned positions—with bows and arrows or slings along the walls, and with any tools they had in their possession below to try to fight off those who managed to get inside.

During those preparations, Renfred regaled anybody who would listen with tales of the battering rams and catapults the crusaders had used to break down Saracen defenses to recapture holy sites in Outremer. At one point, he recalled how the infidel had taken to pouring boiling tar down on the attacking Christians during the siege of Antioch, decimating their ranks. Disibodenberg did not have enough tar to turn into such a weapon; instead, someone suggested having large cauldrons of boiling water at the ready, and women were dispatched to gather brushwood for bonfires to be set up in the square.

Another week went by, and the state of high alert had begun to wane. The emergency plan was still in effect, but taverns and public areas filled again with people eager for gossip and entertainment to take their minds off worrisome thoughts.

Then, at dawn on a Monday, a group of peasants from an outlying village arrived on foot, barely alive with fear and exhaustion, soot covering their faces and clothes. Their homes and granaries had been burned and their bread, cheese, and livestock carried away. They had barely escaped with their lives. Disibodenberg was put back on alert, and just in time because an urgent sound of bells broke the tense quiet of the early afternoon, signifying that the enemy was in sight.

One of the lookouts came running to the abbot to report that a force of about sixty men had emerged from the forest to the west. When they had seen the ditch and the defenders on the walls, they had stopped to confer in the fields about a mile from the gate.

"Are they still at it?" The abbot was composed and efficient, but his face was taut with fear. We had just come out of the vestry of the parish church that had become a headquarters of sorts.

"They are, Father," the boy replied.

I split from the group and hurried up to the infirmary. I climbed a ladder to the roof and perched at the edge. It was a perfect vantage point because it rose above the abbey wall, and I could see over the roofs of the town all the way into the fields on both sides of the high road.

And there, surrounded by yellowing barley gently undulating in the summer breeze, a band of soldiers was milling about as their leaders held council apart, restraining their warhorses and casting occasional glances toward Disibodenberg. These men, I realized, already had innocent blood on their hands and were looking for more. How was such a sin to be redeemed? Certainly not by anchoresses flogging and starving themselves.

Amid such grim reflections, I was nonetheless relieved to see that they looked nothing like the crusaders Renfred had described; instead of shiny plates of armor, shields, and helmets, all they wore were gambesons without even chain mail. Clearly, they had not expected resistance.

"Lucky for us they left their armor behind to keep clean for the big battle." Volmar's voice reached me, echoing my thoughts.

I looked around, startled.

"Here!" He was on the wall above the herb garden, partially hidden by the fruit trees. "Be careful!" he shouted as I turned to face him.

"You too! You know how rotten those beams are."

Volmar grinned. "I'll be fine."

I glanced back toward the fields and felt a twinge of apprehension. The mercenary leaders had rejoined the rest of the group but were careful not to make any gestures that would betray their intentions. I observed them with bated breath, and it seemed to stretch for eternity.

Then they moved, and my heart sank. They came about a quarter of a mile closer and reined in their horses again. Some reached into their saddlebags, pulling out bows and setting out to string them. When they were ready, the remaining men launched a final attack at speed while the archers held back to provide cover. The first arrows flew from the mercenaries' side, and two of our men on the wall fell.

Out of the corner of my eye, I could see Volmar running back to the archers he had posted in the watchtower. *This is not going to work*, I thought desperately. There was no leader to tell the defenders when to shoot, and the timing seemed crucial.

Just then, the first arrows were launched from the town wall, and a few cheers went up. I looked around the edge of the roof as Volmar appeared at the top of the watchtower, and we could see each other across the courtyard. I jabbed a finger toward the town. *You need to move there; they need reinforcements!* But he was scanning the woods for a sign of an assault from there.

I understood why; the knights from Sponheim had spoken of at least eighty men. But I kept shaking my head while pointing urgently toward the town—that was where the attack was *definitely* happening.

Finally, Volmar signaled to his men, and I climbed down and ran into the courtyard just as they were hurrying by. "I am going to organize a watch here and send word if we see anything!" I shouted as they disappeared through the gate.

Volmar's archers had arrived just in time. A few of the mercenaries had been hit on the way, but most had made it to the wall. The hail of stones was keeping them temporarily at bay. The new arrows swished down and laid another five dead, but more than a dozen men came all the way up to the ditch, dismounted, and tried to climb the earth rampart, swords in hand. The angle was too steep for a successful bow shot, but right then a cauldron of boiling water was hauled onto the wall. The sight of the rising steam sent the attackers fleeing, including the ones in the ditch who were now scrambling up the other side.

Renfred, proudly in charge of that part, grinned at Volmar. "These bastards must have heard tales from the crusade. Those armies were full of men for hire too."

His assistants were about to tip the pot over when Volmar raised a hand to stop them. He had, he later told me, an idea. They looked puzzled but obeyed. The attackers were in full retreat, mounting their horses and galloping away across the field. Volmar watched them for a while, then turned to Renfred. "It is better they don't know we only have water here. Let them think it is tar. Maybe this will keep them from coming back."

That evening, the weary but jubilant townsfolk set up tables in the square under the clear summer sky and made a celebratory feast of roasted geese, fried bacon, cheese, and fruit pies, to which they invited the monks. After the meal, I joined the elders' table, where the day's events were being reviewed. The moon had risen, the fires crackled, and the mood, fueled by ale, was cheery. Everyone realized how lucky we had been, for despite the defiant posture, the town was ill-equipped for a siege or a serious fight. Volmar admitted that the archers, though they had had some success in taking out the attackers, had wasted many arrows, and their aim was far from perfect under the pressure of an unfamiliar situation. Fortunately, the mercenaries had overestimated our defenses and had chosen not to risk losses before the main battle.

Renfred offered another reason to be grateful. "Flaming arrows are a horrible weapon," he said, his speech already a little slurred. "They land on roofs and cause fires that can destroy a town from the inside in no time without the enemy setting foot through the gate. I only thought about it after it was all over."

We looked fearfully at one another. A few richer houses were built out of stone, but most dwellings were timber and would have burned up like heaps of twigs. "God protected Disibodenberg from a terrible fate today, praised be His name." The abbot crossed himself.

"Amen!"

"God also chose Hildegard to send us a message of courage!" Renfred exclaimed, emboldened by the ale. "She convinced us to stay and fight. Let's drink to her health!"

They raised their cups with a cheerful noise, splashing some of the contents. Brother Wigbert and Abbot Kuno, drinking wine, took more modest sips as befit their station.

"She also urged me to go into the town and help once the attack began," Volmar added. "She was right that they would not attack up the hill, but at the time I wasn't so sure."

Everyone nodded with renewed appreciation, and I blushed under this barrage of acknowledgement. "Their surprise at seeing our defenses told me they had not expected resistance," I said. "So it made sense that they would not have planned a sneak attack from the woods."

As another toast followed, I noticed Griselda nearby. I excused myself and walked to the servants' table. Someone moved over to make room, and Griselda beamed at me. "Everybody is talking about you."

"It was a common effort."

"Of course." She paused, eyeing me closely. "What's wrong? You look downcast. You must be tired."

"I am." I nodded. Then I took a breath. "Can we talk? Alone?"

We walked to the porch of the parish church, where we would not be overheard.

"Is something wrong?" Griselda repeated.

I cleared my throat, feeling suddenly weary. "I think you should leave the abbey — when it becomes safe to do so."

Griselda's eyes widened, but she said nothing.

"I made inquiries about your family," I went on. "Your father's inn has become quite prosperous." The village was also safe, being located in the opposite direction of where the mercenaries were marauding. "I am sure they will be happy to see you back. You are almost seventeen," I added, for there was still no response, "and you won't be able to keep up your disguise much longer."

I had expected tears, bargaining, perhaps even anger; instead, Griselda's face paled into a look of resignation. "You are right," she said finally. "I have been lucky to be able to pass for a boy for so long, but it is bound to end, and then I will be in trouble."

I was relieved, but the meekness that was so much a part of Griselda's character made it harder.

She dropped her gaze. For a moment I thought she would cry, but she looked up again, almost serene, although her eyes glistened. "I only wish that I had found a way —"

"It was never going to work like that, but don't despair," I said gently. "By putting some distance between yourself and the abbey, you will be able to give it more thought. Who knows, maybe once you return to the world, you will find it more to your liking than before. I know this is what you desire," I hastened to add, seeing tears well up in her eyes as she shook her head. I put a hand on her shoulder. "Don't lose hope."

But in truth, I had no idea how this might be accomplished. I wondered if I should write to my mother to borrow a modest sum for Griselda's dowry, but with the cost of my sisters' marriages, that was probably not feasible. As always, thoughts of my mother — though less frequent these days — gave me a pang of longing, and my throat tightened. Blinking to relieve the pressure behind my eyes, I reminded myself that things had a way of working out in the end—my own life was proof of that.

"I will always think of you as a sister, and I will miss you," I said. "But this is for the best—one day you will see I was right."

Instead of returning to the table, I went back to the infirmary and climbed the ladder to the roof again. The night, like the day before it, was clear, and the near-full moon cast a silvery glow on the fields, making the woods stand out darkly in the distance.

Listening to the muffled sounds of the celebration still going on below, I shuddered at the thought of the horrors that could have been visited on the town had the mercenaries had better knowledge of our defenses. It had been a hard day. I had seen men killed and had assisted Brother Wigbert as he extracted arrowheads from wounds and used cautery to stop bleeding.

As I reviewed the events in my mind, my sadness deepened at the thought that men would so freely endanger themselves and others for no better reason than greed. And I understood that wars had to be avoided at all costs because it was not the emperor or the pope, not even their fighting men, who paid the highest price, but ordinary folk caught in the middle of conflicts they did not understand and in which they had no stake.

But that was no longer true of me. I had had a taste of power and saw that the life I had been born into gave me an opportunity to act in ways that many others could not. And that realization left me breathless with an expansive feeling of freedom I had never known before.

19

September 1122

THE WEEKS THAT followed were tense. People were afraid to venture out of the town even to fetch firewood until news arrived in the early autumn that negotiations at Würzburg had forestalled direct confrontation between the rival forces. Armed men had been ordered to stand down, and anyone caught breaking the peace of the land would be punished severely.

Disibodenberg greeted this with relief, but soon another worry emerged, for the skirmishes had ruined fields and delayed harvest in much of the Rhineland. There was a shortage of laborers too, as those who had lost their homes to the pillaging had picked up what belongings they could salvage and left in search of other places to settle. For the abbey, that meant that all the able-bodied residents, except the anchoresses, were needed to help.

Brother Wigbert helped me obtain an assignment at the orchards alongside Volmar, and together we worked briskly in the crisp air of a September morning, shaking the branches to loosen the ripe fruit, then taking turns climbing the ladder to pick off what was left. As we progressed, I could not help but notice how Volmar had changed from the boy I had met four years before. He was taller than me now, and the golden fuzz on his upper lip had begun to darken and spread to his cheeks. The years of running through the forest and hunting had made him quick, lean, and strong.

We arrived at the edge of the orchard, by the fence that divided it from the vineyards. On one side, the slow-moving band of the Glan shimmered in the sun. It was a secluded spot where we could talk at ease because Volmar had just shared with me confidential information from the scriptorium, where he now trained as a scribe.

"How can you be sure it's not just another rumor?" I was skeptical. "There have been so many these last few weeks, and they all turned out to be false."

"Father Abbot is quite certain this time."

"But the messengers didn't even bring a copy!"

"They were in a hurry to get to Mainz with the announcement," Volmar explained. "It was so urgent they hadn't even waited for copies to be made, but they assured Father Abbot that the archbishop's trusted man would deliver one to us as soon as it was ready."

Apparently, representatives of the emperor and the pope had signed a concordat in the town of Worms, not far from Bermersheim, four days before. The agreement was supposed to regulate the relations between the monarchy and the Church and end the conflict that had torn our land apart for so many years.

"And your task will be to make copies for the abbey?" I asked to confirm. I could barely contain my excitement at the thought of so important a document being available there.

"Yes," Volmar said proudly, "together with Brother Bertolf."

I gazed over the river, thinking. A solution to the crisis would benefit not just the parties involved, but ordinary people who bore its brunt. I wondered about the details of the agreement that managed to satisfy both sides. "Brother Wigbert told me how many privileges and rights the Church and the empire have claimed for themselves over the years," I said. "It seems that what they want above all is to be able to meddle in each other's affairs. I cannot imagine how they were able to reconcile such ambitions."

Volmar shrugged. He did not have much interest in high matters of state and was more absorbed by the prospect of being able to copy the concordat than its contents or future success.

"Can I ask you a favor?" I turned to him, biting my lip.

"Of course."

"Would you let me read your copy when it is ready?"

He hesitated. "It would be difficult to get you inside the scriptorium without anyone noticing." But my gaze must have been so imploring that he added, "I might be able to take it out for a few hours."

I leaped to my feet excitedly, and we went back to work, laughing and chatting until we broke for a midday meal of bread, cheese, and wine. Resting in the shade of a tree, I was suddenly reminded of a trip I had once taken with Griselda to the forest which she had turned into a picnic by bringing a bit of food from the kitchen. She was gone now, having taken her leave after the Feast of the Assumption.

"Brother Wigbert has always been good to me, but until Griselda arrived, I had been lonely." The urge to confide came unexpectedly, and I knew it was my guilt speaking.

"It must have been hard." Volmar's tone was sympathetic. "It was not easy for me at first, either, and I at least had the company of other boys."

"My circumstances were special."

He nodded. My story was in some ways similar to his own. He had also been given to the Church at an early age, but nobody had attempted to impose total seclusion on him.

I shook my head to dispel those thoughts. "But it all turned out rather well, don't you think?" I swept an arm toward the abbey. "This place has truly opened my mind to ideas I did not know existed. I am grateful for that, and I am happy now."

"Despite the attack?"

"Yes." I thought back on that near-disaster two months before. "It was terrifying, but we stayed and fought, and that made me feel strong." I paused, then lowered my head. "Losing a friend is much worse because there is nothing you can do about it."

"I am your friend too." There was a note in Volmar's voice I had not heard before. When he was with the other novices, his voice was as loud and as militant as theirs during the recreation hour when they sometimes played in the courtyard until Prior Helenger came out and put an end to the merriment. But now there was a tenderness in it that made it strangely sweet. "And I am still here," he added, sending my heart fluttering like a bird batting its wings inside a cage.

"I know." I heard my own voice borrowing his emphasis. "You are a dear friend."

His gaze, when he turned his head, made my heart skip a beat altogether. We were sitting shoulder to shoulder, and he shifted toward me so that our faces were closer than ever before. I was frozen in place. The next moment, his lips were on mine, tentative and timid at first, then increasingly more assured, powered by some unseen force. Blood swooshed from my head and seemed to all go into my fingers and toes. I felt dizzy, but there was also a heaviness in my limbs that made me want to melt into the ground.

Volmar's hand found mine, then moved up my arm and stopped at my shoulder, hesitating for a moment before sliding across my chest. My belly tightened into a knot, painful but not unpleasant, and when his fingers brushed my breasts again under the thin fabric of my robe, the knot relaxed and flooded me with a warm and tingling sensation. With effort, I broke away from him. But we remained only inches apart, listening to each other's breaths, before we fell back on the soft yellowing grass under the apple tree.

The river, low after a hot summer and lazily pursuing its course toward the Rhine around sandy shallows, sparkled in the afternoon sun. *So this is how it feels*, I thought, my body still holding on to this novel sensation, my heart slowing from its furious pace. I knew little about relations between men and women, except that they resulted in offspring whose birthing process was of considerable medical interest to me. But it was all shrouded in mystery, sometimes hinted at during those births in code words that were pronounced with embarrassment, or, alternatively, with ribald humor.

I remembered the couple in the alley during the feast of St. Disibod. I had wondered what made them so giddy and impatient, and now I knew. It *was* nice. Then I remembered how the Church — of which I was to become a consecrated member one day — viewed these matters.

Yet how could this sweet, tender thing be wrong? I stole a glance at Volmar, lost in his own thoughts with the serious look I liked so much, and I could feel no regret. He felt my movement and turned to me. For some moments, his eyes traced the lines of my face as if he were about to set off on a long journey and wanted to remember every detail of it. Then he reached and touched my hair, loose after my veil had slipped off. It had grown out long again now that Jutta's frequent illnesses had caused her to abandon her rule about keeping it shorn. "It is like ripe wheat," he said in a marveling tone as he ran his fingers down my tresses.

I closed my eyes, delighted by the comparison, and nestled next to him, basking in the glow that seemed to surround us. Against my thigh, I could feel the pressure of the little box in the pocket of my robe, and I imagined the pure white lump of salt inside, still unchanged even as I had grown and become a woman.

And then words flashed through my mind that sent me into a fit of laughter. Volmar looked at me quizzically but could not help smiling himself. "What's so funny?"

"You won't believe it," I gasped, "but Brother Wigbert once warned me against this when he saw me alone with Griselda. He thought that she and I—"

"I *can* believe it!" He was laughing too, covering his face with his hands.

"Yet it has never occurred to anybody to keep an eye on us!"

The familiar twinkle of mischief returned to Volmar's hazel eyes. "I suppose they trust novices more than they do kitchen boys."

I grew somber again. "That was the real reason she had to go."

"Because they thought that she—or rather *he*—fancied you?"

"That and the fact that she was almost grown up, and it would have been difficult to keep the secret much longer," I said. "I felt it was my duty to tell her that, and she was heartbroken. It is my fault," I added glumly. "I should have been honest with her from the beginning that it was a bad idea."

"She had a few years of happiness thanks to you."

"I told her there might be a way for her to return, but I am not sure I believe it. Not as long as—" I broke off, stunned by what had just occurred to me.

"Not as long as it is not your decision to make?" he finished quietly.

Once again, he had read my thoughts perfectly.

20

October 1122

THE CONCORDAT MAY have been signed, but it was only when the written proclamation had reached Disibodenberg that the town resumed its normal rhythm, with the folk once again going about their business and visiting relatives in nearby villages without fear. At the scriptorium, Volmar and Bertolf worked ceaselessly, and soon I had a copy in my hands which I stayed up all night to peruse.

Awaiting the lauds bell as the gray light of dawn broke over the abbey, I set the parchment aside, rubbed my eyes, and tried to imagine the main characters in this power play. In the palace at Aachen, the emperor, wearing a trefoil crown, was poring over scrolls of vellum, plotting how to retain control over church appointments. In a parallel scene in Rome, the pope, dressed all in white and surrounded by his advisers, tried to determine how to wrest these powers from the monarchy while holding on to as much land as possible. The scope of the struggle was breathtaking, but the document before me seemed to suggest that all that scheming was finally at an end. And yet I was unconvinced.

Later that day, Abbot Kuno convened a special Chapter meeting where a report on the attack would be presented. He had invited me and Volmar, and as the two of us entered the chapter house for the first time in our lives, we found a chamber different from anything else within the abbey. It was round, and the four narrow windows around its circumference let in little light on that rain-whipped October day. Below the windows, tiered rows of seats formed a semicircle that faced an open area occupied by a trestle table and chairs, and illuminated by dozens of candles in iron holders. The abbot had yet to arrive, and a hum of subdued conversations filled the chamber, despite The Rule's exhortation that the brethren keep silent. We took seats in the front row near the door, and a moment later, a snippet of a conversation reached our ears.

"Master Abelard's book was condemned at a provincial synod and ordered burned," a monk seated behind us was saying to his neighbor. "I have it from Hubert von Bernstein, and other pilgrims confirm it."

Volmar and I exchanged curious glances. Herr Hubert was a local nobleman and an abbey patron who had travelled to Compostela in the spring and stopped at St. Disibod a few days before on his way home from the pilgrimage.

"That cannot be!" The other monk was aghast. "By all accounts, Abelard is much revered around the cloister of Notre Dame."

"Apparently, there had been some kind of a scandal. A *love affair*." A sanctimonious note colored the first monk's voice. "And he had already fallen from grace. Then his opponents at Soissons turned the synod into a veritable trial with the Archbishop of Rheims leading the charge."

There was a moment of silence. I would have given a lot to see their faces. Then the second monk asked, "What did they find against him?"

"The judgment said that he had committed heresy by proposing to interpret the dogma of the Holy Trinity by means of reasoning rather than by acceptance and faith."

"God protect us!"

"I wonder if he will be allowed to return to teaching—" He was interrupted by the abbot's entrance. The gathering fell silent as Kuno took his seat at the table, flanked by Prior Helenger, Brother Ignatius, and Brother Odo.

During the opening prayer I could not help thinking about the famous philosopher from Paris who had been bold enough to challenge the men of the Church with new ideas. It was both frightening and exciting, and something told me I had not heard the last of him. But I made an effort to listen when Prior Helenger began reading out the report in a loud, self-important voice. He had been tasked with preparing it and to that end, had spoken with the town elders, with Volmar and his archers, and even with me. I grimaced at the memory of that brief and unpleasant interview, but the report was good—detailed and faithful to what had occurred.

"Thank you, Brother Prior," the abbot said when Helenger rolled up the parchment. "We pray every day for the souls of the five men who lost their lives that our town and abbey might be saved."

The monks lowered their heads. After a few moments of silence, Kuno spoke again. "I believe God sent us this trial as a warning. We must learn from it so we are better prepared next time, for despite the new concordat, we still live in uncertain times." Heads nodded all around. "We do not have military leaders living within our precincts, but Volmar proved to be an able archer and commander. I asked him, therefore, to provide recommendations on how we may cultivate this skill at Disibodenberg." He motioned him to speak.

Volmar stood up and turned to face the monks. There was a barely perceptible tremble in his voice, whether from excitement or nervousness I could not tell. "At Father Abbot's request" — he nodded respectfully toward the table — "I consulted with the town elders, and we believe that from now on, archery should be more than a pastime. We must conduct regular drills for all the able-bodied men over the age of fourteen. The town has ranges set up for competition by the Glan, and I offer to conduct the training myself." A slightly boastful note had entered his voice in a decidedly non-monkish fashion, and I had to stifle a smile. "We will also need to keep a store of arrows on hand. They can be purchased at fairs, but we should also have a resident fletcher. I offer to train him, as I learned how to make bows and arrows at my father's house." A murmur of admiration swept the rows of seats, and many heads nodded again. "Furthermore, we should consider training younger men in swordsmanship. I am not a swordsman myself, but there are former fighting men in the town, and they would be eager to share their expertise."

"These are reasonable proposals," the abbot said. "Does anyone care to comment?" He paused, but there was no response. "Good. Brother bursar will make a note that we need to find funds to support equipping the menfolk with bows and arrows and some swords, and pay those who will train them. And now" — he was eager to move on with the agenda — "I ask Hildegard to say a few words regarding our walls, as a sign of appreciation for her encouragement on the day we learned about the danger facing us."

Sitting to his right, the prior had so far ignored me but now turned resentful eyes in my direction. I rose, and although I had treated many of the monks, they seemed uncomfortable and shifted uneasily in their seats. But there were a few curious faces too, and Bertolf's was positively friendly as he gave me an encouraging nod.

"Brothers." I inclined my head. "I have talked to pilgrims, merchants, and journeymen about the defenses they had seen elsewhere, and it has been very instructive." I sought to inject an extra dose of assurance into my voice. "It appears that wooden walls are becoming obsolete, as towns are choosing stone as a longer-lasting and sturdier material, not to mention less prone to catching fire. I recommend rebuilding our walls in the same fashion."

There was an eruption of voices from the tiered seats, and the abbot raised his palm. "Silence! If you have opinions or comments to offer, do so one at a time. Brother Ordulf?"

The matricularius stood up. "Wood is a perfectly good and time-tested building material and is available in abundance," he said. "New Benedictine houses like the Laach priory have used it. We should mend and strengthen the existing walls instead of incurring the expense and nuisance of tearing them down and raising new ones," he concluded, staring at me down the length of his nose.

"I agree." Brother Ignatius, the treasurer, chimed in. "There are ongoing renovations that still need to be paid for."

I saw that this was going to be about money and the vanity projects the abbey had under way. A lavish new chapel was being constructed, paid for by an endowment from a wealthy landowner. The treasurer was already salivating at the idea of the relics, precious vessels, and ornaments that would have to be acquired to fill it to the glory of God. One glance at the abbot told me that he shared that view. It was hardly surprising; Kuno had been on a quest for new relics for months now, huddling with itinerant sellers in search of the perfect set that would attract more pilgrims to the abbey.

"Brother bursar, what say you?" He turned to Odo.

"I would have to know the estimated cost to make a definitive judgment, of course," the bursar replied deferentially, "but I suspect it wouldn't be cheap. Our income is not likely to allow for this kind of expense."

The abbot turned to me. "We shall keep your suggestion in mind for when we receive a new endowment. In the meantime, we can set smaller sums aside for repairs."

My heart sank. Had he forgotten our narrow escape? He had just talked about the need to learn lessons but was already thinking of half-measures. "But Father, if I may — you have said that these are uncertain times. Solid and reliable walls are a life-saving priority, not a luxury, and we forego them at our peril!"

Kuno did not miss my emphasis on the word *luxury*. "We are not a wealthy house," he replied coolly. "A new chapel and new relics are our gift to the saints that they may continue to protect us."

I sat down, defeated. I knew better than to argue, but it was a bitter pill to swallow. It was worrisome too, because as long as the peace held, however fragile, there would always be a more important vanity to indulge before practical considerations.

The abbot's voice rang out again, "Now let us turn to the matter of the agreement recently signed at the Worms cathedral." Forgetting my disappointment, I was suddenly all ears. For a moment, I expected to be asked to leave, but the abbot continued. "As many of you know, we received the text of the agreement struck between His Holiness Pope Calixtus and Emperor Heinrich, and our scribes have made copies, one of which will be kept at the library if you want to peruse it. My purpose today is to inform you of the chief benefits of the concordat for our Holy Church." He paused for effect, and the tension in the room was palpable as all eyes watched his lips. "From now on," he resumed, "the election of bishops and abbots will be left to their constituents — that is to say, cathedral canons and monks, respectively. No more arbitrary appointments of the emperor's men and other loyalists." An excited murmur rose over the chamber. "And the Church has been freed from the noxious control of secular authority by removing the right of kings to invest bishops with the insignia of spiritual power — the ring and the crosier."

I glanced over my shoulder and saw the monks nodding with satisfaction, no sign of skepticism on any of their faces. I waited for someone to offer a comment or ask a question, but nobody did. The abbot's complacent look suggested that he was not about to qualify his statement any further.

Before I knew what I was doing, I bolted from the bench as if pushed by an invisible hand. "But Father Abbot," I protested, "the emperor retains the right of arbitration!"

A ripple of gasps swept the chapter house, and I felt Volmar tugging at my sleeve. The abbot frowned. His intention, it seemed, had been to present the concordat as a complete success of the papal faction. Still, he answered patiently enough. "That is less privilege than what the monarchy had previously enjoyed. It returns the emperor into the ranks of laymen and allows the Church to govern itself."

That was true. The agreement was a defeat of the notion that kings were God's anointed and as such imbued with the divine right to influence ecclesiastical affairs. Yet giving the emperor the right to have the final say in *disputed* elections was akin to preserving his right to appoint men that suited him, for, as everyone knew, episcopal contests were notoriously fractious. "The emperor will still invest bishops with the lance, after having witnessed their election in person or through his representatives, and perhaps having cast the deciding vote," I persisted, firm in the opinion I had formed last night. "He effectively retains the power of appointment, and that means that little will change — his successors will take advantage of this right whenever possible, and the conflict will continue. This agreement solves little."

A profound silence descended on the gathering as all eyes turned to the abbot, except Brother Wigbert's, whose pleading gaze was trained on me from across the chamber. As Kuno weighed his response, a range of emotions crossed his face from irritation to amazement to impatience.

Prior Helenger, on the other hand, had no trouble deciding. "How dare you speak without permission?" He was barely able to contain himself. "We will not sit here and listen to your opinions on matters of state!"

"Chapter is a forum for an open discussion, and I was asked to attend, so I assumed that I had the same right to speak as anyone else," I replied, lifting my chin. "And I have doubts whether this concordat will help the Church achieve a separation and autonomy from the empire."

The prior scoffed. "You *obviously* don't know what you are talking about. The Church does not want to be separate from the state. The Church must oversee the state because all power proceeds from God, and it is our task to ensure that the monarchy conducts its affairs based on Christian principles."

In a flash, I remembered Brother Wigbert's explanation of the origins of the conflict and how the fault lay on both sides. It suddenly made sense. Helenger's words had revealed a complex game on the part of the Church, the mirror image, in fact, of the monarchy's ambitions. After all, had not Pope Gregorius excommunicated the emperor's father, denied his sovereignty, and instigated the appointment of an anti-king? The Church had been fighting for the same thing — the entirety of power, rather than its own separate domain. And this despite Christ's admonition that His kingdom was not of this world.

Abbot Kuno, as if guessing what was going through my mind, said in a tone that was almost gracious, "We must rejoice that the investiture settlement gives the Church a spiritual autonomy. It will also ensure peace throughout the realm."

"I am not sure about that, Father." I pulled my arm discreetly against another tug from below. "The emperor will still be able to put pressure on the clergy as he did to Archbishop Adalbert when he put him in prison."

The abbot grew suspicious. "How do you know so much about the concordat?"

I faltered, belatedly realizing that I might get Volmar in trouble. But then Helenger renewed his attack. "How?" he snarled. "It's obvious — she's a witch! The Devil let her into the scriptorium at night and she read the copies!" His voice rose hysterically.

For the first time, I saw the abbot redden with anger. "I will not have this kind of talk in Chapter or anywhere else within this abbey! This meeting is over!" He turned to the monks. "You are dismissed. And you" — he pointed a finger at me — "will see me in my parlor."

He exited hastily, and the monks followed at a more leisurely pace amid a buzz of talk and occasional glances at me. Rising from the bench, Volmar gave me a reproachful look. I held my hand out in an apologetic gesture, but he walked away. As the chamber emptied, Brother Wigbert came over, shaking his head resignedly. "I will go with you," he said, "and you better show some contrition."

The fire crackling in the hearth banished the autumn gloom and spread a pleasant warmth throughout the parlor. The abbot was sitting at his desk, and the prior occupied the usual place at his right shoulder, standing with his hands folded inside the sleeves of his robe. The orange glow danced on their faces, one weary and the other maliciously alert. When I walked in, the abbot asked without any preamble, "Are you aware that novices are not allowed to speak up during Chapter meetings unless specifically invited to do so?"

"I am now, Father," I replied humbly, mindful of Brother Wigbert's admonition, although it was all I could do to stop myself from reminding him that I had, in fact, been invited to speak — just on a different subject. "I beg your indulgence."

"This was your first infraction, so I am going be lenient. You are not to leave the convent for three days, and you will lie flat through each service of the Divine Office as penance during that time."

"Yes, Father."

"You should thank Father Abbot for not putting you on bread and water," Helenger growled, unhappy with so light a sentence. "Still, this will teach you not to speak on matters you don't understand. Who do you fancy yourself to be now—a papal representative?"

"No, but neither are you."

The prior's face paled. "This level of insolence is not to be tolerated!" His whole frame was shaking.

I thought the abbot's chin twitched before he composed his features into a stern look. "I am concerned that you do not know your proper place, Hildegard."

"Father, if I may," Brother Wigbert interjected. "I will gladly remind my assistant what her role is. She has had much success in the infirmary and may think that it entitles her to express opinions on other issues and in other forums. It won't happen again."

His intentions were good, but I was stung nonetheless. How could he talk so dismissively about me, and as if I were not even there? I remained silent, but inside I nursed a great sense of injustice.

Helenger would not let the opportunity slip. "Why is she still allowed to walk freely around the abbey, I wonder?" His voice rose shrilly again. "Shouldn't she be confined to the enclosure to prepare for her vows? She is of age, and her continuing presence is a distraction and a bad influence on the monks. I have seen how some of them look at her—"

"Prior Helenger!"

"Forgive me for speaking so bluntly, Father, but the second year of her novitiate is coming to an end, and instead of retiring to the convent to become an anchoress, she is taking trips to the town and usurping Sister Jutta's role as *magistra*."

"I am not usurping anybody's role!" I protested vehemently, my cheeks burning with anger and shame at his insinuations. "Sister Jutta remains our superior."

"You see, Father? All she does is argue like a lawyer at the emperor's court. She needs to learn her place. There is no room for insubordination in a holy community."

"Speaking up at Chapter without an invitation is not a grave violation of The Rule, and she has been reprimanded," the abbot reminded him with a touch of impatience.

"She went to the fair three years ago. Alone." The prior's voice was suddenly calm, but it cut like a blade. "Ask Brother Wigbert if she had his permission."

The infirmarian looked at me quizzically, and the abbot frowned. "Is that true?"

"Yes," I admitted contritely, sending Brother Wigbert an apologetic look.

The abbot did not seem eager to pursue this further — it was a long time ago, after all — but the prior was not done. "She was also overheard questioning the validity of the Augustinian doctrine."

My memory reeled back to the day when I had talked with Brother Wigbert about Church Fathers as he tended to the ailing cobbler. The monk with jaundice on the neighboring bed must have reported it to Helenger. Icy sweat broke all over my body as I realized that my suspicions were correct — the prior had spies everywhere.

"I was not yet fourteen, and I was learning about the Church." I tried to retain my composure. "Surely you are not going to accuse a child of heresy?"

"You are not a child anymore," Helenger snickered, "and who knows what views you hold now?"

"That's enough." The abbot rose with surprising energy, his chair scraping across the stone floor. "I will not hear another word of it. I am not going to investigate heresy among my novices. However" — he turned to me wearily — "it is true that your novitiate is almost complete, and you must prepare for your vows. You will return to the convent and stay there."

"But Father Abbot, the infirmary!" Brother Wigbert protested.

"It worked before she arrived," Kuno said firmly, "and it will work after she is gone."

21

February 1123

"*O* NOBILISSIMA VIRIDITAS, *que radicas in sole et que in candida serenitate luces.*" The chant, my favorite, reminded me that nature — steady and reassuring in its timelessness even when the world of human making seemed to be falling apart — possessed an unfailing power to lift our spirits. "O noblest greenness, you are rooted in the sun, sparkling with bright serenity."

"*Tu rubes ut aurora et ardes ut solis flamma.*" Among the chorus of voices was a new one, and it belonged to Gertrude, a girl of fourteen who had made the perilous winter journey from Swabia shortly after Epiphany to join our convent. She was quiet and obedient, but when it came to music, she filled the chapel with a pure and sublime sound. She had received a musical education at home including the principles of notation, and I hoped to use her talent to expand our repertoire of chants. "As morning's dawn you glow and burn like the sun's flame."

The final notes climbed to their wavering heights when a loud knock on the gate reverberated throughout the enclosure. I rose and stepped into the sunless light of a February afternoon. The world around me had nothing of the verdant luxuriance praised in the chant, but I hoped the music would see me through the winter until the sparse vines animated with new leaves. Would my life be better then?

Since the previous autumn, I had been confined to the convent and found the long periods of silence broken by prayers hard. My vocation was meant to be an active one that would allow me to constantly improve my mind and better the lives of others in practical ways. But my existence was constrained and quiet, and it was not good for me.

The knocking resumed, sounding more urgent. I slid the bolt and saw the anxious face of a young monk through the grille in the door. In a nervous voice, he explained that I was to come see Brother Wigbert immediately. I asked no questions as I hastily wrapped myself in my cloak and followed him.

In the infirmary, he ushered me straight into the surgery where Brother Wigbert waited with a patient, a gangly teen with a broken arm. My medical instincts stirred immediately as I noted that the bone was dislocated but had not pierced the skin. The young monk stood quietly next to me, his eyes downcast and his face pale green.

"Thank you, Brother Edwig, that will be all." Wigbert's voice was calm, but I detected a note of irritation in it.

The monk withdrew hastily, and the infirmarian shook his head. "The boy has a weak stomach, and he cannot make drafts that would at least bring patients some relief as recompense for their poor taste," he sighed.

"I am sorry to hear that." I was struck by Wigbert's decline. Since last I saw him, his movements had noticeably slowed. As he rubbed his joints, I noticed with dismay that his fingers had become more gnarled.

Our eyes met, and I knew that he had guessed my thoughts. "I sent for you," he said, "because I can no longer set bones safely. I had hoped to guide Edwig through the process, but he almost fainted." His face was serious, but his eyes shone with affection. There was also a glimmer of pain in them, and it was more than the physical ache of his sore joints. It betrayed the realization of fading away as a physician, a role he had embraced for most of his life which was probably more important to him than that of a monk.

I averted my gaze and set out to prepare for the procedure. Moments later, I was working under Wigbert's experienced eye, although I had assisted him so many times, I would have been able to do it alone. When the bone was back in its place and the patient sent on his way, the infirmarian motioned for me to follow him to the workshop.

"I am glad to see you." He lowered himself on to the bench with a groan, relieved to be off his feet. "You are the best student I have ever had."

I flushed with pleasure at the compliment, and at the sense of our old camaraderie that I missed so much.

"Poor Edwig is trying hard, but he has two left hands with my glass vials," Wigbert went on. "He cannot begin to comprehend the first thing about the balance of humors, and urine analysis repulses him. He is too soft." He sighed. "Meanwhile, your talent is going to waste."

My throat tightened, for he had echoed a frequent and desperate thought of mine over the last four months. "I am content." I tried to sound convincing. "I have a great deal to do at the convent." That part was true at least; Jutta was almost always ill with fever, and Juliana preferred that I lead them during services, even though she was my senior. And we were constantly receiving letters from candidates, which it was my job to review before passing any recommendations on to the abbot. "Sister Jutta needs me."

But the old monk was not fooled. "It is a *waste*," he repeated, waving his hand. "And as for Jutta, it is only a matter of time before she loses her life to those practices."

"She may be misguided, but few women deserve to be called holy more than she does."

A mixture of surprise and amusement crossed Wigbert's face. "And to think that only a few years ago, you were rebelling against the self-flagellations while I was the one attempting to justify them."

"I try to understand. It doesn't mean I approve."

"Are you taking a more indulgent view of St. Augustine now too?"

I shrugged. "His teachings on the virtue of moderation are similar to those of our founder, and I agree with them. But I find his stance on the issue of infant baptism unjust and unmerciful."

"You are a thinker." Brother Wigbert smiled. "And that is why I need you back here."

My heart fluttered with a tiny glimmer of hope, but my reply was sober. "Father Abbot will not permit that."

"He already has. We have had enough mishaps to draw his attention. Two weeks ago, a woman suffering from an excess of yellow bile almost died when Edwig made her a draft of milk thistle, black pepper, valerian root, and I don't know what else. She convulsed on the floor, and it took two of us to hold her down to prevent her from choking. But I don't blame the boy," he added in his usual kind-hearted way. "He did not volunteer. Prior Helenger sent him. I should have overseen him better, but I am old and it is hard for me to keep an eye on everything."

"I am sure you are still of great help to your patients."

Wigbert shook his head. The pain in his eyes was gone, replaced by the same serene resignation I had seen in Sister Adelheid when she had faced her mortality. I wondered if I would have the same courage to accept the inevitability of passing when my time came.

"I am becoming useless," he said, speaking over my attempt to protest again. "If we are to be able to fulfill our Benedictine duty to the sick, you must come back. The abbot recognizes that and has authorized your return. Besides" — he smiled with pride — "patients are asking after you."

I could not help smiling back. "If I am needed, I will gladly accept the task."

"It is decided, then." He was visibly relieved, though his relief could not have been greater than mine.

"Brother . . ." I hesitated.

"What is it?"

"There are things we need at the convent — like charcoal and lamp oil — that we are unable to procure ourselves. We are out of funds."

Wigbert looked dismayed. "I will have them sent today. Is there anything else you need?"

"Fresh rushes and some wool to mend our winter robes would be good too." Then I added, "I don't understand why we have no money, especially as Gertrude brought fifty silver marks with her not two months ago."

I was certainly not prepared for what I heard next. "Sister Jutta cedes the anchoresses' dowries to the abbey," the infirmarian said. "I thought you knew," he added, seeing my mouth fall open.

My mind reeled. Why would she do that? But I already knew the answer; Jutta believed in utter poverty and cared nothing for comforts. Yet her stance would only hurt us in the long run. "I must speak with Father Abbot," I said, gripped by a sense of desperation. "Can you arrange that, Brother?"

"Speak about what?" He blinked.

"A permission to enlarge the convent." I knew I did not have the authority to make such a request, but Jutta was beyond caring, and the convent could not go on like this for much longer.

To my surprise, he did not object to my raising the idea — perhaps the monks already understood Jutta's waning role—but that did not mean that they would accommodate me. "I doubt he will agree."

"Why not? It is too small for the four of us; we sleep, eat, and study in the same room."

"You are arguing about the convenience of women who have chosen to lead an anchorite life."

He had a point. "What about future income?" I asked. "There is much interest in our convent, and we could admit more novices if we expanded our quarters. And as things stand"—I could not help the bitterness in my voice—"the abbey would benefit the most."

Wigbert chuckled. "Now *that* is an argument that might convince Father Abbot."

Thus I returned to the infirmary. Brother Edwig was relegated to menial tasks, which he was only too happy to perform. I came every afternoon, and although I was no longer allowed to go into the town, I was nonetheless grateful to be able to practice medicine again. The abbot heard my plea for the expansion and promised to think about it, but if the abbey wall was any indication, nothing was likely to come of it any time soon.

All through those months Griselda was never far from my thoughts. I finally wrote to my mother to ask for a small loan to secure Griselda's admittance. Afterwards, I sat listening to a May shower pattering on the roof, and my thoughts drifted back to my first year in the convent when I had been lonely and homesick. Those feelings had abated over time, but I still felt nostalgic every Christmas when the annual letter from Bermersheim arrived. The news had been mostly good: marriages, new nieces and nephews, good harvests, and salt production from the Alzey mine that continued to provide the family with a respectable income.

There had been only one mournful letter in those eight years; it had announced my father's death the previous winter. My eldest brother Drutwin had taken over the management of Bermersheim, and my mother lived with his family on a small income from her widow's inheritance. As I sealed my letter, I recalled one of the last conversations I had with her, about how unfair it was for poor people not to be able to pursue a religious vocation in the same way that wealthy ones could. A surge of pride welled inside me that I always felt when I thought about my mother who—even if she did not often get her way—had never been afraid of making her opinions known.

I smiled as sunshine pierced through the clouds, wondering whether my own stubbornness had come from her. It had to have, because my father, God rest his soul, had always preferred to stick to familiar traditions and the surety of unquestioned beliefs.

After the midday service I went to the infirmary. It was quiet, and Brother Wigbert informed me in a matter-of-fact tone that Volmar had just been there asking for me. "I told him to see if you were in the workshop," he added as he disappeared into the ward with a bottle of gout medicine.

I turned on my heel and hurried to the herb garden, for I had not seen Volmar in months. But I was not prepared for my reaction when I turned the corner and almost ran into him.

How can I explain it? My throat went dry, and I felt so light-headed that for a brief, stunning moment, I thought my legs would buckle under me. The realization of how much I had missed him crashed over me. "You wanted to see me?"

He nodded, and I noticed how serious he was, almost grave.

"Are you unwell? You should have asked Brother Wigbert—" I broke off as he shook his head, tightly but firmly.

"I wanted to talk to *you*."

"Of course." I moved past him, my puzzlement growing, and he followed me into the workshop.

By now there was not a cloud in the sky. As we stepped inside I inhaled the aromatic air, a mixture of dry herbs and old timber warmed by the sun. We sat facing each other across the table where I had spent so many hours studying medical texts. Volmar's freckles had faded now that he was spending much of his days in the scriptorium, but his brown hair shone golden where sunlight touched it, just like it always had. It also curled slightly above his ears, a sight that made me feel inexplicably tender.

His expression remained impenetrable, and it made me nervous because I was usually able to guess his moods. "Are you unwell?" I repeated, feeling immediately awkward. He had already said he was not. "Can I make you a draft?' The second question was even worse.

"I'm fine," he replied distractedly. He seemed to be considering something.

I jumped from the bench. "Do you want some wine?"

"Thank you."

I poured two cups and returned to the table. Volmar's closeness increased my nervous excitement, and the robust scent of spring wafting from the garden did little to mitigate it.

Since that day at the orchard the previous autumn, the way I thought about him had changed. It was not the simple joy of our early trips that I recalled; rather, a flash of a smile or a hand gesture would intrude on my thoughts during my studies, in the chapel, or when I was boiling roots, and it would make me feel hot and breathless even on a cold day. I closed my eyes and took a long sip of the wine so he would not guess my thoughts.

But before I put it down, he said abruptly, "I have come to ask you about your vows."

I swallowed. "My vows?"

"Yes. Are you preparing for them?"

"Uh, yes . . . though I have still much to do." I rolled my eyes in mock despair, but he did not seem amused. "I have been so occupied with medicine these last few years that I have much ground to make up in theology," I explained.

"It can be tedious."

I laughed more loudly than I intended. "It certainly can, but it has made me think of ways to combine nature and healing with God's teachings. I believe" — I leaned forward, warming quickly to my theme, as I did whenever I discussed my studies — "that He left us clues as to His purpose and our destiny in the way He organized the world. There is still much I don't understand, but perhaps with time it will become clearer."

I thought my excitement would lift Volmar's mood, but he only arched his eyebrows. "You have no doubts, then, that this is the path you want to take?"

"No," I said, surprising myself with a slight hesitation. "Do you?"

"I have . . . some." His gaze darkened as it wandered to the window, faint color rising to his face. "There are many ways a life can be lived worthily, and they all have their appeal and also their price," he said reflectively. "Right now, I don't know if the monastic life is right for me. I don't know if my calling is genuine, if this is what I want, or if I am only fulfilling my parents' wish. I used to think that it was desirable, but now" — he looked me straight in the eye — "I am not so sure."

My breath became painfully shallow. "I cannot imagine a different life for myself," I said, feeling a clutch at my heart. "This is the only path that will allow me to do what I want to do." I saw a shadow cross Volmar's face. "There is no denying that it is hard; if you have any doubts, you should not undertake it. People who take vows against their conviction condemn themselves to a life of misery that can make them drift as far away from God as the most unrepentant of sinners." I paused, finding my next words difficult but necessary. "So if it is a different kind of life that you desire, if it is marriage that you are made for, you should return to the world. Only then will you be truly happy." I looked down at my hands, blinking to relieve the pressure building behind my eyes.

"What about you?" he asked vehemently. "Is love nothing to you?"

My heart stopped, and for a long moment I could not trust myself to speak. When I did, my voice was barely above a whisper. "My greatest love is for my studies, and for helping those who cannot find help elsewhere." I could not look him in the eye, afraid he would read the whole truth in it. "I want to improve lives. I don't want to be just an observer. And I won't be able to do it if I take a husband." I heard a tremble in my own voice as I realized that I was likely to lose Volmar. Yet married women were forever chained to the family hearth, giving birth and running the household, and I knew I could not live that life.

Silence stretched between us, and it was not the familiar, companionable silence of our early days; rather, it was tinged with a sadness I had not known since the night my parents had left me at St. Disibod. It began to fill the corners of the workshop with premature darkness, even though the sun was still high in the sky.

Volmar's face was drawn, and his fingers squeezed the wine cup so hard his knuckles had gone white. "I know you want things that other women don't care about," he said at length, "but there is only so much you can achieve in this place." He made a motion with his hand to encompass the workshop and the abbey.

"Even at St. Disibod, monastic rules give women more freedom that the obligations of marriage," I countered.

"The prior nearly succeeded in enclosing you already. I heard him say to Brother Fulbert that it is an outrageous violation of nature for women to pursue activities of the intellect." He paused to let it sink in — Fulbert was the abbey librarian. "Do you expect it to get better when you have taken the veil, or when Abbot Kuno is no longer at the helm?"

He was right. Everybody knew that Bother Wigbert brought me books from the library, and as long as Kuno was alive, my access would be assured. But afterwards? I had no idea, and I preferred not to contemplate it. "I am needed in the infirmary," I said instead, feeling on firmer ground. "My skills will be enough to grant me sufficient liberty."

"They will never give you what you want." He shook his head. "You will be an assistant, a herbalist, always at risk of being replaced by the first monk who comes along with any medical training. They will never call you a physician, even though that is what you are." Despite everything, indignation colored his final words, and I felt the familiar comfort of having him on my side. Would I be able to do without it?

Suddenly, the notion of leaving the abbey, of sharing my life with Volmar on our own terms, stood in my mind as a possibility. I would be a doctor, I would write, I would not stay at home to supervise cooks and maids. And he would accept it. But even as I let myself entertain this fleeting fantasy, I knew that it would not work. The world would not allow it.

"My place is here." I said, and each word was like a knife thrust into my own heart.

Volmar lowered his head. When he lifted it again, I saw acceptance in his face but also deep pain. It was all I could do to stop myself from embracing him, from holding on to him for a little longer. "I am sorry," I said, my words distorted by a sob I could not suppress. "I really am." I covered my mouth, feeling the wetness on my face work its way between my fingers.

He rose from the table. "I should go."

I nodded, unable to speak.

A moment later I listened to his footsteps outside. When they faded, a silence that had an awful finality to it fell on me with a crushing weight. Unable to bear it, I ran outside and followed Volmar, but when I arrived at the crossroad outside the infirmary, something stopped me again. I watched his lithe figure until it disappeared through the arched doors of the church.

Then I turned and pressed my palms to my eyes, pausing one more moment before I returned to my duty — and my truest calling.

22

June 1123

I BECAME ILL again. As the pain pierced me to my core, a vision of the Church as a great nourishing body, a nursery and a refuge, stood before my mind's eye. I still wanted to enter the consecrated state but was forced to acknowledge that it was not my only desire, and each day threatened to take me before Sister Jutta to announce my decision to leave the convent for a different life. When my headaches finally subsided, it was in St. Augustine, ironically, that I found solace, rereading the account of his own struggle against temptation.

I also began to compile my notes into a medical guidebook. I first sat down to it the week before I was due to take my vows, during one of those sleepless nights when my resolve seemed to be at its weakest.

My hand moved quickly, the pent-up emotions finding a channel at last.

"Et ut mundus in prosperitate est, cum elementa bene et ordinate officia sua exercent sic etiam, cum elementa ordinate in homine operantur, eum conservant et sanum reddunt."

As the earth prospers when the four elements exercise their offices properly, so when they work properly in a person, they preserve and return him to health.

The soft scratch of the quill on the parchment, reassuring and familiar, quieted my mind, and a sense of clarity descended on me.

I wrote for hours until the sky blushed pink with the first hint of dawn. I put the sheets aside and went out into the courtyard to find the disk of the sun, still tinged with the pale red of the early morning, rising above the eastern wall of the convent to the trill of a nightingale, a lonesome fanfare. In that moment, I longed to have Volmar with me to welcome the new day.

If I took the vows, that would never happen, and right then it seemed an unfathomable loss. What if this was not a temptation but a gift, and I was refusing it? Was I any different from Jutta squandering her health, another divine blessing?

I stood there as the battle of two contradictory elements inside me — fire and earth, choler and melancholy — rendered me miserable. I was being forced to question everything for which I had strived and in which I believed, and I had nobody to share that burden with me. If Griselda had not left, I would have someone to confide in, and I knew she would understand. But she was gone, and I was utterly alone.

On the eve of the feast of St. Disibod the following Sunday, I stood before Archbishop Adalbert of Mainz, exhausted from lack of sleep and poor appetite. Jutta had remarked on my wanness earlier that day and praised it as proper and fitting for my soon to be holy state, but Juliana had remained silent, regarding me with what I thought was pity. Yet she had no way of knowing what was in my heart.

The ceremony was held at dusk as the profession of anchorite vows was meant to symbolize a death in life akin to a burial. I had remained inside the convent all day until Abbot Kuno had come to escort me to the church. The evening was overcast, with none of the Rhenish sunset glory. That disappointed me, for I would have liked the fiery light that normally flooded the courtyard at that hour to usher me into my new life.

I entered the church barefoot and clad in a white robe, hoping fervently that the imminent shield of my vows would protect and deliver me from the anguish once and for all.

The interior was dim, the only light coming from the tapers flickering around the chancel where the monks had taken their seats, their shapes outlined against the wood panels of their stalls. As they intoned *Veni Creator Spiritus*, I glanced up at the small gray squares of the clerestory windows; by the time my new life began, they would be completely dark.

I approached the altar. *Uphold me by your promise and I shall live; let my hopes not be in vain,* I recalled the words of a psalm in which I wanted desperately to believe.

I lay prostrate while Brother Gottlieb read from the Scriptures. "If you make a vow to the Lord your God, do not be slow to pay it, for the Lord your God will demand it of you." The words reflected hollowly off the stone walls, acquiring a quality of admonition for which I was grateful. "Whatever your lips utter, you must be sure to do because you made your vow freely to the Lord your God."

With that exhortation ringing in my ears, I bowed before the archbishop as he sprinkled holy water, blessed me with frankincense, and gave me a white veil. "Then he said to them:" he quoted from an evangelist, "Whoever wants to be my disciple must deny themselves and take up their cross daily and follow me."

The symbolic funeral rites commenced with an anti-phon followed by psalms from the Office of the Dead before the monks led me back to the convent. The archbishop sprinkled the doorstep with holy water, and as he did so, the words Juliana had spoken in the midst of a dark night of despair came to me: *And now I am left alone, sealed in this tomb!*

Before I crossed the threshold, I kneeled and prayed aloud, aware of the faint tremble in my voice. "For the Lord has chosen Zion; he has desired it for his dwelling place. This is my resting place for ever: here I dwell, for I have desired it."

The next day I went to work at the infirmary as usual, and Brother Wigbert informed me that Volmar had left the abbey without professing his vows.

23

December 1124

JUTTA'S PRACTICES FINALLY caught up with her in her thirty-third year. Brought to a state of enfeeblement well ahead of her time, she looked like a frail old woman, and the periods of convalescence between her bouts of illness had grown increasingly shorter. When her fasts had turned into a refusal of all food, accompanied by extended vigils, I knew that she would not rise from her bed again. It was the winter of the year 1124.

I still did not understand what had made Jutta choose to use her time in this world—full as it was already of violence, want, and disease—to make her life more painful than it had to be. Four days before Christmas, when there was a stillness in the air that usually portended snow, I went to bathe her forehead with yarrow water and found her sitting on her pallet. It was the only concession to comfort she had made during her illness but she had insisted it be strewn with ashes. Jutta's eyes were shining with an unnatural light, something I had seen in gravely ill patients before, and it bode nothing good.

"You are weak, Sister; you should not exert yourself," I said as I put down the bowl.

"I must keep vigil for the coming of my Heavenly Spouse. The moment is near."

I touched the towel to her face and felt the fever through the cloth.

"My only care as I depart this life," she resumed, "is to leave the convent in reliable hands."

There was an opportunity in this admission, and I took it. "If you let me bring you some food and water, you will strengthen and such a transition won't be necessary just yet."

"The time is short." Jutta repeated, excitement bubbling under the surface of her voice. "I want you to take over when I am gone."

My hand froze midair. "But I am not the next in line. Sister Juliana—"

"Juliana never wanted this life." She waved her hand dismissively. "Even so, you are worthier than anybody I know." She gazed at me with her usual intensity, and I looked away. If she was asking me, who was so averse to asceticism, to uphold the convent's reputation in that area, I was not going to make that promise.

"I don't think I can follow your example." I admitted honestly.

Jutta's gaze did not waver. "You can do more than I did . . . I have mortified my flesh, but it is to you that God chose to speak." She was tiring, and her voice dropped to scarce above a whisper. "Use all you have learned for the elevation of the people to help them understand . . . " she trailed off.

"I have been working on a book of medical treatments," I confessed on the spur of the moment.

"That is good. You have a lot to teach others, but don't stop there."

"You don't mean" — my eyes widened — "that I should write about matters of faith?"

A barely perceptible nod.

"But how? Will I even be allowed?"

"It will not be easy to make your voice heard, but that is not a reason not to try." The effort of speaking was becoming too much for her. "But now, promise me that if the sisters elect you, you will accept the burden."

I considered this for a long moment. I knew this day would come, but I would have preferred more time to prepare. "I promise," I said nonetheless, for the timing was beyond my control. If this was how it had to be, I would do it; otherwise, who knew what would become of us?

I dipped the towel in the water again and set out to wash her hands and feet. Her body trembled slightly, as if her *viriditas*, so weak and languid just a short while ago, had suddenly stirred and began to boil under her skin, ready to burst out of that unwelcoming dwelling and return to the world. "Are you not afraid of death, Sister?" I asked as the window shutters rattled in their hinges, the wind picking up ahead of the snow.

"Fear is of this world." The corners of Jutta's mouth curled up in a rare smile. "Yet the world is only a thoroughfare, and we pilgrims upon it toiling on the way to our sacred destination. Death puts a blessed end to all sorrow, so why should I be afraid? I long to be dissolved and to be with Christ."

"I hope that when the time comes, the passage will be easy for you. You have suffered enough."

"There is no such thing as enough suffering because the flesh turns to sin the moment you stop chastising it. I welcome it." There was a peculiar gleam in Jutta's eyes, and I was stunned to see that it was one of pleasure — it was sensual.

Suddenly, it all made sense. Instinctively, my hand went up to my brow as if to shield myself from the shattering realization. *May God have mercy on her when she finally stands before Him*, I thought. *May He not hold her sin against her as He would a thief's or a murderer's because she may not have been responsible for what she had done.*

In my years in the infirmary, I had seen people who did harm to themselves or others prompted by a disease of the mind that robbed them of free will and sound judgement. It was due to an imbalance of humors in the brain, of a mysterious origin, and extremely hard to treat. Why had I not seen this before?

"I would like to confess." Jutta's voice reached me through the fog of my stupefaction.

Pity hollowed out my chest. "I will arrange that with Father Abbot."

I wrapped up the ablution, for there was not much time left. For all the purity of her life, Jutta must not die unshriven.

An hour later, we carried her to the gate. Snow was already falling, and the abbot's cowl sparkled in the quivering candlelight as we opened the grilled window so he could hear her confession. When it was over, he passed us a viaticum and a vial of blessed oil to be put on seven parts of Jutta's body. The rite completed, she donned the white veil in which she had taken her vows and asked us to keep vigil with her. We prayed and sang together as the snowstorm intensified, and in the small hours of the morning, Jutta von Sponheim drifted off to sleep never to awaken again.

Tradition called for all sisters to be involved in the washing and preparing of the body of one of their own for burial, but I decided to do it alone. I removed the sackcloth robe that had been Jutta's only earthly attire and found a hair shirt underneath. Not altogether surprised, I took it off too, but, as the marble-like nakedness of the body unaccustomed to the rays of the sun came into view, I felt cold sweat break out at the base of my neck.

Leaning on the edge of the table, I closed my eyes and thanked God for having had the foresight to exclude Juliana and Gertrude from the rite because fastened tightly around Jutta's right thigh, a metal chain was sunk deeply into the flesh that was horribly inflamed and infected. It had to have been there for years because scar tissue had grown around parts of it while other areas were covered with blisters—crimson, hot, and pus-oozing in life, now bluish-purple and dry. An awful smell rose from the wound, and to be able to proceed, I had to tear up a linen towel and tie a strip around my nose and mouth.

It took some searching to find the clasp that held the cilice together, and I unhooked it with effort. My stomach pitched into my throat for one dreadful moment, but I steadied myself with a few breaths, for I was determined not to leave that terrible instrument buried in Jutta's body. I pulled firmly, and the band began to come out one link at a time, the inward-facing spikes emerging with awful regularity from within the withered muscle with a soft tearing sound.

When it was all out, I turned the body on its side to examine the back. The old wounds had scared over so thickly that they had long since stopped bleeding under the lashes of the whip. So that was it. The festering mutilation on the thigh was the true cause of Jutta's recurring fevers, her steady weakening, and eventually her demise. It was nothing short of a miracle that she had lived so long. What unimaginable pain it must have been! This was why she had never allowed me to tend to it—she had not wanted it to heal.

As I stood staring at the ravaged thigh, a conversation I had had with Brother Wigbert came back to me. Soon after I had started working in the infirmary, I told him that Jutta, who had never indulged in any condiments with her meals, had begun to ask for more salt from the kitchen. Wigbert had seemed disturbed, and now I understood why. Salt . . . as the implication sank in, I felt sick again.

I went to the window and stared at the thick layer of snow sparkling in the midday sun, letting the sight purify my senses. I felt tainted, and the pristine landscape soothed me, but when I returned to wash the body, its contours began to blur and heavy tears spilled down my cheeks. Grief welled inside me like water filling my lungs and choking the breath in my throat. Jutta had effaced herself but she had allowed me to thrive—one word from her, and I would never have worked or studied with Brother Wigbert. And while I had shown my gratitude to the old infirmarian many times, I regretted never having properly thanked her.

Wiping my eyes with my sleeves like a child, I wrapped the body in a shroud, placed a candle by its head, and kneeled by the bier.

Requiem aeternam dona ei, Domine
Et lux perpetua luceat ei.

Jutta was buried in a side chapel of the church because the snow had made it impossible to dig a simple grave in the cemetery that she had wanted, and where we would move her in the spring. Yet despite the snow, ordinary folk had trudged from as far as Böckelheim and Sobernheim to bid farewell to the famed anchoress of St. Disibod. I had never seen so many people in the abbey at one time, thronging both courtyards and spilling through the gate despite the cold.

The next day, Abbot Kuno summoned me to discuss the transition at the convent. For some time, I had been feeling blind in my dealings with the monks because Brother Wigbert's increasing forgetfulness—he would miss church services without knowing it, or stare at me helplessly when presented with a complicated bone fracture—meant that I knew less and less about what went on inside the abbot's lodging. My nerves were taut when I went to the meeting with no inkling as to what might be planned and no advice on how to handle it. Important decisions about the future of our community might be in the making, but unable to anticipate and prepare for it, I felt uncertain and acutely alone.

I did not fear for the convent's survival because we were too profitable to the abbey, the endowments Jutta had ceded over the years having paid for various renovations and additions. The church alone had been outfitted with new statues, a gilded cross, and a reliquary containing a splinter from the Holy Cross. And those were the things I was aware of; who knew what else had been stashed away in the treasury house, which itself had been expanded only the year before?

What worried me was how the monks would treat us after Jutta's death. Would we continue as a fief that supported their lavish spending, or would we be allowed to function as an independent entity that used its property as it saw fit? From what I had been able to gather, we were entitled to our income—as evidenced by Jutta always ceding it voluntarily—so the convent must have been founded as an autonomous house, bound to the abbey only by its common allegiance to *Regula Benedicti*. Under Jutta it had shifted into an obscure dependency, but there was no reason why it should remain that way when she was gone.

I entered the abbot's parlor, where the air felt tense from Prior Helenger's presence even before the first words were spoken. Pale winter daylight filtered through the window but failed to dispel the shadows from the chamber's corners. The fire from the hearth provided more light, but it caused the prior's tall shadow to hover ominously on the wall, its top breaking where the wall met the ceiling to make it seem like he was looming over us.

The first thing Abbot Kuno wanted was an account of Jutta's last days. I told him of my discovery of the hair shirt and the cilice, which left him visibly shaken. Helenger, on the other hand, listened with avid curiosity, his eyes shining not unlike Jutta's when she was alive. When I had finished, the abbot shook his head. "The extent of her bodily mortification was greater than we had all thought."

"Yes."

"Is that what caused her death?"

"Ultimately. The infection was responsible for the recurring fevers that sapped her vitality in the end."

"She was a holy woman." Helenger's voice rang out, strangely thick. "We need more martyrs like her."

I ignored him, keeping my eyes on the abbot. "I have not read the convent's charter since Jutta became enclosed fifteen years ago," he said at length, "and I have forgotten the details because my memory has grown weaker, as has my vision. But Brother Prior"—he gestured toward Helenger without looking at him—"took the pains to reread it, and he informs me that the document leaves it to me to choose the manner in which her successor will be selected."

So we were not exactly an independent house. "How so?" I asked, trying to hide my disappointment.

"I can make a nomination, or I can leave it entirely to the sisters to select their *magistra*."

"And I have advised Father Abbot to nominate Sister Juliana, who is the most senior member of the anchorite community," Helenger hastened to inform me.

Of course you have, I thought, still looking at Kuno.

"It is true that Sister Juliana is the next in line," the abbot said, "but I want to know if Sister Jutta expressed any wishes as to who should succeed her in her duties."

"She has, Father." I straightened my spine reflexively. "She wanted me to take over."

Helenger gave a snort. "You cannot prove that."

"Are you saying that Sister Hildegard is lying, Brother Prior?" The abbot raised an eyebrow in his direction.

"I am *saying* there is no proof," he repeated petulantly.

"There is no proof because we were alone when she expressed her will," I said. "I suggested Sister Juliana myself, but Sister Jutta did not believe she wanted it."

"It is not a matter of choice but of duty."

"We cannot force anybody to lead a community against their will." The abbot spread his arms. "It is too important a role. Sister Juliana's stance on the matter will be easy enough to verify," he added for the prior's benefit, then gave me a considering look. "And what was your answer?"

"I said I was ready to lead if they chose me."

"Father Abbot, she lacks the experience. It would be an insult." The contempt had left Helenger's voice and was replaced by a ring of frustration that I knew would give way to anger next.

Kuno leaned on his desk and steepled his fingers under his chin, contemplating me. In that moment, I saw how he, too, had aged. His face, once round and red, had thinned and become more lined, folds of skin hanging on the sides of his jaw. His hands were covered with brown spots, their knuckles more prominent than I had remembered.

"I will nominate you," he said, raising his hand as the prior opened his mouth to protest, "but a nomination does not assure an election. The anchoresses will have to vote, and if there is a tie, I will break it."

"But Father Abbot—" Helenger's eyes widened as if to say, *What about that other matter?*

I guessed immediately what was on his mind but took care not to reveal it.

"I have made my decision," Kuno said wearily.

"Can I make a request, Father?" I asked, encouraged.

He nodded cautiously.

"May I read the charter?"

"If you are elected, you will be entitled to have access to it."

He rose and I followed, feeling lighter. The charter had the final answer to the question of who controlled the convent's finances, but I was not worried anymore; Helenger's reaction had been eloquent enough. All I needed now was the votes.

"One more thing . . . Sister." Helenger's voice reached me on my way out the door, and his emphasis was loaded with cold fury. I stopped, and as our eyes locked, I saw implacable hostility in them. "Whoever succeeds Sister Jutta will only be entitled to be called *magistra*, not prioress, because the convent ranks lower in the hierarchy of the abbey. It is not an equivalent house."

As the caveat was unnecessary, I inclined my head and was about to turn away when a dismal thought struck me: if I were elected, I might one day have to deal with an Abbot Helenger. He had tried to throw obstacles at my feet for years, and when Abbot Kuno was gone, he would unleash everything in his power to relegate me to an anchorite oblivion. He must have read all that in my face, because as I gave him one last look, his mouth twisted in a mirthless smile full of malice.

A week later, on the first day of the year 1125, I was duly elected *magistra* of the convent of St. Disibod.

24

October 1125

I DID AWAY with many of the rules by which Jutta had governed the convent. I asked the kitchen to send us fresh fruits and vegetables along with our normally bare rations of bread, water, and milk, and to add fish on Sundays and holidays. With Brother Wigbert's help, I procured larger braziers for the dorter and the chapel so they were finally properly heated, and fresh rushes were now regularly spread on the floors. It was no longer required of the sisters to kneel for hours in front of the altar; instead, I let them choose the way they wanted to perform their devotions.

Next, I turned my attention to our robes. We had always worn habits of coarse wool bought locally, but now I decreed that we could receive cloth from home — soft wool for the cold season and linen for the warm months — in colors other than gray. Juliana opted for black, while Gertrude chose white with a short silk veil. She looked very becoming in it too, as I had done away with the practice of having our hair shorn four times a year. If anyone had been allowed inside the enclosure, they would have often found us with our hair unbound and streaming over our shoulders as we went about pruning the vines and tending to our newly-planted rosebushes. How we had changed in just a few months! Never before had our cheeks been so rosy, nor our sense of camaraderie so deep. In Jutta's time none of it would have been possible, and it gave me a bitter kind of satisfaction.

But it was not an easy transition, plagued as I was by Helenger's constant complaints and an ongoing lack of funds. To make matters worse, Brother Wigbert's decline had quickened after I had become *magistra*, and soon I was running the infirmary by myself, setting bones, lancing boils, and dispensing medicines, with ever-changing novices for assistants.

Before the first year of my tenure was over, Wigbert was confined to bed and no longer recognized anybody. I was the only one whose presence sparked a glimmer of awareness in his eyes, as if my voice managed to shed a momentary light into the darkening recesses of his mind. And I grieved for the old infirmarian, for in him I was losing a teacher and a friend whose guidance had opened my mind and made my success in the practice of medicine possible.

Whenever I had a free moment, I would sit at his bedside, hold his hand, and tell him news from the world.

The year had been an eventful one, and many throughout the Rhineland — from the heights of princely and ecclesiastical courts to the merchant shops of port towns — were looking forward to its end with hope for quieter times. The simmering conflict within the empire had flared up again, ravaging commerce and weakening the nobility's grip on their lands. Emperor Heinrich had died without producing an heir with his English wife, which precipitated a brief but fierce struggle for the throne. Duke Frederick of Swabia, his nephew, was a natural successor, but the Archbishop of Mainz had thrown his support behind the Duke of Saxony, Lothair of Supplinburg—according to some because Frederick was one-eyed, but more likely because Lothair had soundly defeated Heinrich at Welfesholz ten years before. He was therefore a potent symbol of the papal faction's struggle against the Salian dynasty and offered the best hope for a more pliable monarchy.

Predictably, that choice had run into opposition from the late emperor's kin, and the conflict might have turned bloody but for the fact that Frederick's younger and more ambitious brother Konrad, Duke of Franconia, was in Jerusalem during that time. Frederick lost the election to Lothair and never managed to rally enough supporters to attempt to take the throne by force.

I had followed those developments closely through intelligence gathered from our visitors, and it seemed to me that the concordat had done nothing to quell the proclivity of the temporal and spiritual powers to use elections, whether ecclesiastical or royal, as an opportunity to ascertain more control over the other's domain.

"And no, there had been no comet in the sky the night the emperor died," I whispered after I had recounted the events, smiling even as I swallowed a lump in my throat. Wigbert's expression was as serene and trustful as that of a child listening to a bedtime story.

I blew out the candle, added charcoal to the brazier, and left for the convent. Often, that late night walk was the time when I felt most lonely, and when my thoughts instinctively went to Volmar. He had been gone for more than two years, and although I did not know where he was or what he was doing, I hoped that he was safe and happy. I still missed him, but I no longer felt the acute sense of loss that had followed his departure. Nowadays, the thought of him brightened my mood and helped dispel my solitude, even though there were times, especially when Wigbert was faring worse, when

I wished he was there to offer words of comfort and courage for what lay ahead.

But that autumn night, I had reason to feel hopeful again, even excited. Just five days before, our convent had grown. It was not exactly an expansion—my plea for renovating and enlarging our premises had yet remained unanswered—but Jutta's vacated place had allowed me to accept a novice, and I made my choice carefully. Elfrid was unlike the rest of us; she was a small, plump woman in her middle thirties, she had lived in the world before she had joined us, and she possessed a restless energy in her movements that betrayed a force to be reckoned with. She also had a worldly skill.

I knocked on the door, and from the short, rapid steps on the other side, I guessed that she would be the portress. Perhaps she had just returned to the enclosure herself. Indeed, as the gate squeaked on its rusty hinges, there she was, welcoming me with a bright smile on her wide face.

"How did it go?" I asked, alert despite my weariness. Everything about her was sure and lively, two traits absent from the convent. Her *viriditas* made my heart lighter.

"With God's help, the babe was delivered safely and is living, though she is tiny and will require much care to thrive," Elfrid replied. She had been a midwife in Rüdesheim and had decided to spend her widowhood as a nun. Her dowry—the money she had inherited from her mildly successful merchant husband—had been only fifteen silver marks, much less than a daughter of nobility would have brought. But I had not hesitated, for here was a chance to do something about the poor quality of maternity care that made the risky business of childbirth more dangerous still.

Surprisingly, Abbot Kuno had given his leave for Elfrid to go on house calls, though it was only because he wanted to avoid a battle over allowing women to deliver in the infirmary, an option I had deliberately suggested first. "It took so long that I had to use three measures of henbane to help her through it." She reached into her scrip and took out an almost empty bottle to show me. Elfrid was also a competent herbalist, and her infusion of henbane in wine was highly effective in easing labor pains. "There was some bleeding afterward, but I put pressure on her stomach and held it for thirty Hail Marys," she added. "In two days, she will be back on her feet."

I was greatly relieved because the patient happened to be Renfred's only daughter, the babe his first grandchild, and the old man deserved some cheer after he had buried his wife in the spring. I thanked Elfrid and turned toward the chapel to say a quick prayer before retiring; I had missed compline again. Elfrid headed for the dorter, but not before informing me excitedly, "Tomorrow, if I am not called to another labor, I will work on a remedy for husbands who suffer from marital difficulties. I have heard several women complain about it, and I have not been here a week."

My hand flew to my mouth to cover my shock and a simultaneous urge to laugh. Then I composed myself, for the physician in me was curious, "What kind of remedy?"

"It requires the seeds of watercress, leeks, and carrots which are bound into a honey paste mixed with spices. There is ginger and a little bit of cinnamon in the workshop, but if we could get our hands on some cloves and pepper, we could make a lot of people happy." She winked and was gone in a flurry of robes.

I reached the chapel door, pondering on how important it would be for Elfrid to abandon her worldly way of speaking, and on how refreshing it was that she had not done it yet.

When I came out, gusts of winds where swooping overhead like swallows before rain, shaking the tendrils of the vine and tearing off its drying leaves. The clouds were scudding fast across the sky, and together with the sharp breeze, they portended a change from the mild weather of the past few weeks. I was not halfway to the dorter when another gust sent a shutter of one of the windows swaying in its hinges. Before I could go inside and close it, a final blow loosened it out of the wall altogether, and it landed on the beaten earth with a thud.

I gritted my teeth in frustration. The convent's buildings needed repairs badly, and it was time to bring it up with Kuno again. I would send a message first thing in the morning to ask for a meeting. But that night, at least, we would be shivering in our beds.

In response, I received an invitation to the Chapter meeting the following day. My last appearance at the monks' gathering had ended with an attempt to shut me permanently inside the convent. As *magistra* my position was different, though I was still nervous.

On my way to the chapter house, I took stock of the improvements that had taken place over the years, many of them paid for with our money. The new tiles on the roof of the church glinted red in the October sun, providing a lively counterpoint to its bulky gray mass. Inside, there were new relics, a richly decorated Bible, and fine wall hangings rumored to have arrived all the way from France. I had also heard that the monks' cloister now boasted a fountain carved out of marble, a stone prized for its beauty and durability by the Romans. If it was true, it would have cost a small fortune.

But our walls had seen no major work done since the attack three years before, even though the empire's affairs were as volatile as ever under King Lothair. As the abbey had grown richer, the main safeguard of its prosperity had gone unaddressed. We were protected by the same wood-and-earth palisade that was full of rotted beams only provisionally patched up. The monks had been lulled into complacency, and I could not keep my head from shaking as I reached the chapter house. It, too, was fitted with sturdy new oak doors bound in intricately carved iron.

The obedientiaries had already taken their seats at the table, but it was Helenger who was presiding over the assembly. All at once I remembered that Kuno had been planning to visit a priory north of Mainz that was in the middle of trying to achieve independence from its mother house at Affligem.

"Father Abbot is gone to Andernach to lend his support to Prior Gilbert." Helenger confirmed my fears with a wolfish smile. "I have been given full powers to conduct business in his absence."

With a sinking feeling, I realized I had walked into a trap. My plea might have worked—just—with Kuno, but there was little chance I would get what I wanted from Helenger, and there might be gratuitous humiliation in store for me besides that.

For the first hour, he went down a tedious list of business, although I was interested to hear the report on the income from that year's harvest. It amounted to a respectable sum of three hundred twenty-five marks, far higher than the one hundred marks the abbey used to earn when I had first arrived, and a reflection of how its fortunes had risen along with the convent's reputation. That list, I thought in frustration, included the bounty from the two dozen acres of oak forest and another ten acres of arable land Gertrude had brought with her.

A murmur of subdued conversations brought me out of my musings. Helenger had arrived at the end of his agenda, and the monks took advantage of the break to comment amongst themselves. When the ripple died down, he turned to me with affected politeness. "Sister Hildegard has requested a meeting, and even though Father Abbot could not be here today, we will gladly hear her business."

I did not relish the idea of presenting my petition in a wider forum, but on reflection I realized that it might be beneficial. The monks, on the whole, respected the convent— some had even been admirers of Jutta's ascetic ways. Perhaps

Helenger would have a harder time refusing me in front of them. "I would like to submit for the abbey's consideration," I began without any preliminaries, "a request to renovate and enlarge the convent's buildings."

The prior regarded me with an impassive face. "What exactly do you have in mind?"

"It would be of great benefit to our community if our wooden dorter was replaced with a larger one built of stone, with separate sleeping and refectory quarters."

"The enclosure is too small to fit a larger building," Helenger said complacently.

"It could be easily expanded by incorporating a part of the smaller courtyard that is used by nobody except the servants and messengers between the abbey and the convent."

A smirk curled the corners of his lips. "I don't understand," he said, feigning astonishment. "The anchoresses vowed to live out their days in simplicity and poverty, and you are asking us to build a sumptuous residence for them?"

"Hardly sumptuous, Brother Prior," I replied evenly. "Rather, a more dignified place that meets our basic needs so we can fulfill our mission for the benefit of the people we serve and the glory of God."

Helenger's face remained set; it was clear that my plea was not a welcome one. I wondered whether he was truly so shortsighted as to keep the convent from growing. But his next words took me by surprise, for rather than refusing outright, he decided to attack me. "Troubling news has reached us regarding—shall we say—a certain relaxation of manners at your convent. There are rumors"—he wrinkled his nose as if he had smelled something foul—"of women wearing their hair long, going about with uncovered heads, and wearing fanciful garments. I fear that you are in breach of The Rule and that you will bring God's wrath upon us with this sacrilege."

His approach was to undermine my credibility, then. I regarded him with what I hoped was an equally icy look as the chapter house fell silent. "Would you care to name those offended that I may assure them they have no cause for concern?"

Helenger waved his long hand dismissively. "I am not going to name anyone, but I *will* say that I fully share those misgivings, and put it to you in front of these witnesses that you are not a fit leader for the convent, and therefore in no position to make any demands."

A murmur of voices rose again, and I saw heads shaking and disapproving glances cast toward the prior. For the first time, I wondered about his personal popularity among the monks.

I turned to face the tiered seats, and said loudly, so my voice would reach the back rows, "I assure you, Brothers, that we fully respect The Rule in all of the convent's activities. Sister Jutta had imposed, as was her right, stricter regulations regarding hair and attire than those recommended by the Blessed Benedict. I have a different view in this matter, for I saw that shearing off the hair saddened and subdued the women, and there is no need for that. A religious calling fulfilled with serenity and without needless suffering is more pleasing in God's eyes."

I paused, taking stock of my audience. Most of the monks listened with polite attention; only a few, whom I knew to have a sycophantic streak, were eying Helenger, ready to take their cues from him. "Regarding our robes, there is *nothing* fanciful about them," I went on. "I wear a simple white one, as you can see, and so do Sisters Elfrid and Gertrude. White is a symbol of innocence—and thus we are like Eve in Paradise before the Fall—and of chastity, which makes it suitable for brides of Christ"—Jutta's favorite metaphor for our consecrated state—"therefore it cannot be immodest, much less sacrilegious."

Heads were still nodding in approval when the prior's voice thundered from the dais. "Under your oversight, the convent has departed from its anchorite ways and become an insult to God and the Church. You will be called to answer for that!"

The accusation sent my blood boiling. I'd had every intention of dealing fairly with the abbey, but if they believed they could continue to exert unlimited control over the convent, they would have a rude awakening. "You seem to forget, Brother Prior" — I eyed him levelly — "that you are not talking to a child oblate anymore. I hold a rank as the head of the convent, and our charter gives me prerogatives which I intend to fully exercise to fulfill our mission."

The silence was so complete that it seemed nobody dared to breathe. Helenger looked incredulous as he opened his mouth, but no words came out. I saw that despite his anger, there was a calculating glint in his eyes. He was aware that what I had said was true.

"Are you going to build a new convent without the abbey's permission, then?" Derision distorted his features.

"Of course not," I scoffed at this weak attempt to ridicule me. Then I smiled in as friendly a way as I could manage in front of him. "Our current size allows me to accept one more novice, and there are dozens of women from wealthy Rhenish families that I can choose from. I assure you the new entrant will come with a sizeable endowment over which — as you well know — I will have full control under the terms of our charter."

I let the unspoken implication sink in, trying to exude a posture of certainty and defiance, though, in truth, I felt neither. A fifth sister would be a big inconvenience in our already cramped quarters. I also hated having to make this argument, which amounted to blackmail, because it was beneath the dignity of my state, my office, and myself as a person.

Helenger was still gathering his wits when Brother Peter, who had replaced Ignatius as treasurer, spoke up. Peter was relatively young for such a senior post, being only twenty-five, and he was handsome and soft-spoken with an honest, intelligent face.

"Brother Prior, if I may," he addressed Helenger. "I think we should consider Sister Hildegard's petition. It is true that there is much interest from women in joining the convent, and little room to accommodate them." I studied him, wondering if he was concerned with our welfare or merely worried about a source of income drying up, the more so since the expectations for generous gifts from local nobles had not come to fruition, as King Lothair had raised their taxes to refill the empire's treasury, exhausted after his predecessor's wars.

The prior turned to Peter, but instead of a fury I had expected, there was an almost anguished look in his eyes. The young monk shifted uneasily under the intensity of his gaze. "I think perhaps we should consult the brethren." Helenger's voice sounded strangely subdued, as if he had a hard time filling his lungs with air. "Does anyone have a view on this matter?" He turned back to the monks and cleared his throat. "Brother Hippolytus?"

The monk named Hippolytus rose and pushed the cowl off his head. He wore a stern expression and avoided looking in my direction. During his visits to the infirmary, he had always refused to be treated by me, insisting on speaking only to Brother Wigbert. Now that the infirmarian was incapacitated, he had stopped coming altogether, sending novices to request remedies for his various—and mostly imaginary—ailments.

"I do not like the idea of expanding the convent," he said unhappily, bringing a satisfied smile to Helenger's face. "In fact, I don't think we should have a female community here at all. It was a mistake to allow Sister Jutta to establish herself at St. Disibod in the first place. Women are nothing but a source of temptation, sent among us by the Devil to confound us and turn us away from—"

"Thank you, Brother!" Helenger interrupted sourly. He may have been as grated as Hippolytus by our presence, but even he understood its benefits. "Anyone else?"

As nobody spoke up, he hastened to close the Chapter. "I will defer to Father Abbot on this," he said, looking somewhere above my shoulder. "You will have your answer soon enough."

That night I asked Juliana to lead compline in my place, and as they sang, I reviewed the meeting again in my head. By degrees, it became clear to me that even under the most benevolent abbot—let alone Helenger, whose succession seemed a foregone conclusion—there would always be tension between us and the abbey.

And at the center of it would be money.

25

January 1128

T HE EVENING BEFORE the feast of the Epiphany was typical of a Rhenish January: blustery and cold but bright
from the fresh snow underfoot and the clear stars overhead.
Since I was a young child, the wintry aspect of the sky had
made me wonder about those far away bodies and the source
of their illumination. I was now convinced that it had to be
the same as on earth, where God's breath infused *viriditas*
into stones and creatures alike, and that force was transferred
from one body to another, from one object to another, in the
never-ending cycle of rebirth and renewal.

As I walked to the abbot's house it occurred to me, not
for the first time, that the light of the stars must reflect that of
the moon. And the moon? Its brightness could only be animated by the sun's fire. Everything served something higher,
and nothing exceeded its due measure.

I shook a few stray snowflakes off my cape as I entered the parlor. Tonight we had our monthly supper, an arrangement we had recently started so the abbot could stay abreast of the convent and the infirmary's affairs.

The fire was burning brightly, and I crossed to the hearth to warm my hands, my eyes alighting on a pair of new wall hangings depicting the Annunciation and the miracle of the loaves and fishes, finely woven with colorful thread. I turned my face to hide my resentment; the abbey acquired new ornaments and relics regularly — all in the hopes of attracting more pilgrims, the abbot said — but no work had yet been done on the convent, although Kuno had given his preliminary consent the previous winter. I had even accepted a new novice, Burgundia, and ceded a third of her dowry to the monks as a sign of goodwill. But that was in the year 1127. We had just welcomed the new one, and all five of us were still living with no room to spare, a community that could grow no more.

As we sat down to a savory dish of veal stewed with carrots and onions, I took a long sip of spiced wine, letting its aroma pervade my senses as it warmed me. After a few moments, I felt the welcome sense of mellow detachment that only good wine can bring, but then a wave of nostalgia swept me.

"Brother Wigbert always looked forward to his suppers with you. They made him happy," I said, emotion swelling in my chest. The old infirmarian had died the previous November, and although his spirit — that which had made him Bother Wigbert — had departed long before that, I felt the loss keenly. "I miss him."

The abbot's eyes glistened momentarily. "He is with God now and intercedes with Him on our behalf. We can only be grateful that he died so peacefully."

I agreed. I had seen my share of death, and the way it had taken Wigbert, without the awareness of the end approaching, seemed the more merciful way.

"When a companion passes away, especially one not much older," the abbot spoke again, "it puts mortality in a new perspective. It becomes less abstract, more personal." There was a faraway look in his eyes. He was in his fifties, and I wondered what it must be like to be looking *back* at one's life, rather than *ahead*. Was he proud and content, or were there things he regretted? He performed his duties well and had saved the abbey from oblivion, but he had also kept Helenger close all these years, tolerating his temper and behavior, which brought him into intermittent conflict with the other monks — and at times also with me.

The abbot shook his head as if to dispel the somber reflections and brought the conversation back to more mundane business. "Are you satisfied with Sister Elfrid's work?"

"Greatly, Father. She is an excellent midwife and a competent nurse. Without her, I would not be able to manage the infirmary."

"It is certainly busy." There was satisfaction in Kuno's voice. Our reputation was unrivaled in the Rhineland, and although in accordance with *Regula Benedicti* patients were treated for free, the wealthier ones always left gifts for the abbey. "I want to ensure that you have as much help as you need. I understand that Brother Edwig" — he was referring to the latest of my assistants — "is better suited to menial tasks than medical procedures?"

"Indeed. Not everyone has the calling for it."

"That is why I am going to send Brother Fabian to you for training. He is a novice who joined us six months ago and has expressed a great deal of interest in medicine."

An assistant with a disposition toward healing? That would certainly be a novelty. "Anything helps," I said, "and if he turns out to have a talent for it, it will only benefit the abbey." I had no illusions as to the self-serving nature of the offer. Kuno needed me and the infirmary more than ever.

"Quite," he hastened to agree.

I decided to take advantage of the situation. "Father, I must ask again if you have given any more thought to the convent's expansion. We see much interest from candidates but have no way to accommodate them, and as *magistra*, I cannot allow this potential to go to waste."

He regarded me with an almost apologetic expression, and it occurred to me that it was probably the prior and his backers who had been holding it up. I felt a pang of sympathy for Kuno, caught as he was between competing interests. But he was the abbot and he would have to make a decision, and I would not back down from what was best for us.

"I have," he said. "We can spare a part of the smaller courtyard up to the old watchtower to enlarge your premises. I will make the announcement at the end of the month."

I sat back. "Thank you, Father. I know how difficult it will be to justify this to . . . some of the brothers, but I assure you it will benefit all of us."

Kuno closed his eyes in subtle acknowledgement. "We will use timber for the new buildings, as stone would be too expensive. Unless, of course, you want to pay for it out of Sister Burgundia's dowry."

"You know it would not be enough," I replied coolly, ignoring the sarcasm and refraining from reminding him of my own gift to the abbey. But I was glad nonetheless; under the circumstances, just seeing the convent rebuilt and expanded would be a success.

"I am glad we understand each other, Sister. I am going to hire Master Albert." He made a gesture to encompass his comfortable lodgings. "His skill and reputation are excellent." The master builder, who lived in Disibodenberg, had supervised the construction of the abbot's new house three years before.

"I will prepare a sketch of what I have in mind," I said, reaching for a piece of pear baked in honey that had been served for dessert. "Perhaps we can discuss it at our next supper."

"That would be good. Then construction can start as soon as the spring rains are over."

As I walked back to the convent later, snow crunching under my feet, I wondered again about Kuno's motivations. For unlike Helenger, whose hatred for me was clear, the abbot had been mostly kind. Fundamentally, he was a good man, but the abbey's rising stature and the reputation of his table — both of which were costly to maintain — were important to him. Whatever it was, as long as he remained in good health, my relations with the abbey would be manageable enough.

By June, the new construction was underway, and I decided to make a journey to Jutta's ancestral home at Sponheim, which I had wanted to do since she had died. It would be my first trip outside Disibodenberg in thirteen years, and I looked forward to putting some distance — if only for a few days — between myself and the place of so much recent grief.

I brought Gertrude with me, and we set out on the high road in the early morning the day after the feast of St. Johannes the Baptist. Our path took us between the still green barley fields before we entered the forest and turned northward. For protection, I hired Arno, a former man-at-arms who had recently quit the archbishop's service after ten years of soldiering and now made a living escorting merchants to Trier and Mainz. The clear sky promised a serene day, and sparkling dew hung from the tips of the leaves, from which it fell like soft wet crystals on our heads. Even before we crossed the Nahe, I stopped our progress twice to collect a quantity of herbs, which I tied with strings and hung on the sides of the wagon to dry.

From the bridge, I looked back on the orchards and vineyards stretching along the river, its gleaming waters vanishing around the bend of Mount St. Disibod, crowned with the tower of the abbey church. On the other bank, the road sloped upward among the green hills of the Uplands, covered thickly by oak forest. By noon the breeze had died down, and a hot midsummer day settled over us. Each time we emerged from the shade of the woods onto a clearing, the heat drenched us in a dazzling cascade of white light, and the sawing of cicadas seemed to reach a fever pitch in the still air. With the weather so fine, we were likely to reach Sponheim before nightfall unless I found more herbs to collect.

Moving through the undulating country, whose forests were crisscrossed by narrow streams and broken up by meadows, I was reminded of the journey I had made from my own home all those years before. It had been cold then, a scent of winter in the air, but today was more like those carefree days I had spent with my siblings in the Bermersheim forest, vast and overflowing with a secret life, vigorous and green in the sunshine. I thought of Uda, who was still with the family, caring for the grandchildren now. I would never partake in their lives, but reaching into the pocket of my robe, I felt the small box with the lump of salt, my link to them through distance and time.

As we entered the County of Sponheim, the road became flatter for a while, but the hills reappeared as we moved along the northwesterly course. We reached the town shortly before sunset, and I was impressed by the size of the Benedictine abbey Count Stephan had founded more than twenty-five years before that dominated the town with a gray octagonal tower. I had considered lodging there but decided to stay where Jutta had grown up. The last several hundred yards took us up a steep path toward the family's seat—a solid-looking fortress protected on one side by the Ellerbach, a tributary of the Nahe, its walls shining wetly from an afternoon shower.

Our wagon rolled into the bailey. The keep was smaller in width than I had imagined, but at three storeys high, it had the appearance of a tower. Moments later, Countess Sophia appeared in the doorway. I had met her once before, on the night she and her late husband had visited Bermersheim and my future was decided. She had been a great beauty, and I still remembered the cascade of auburn hair that had framed a face of radiant complexion, making her seem like a celestial being from my mother's illustrated psalter. Sophia's low-girdled dress of green velvet, with a bodice sown with pearls and hemmed with golden thread, was still etched in my memory. Much older now, though still handsome, the dowager countess dressed more somberly these days, wearing a plain brown dress of fine linen, her head covered with a cream-colored silk veil that fell in long folds down her back and was kept in place with a silver circlet.

She was accompanied by a stoutly-built man in his early thirties who must have been her eldest son and Jutta's brother, the current Count von Sponheim. "You do us great honor, Sister." The countess opened her arms.

"We are grateful for your welcome," I replied. There was something maternal about the way she embraced me, and it brought back another childhood memory that made my throat tighten. "I trust you and your family are in good health."

"We are, God be praised." Sophia beamed. "This is my son Meinhard. He will be married this autumn, and I look forward to bouncing my first grandchild on my knees soon."

Meinhard inclined his head courteously. "We know how close you were to Jutta, and we assure you of the same welcome we would give our kin."

"That is generous of you, my lord," I said, noticing a grimace of pain flashing across the countess's face at the mention of her daughter's name.

"We should let our guests rest," she said in a suddenly hoarse voice and motioned us to follow her toward the guest quarters.

Our room was furnished simply with two beds, an oak table with an oil lamp, and a chest, but it seemed luxurious in comparison with our enclosure.

"Before your nurse took you away to bed that evening at Bermersheim" —Sophia turned to me on her way out, her emotions seemingly under control again—"you said that my dress was the color of the grass in your garden in spring."

I nodded, the memories rushing back again.

"I promised to show you *my* garden one day, and I am going to do that tomorrow."

I joined the countess in the main hall for breakfast the next morning. It was the finest place I had ever seen, with brass and silver wrought candelabras gracing the corners, rich tapestries depicting hunting scenes, and numerous swords, shields, and other manner of armor once worn by the von Sponheims displayed on the walls. It reminded me of the hall at Bermersheim, much smaller and more modest, but also decorated with breastplates and weapons my forebears had worn while fighting the Christian cause in Damascus and Palestine.

After the meal, Sophia led me across the courtyard. It was bustling with soldiers marching in and out of the lookout towers, peasants hauling carts of vegetables to the kitchens, and servants carrying loaves of freshly baked bread and rolling barrels of beer out of the brewery. There was a sense of domesticity in the commotion, in the smells of cooking, even in the clanking noise of metal from the smithy somewhere on the other side of the keep.

We walked to a small ironbound door which Sophia unlocked to let us into a walled garden, surprisingly quiet for its proximity to the busy household. It was exquisitely maintained. Flowering rosebushes and beds of eyelets, peonies, lilies, and irises lined the gravel paths. In the center, a fountain trickled with water like molten silver in the sunlight, and along the perimeter there were benches and thick vines draping over the walls behind them.

I gazed around in delight. "This place is truly divine." I breathed in the heady scents. "Nature is God's gift that we must cherish and care for. And when we do, it repays us with such beauty and bounty."

"I hear you have an impressive garden of your own at St. Disibod."

"It is a working garden." I tried to sound modest, but I could not keep a note of pride out of my voice. "I grow herbs for medicines. It is not nearly as pleasant as yours, but I enjoy working in it."

"My gardener does most of the work, though I do a little bit myself." The countess started down a path, rubbing her knuckles in the same manner Brother Wigbert had used to. "But I fear it won't be possible much longer because I am getting old." Walking beside her, I noticed that despite strands of gray in her hair and the wrinkles in the corners of her eyes, she still carried herself straight and walked with the same graceful gait. And her skin, though no longer as supple, had retained a great deal of its luminosity.

"I will send you a bottle of aconite oil," I said. "It is very effective at alleviating discomfort of aching joints."

Sophia smiled lightly. "Your reputation as a healer reached us long ago, and I must say I am not surprised. Already when I first met you, a little child that you were, I was struck by your cleverness and judgment that were far beyond your years. I was overjoyed when I learned of your rise to the head of the convent."

I blushed. "You do me too much honor by speaking so highly of me, Countess. Surely your daughter is far better known around these parts, as she should be."

"It is true that Jutta's reputation here is excellent." Again, that strange shadow crossed her features. I would have expected more enthusiasm from a proud mother, but it was lacking in her tone. "She is best known as a martyr, and that pains me greatly." Sophia kept her composure, but I could sense powerful emotions beneath the surface. "The news of her bodily chastisements broke my heart because no mother can remain indifferent when her child suffers harm, and by their own hand!"

She gazed at me directly, looking suddenly older. "I don't know what compelled her. She had been such a happy child, but then the brain fever came and she was never the same afterward. The first thing she vowed upon recovery was to know nothing of the marriage bed. All she wanted was to found a convent, even though my husband had just established an abbey here in Sponheim." She fell silent. "He was a pious man and only happy to indulge her whim" — her voice was hard with resentment when she spoke again — "but even *he* had never imagined what was on her mind. It is better he died not knowing of it," she added bitterly.

I felt both admiration and pity for this dignified woman. "Perhaps you can find consolation in the thought that your daughter lived — and died — the way she desired, and that in her own way she was content."

But Sophia did not seem to hear me. "Is it true? Did she really whip herself until she drew blood?" Her body shivered, and she grasped my arm. "Did she constantly fast until she grew too weak to walk?" Her eyes, full of pain, were fastened on mine, and I knew she desperately wanted me to deny it.

"There *was* evidence of mortification." I chose my words carefully and put a comforting hand on her shoulder. It would have devastated her to know the whole truth. "But it is no use dwelling upon it. Jutta is with God now, and she is happy." I wanted to believe it just as desperately.

The countess's heaving chest began to slow down. "You are right." She nodded repeatedly as if trying to convince herself. "But tell me one more thing — was it hard being cloistered with her? You seem to have such a bright outlook. It must have been difficult for you."

"Not as hard as it might seem." I hesitated. "In the end, Jutta accepted me the way I am, and for that I owe her a debt of gratitude."

"Are you keeping an eye on the sisters now that you are *magistra*?" Sophia's mind was still fixed on the mortification.

"Yes," I assured her. "I modified the rules so the life that is already demanding of sacrifice doesn't warp their minds and tempt them to engage in unhealthy practices."

"I am glad to hear that," she said with genuine relief. We walked in silence for a while, listening to the trills of a blackbird in the trees. "I know it is no use asking," the countess resumed at length, "but I would give anything, and I mean anything" —she swept her arm to encompass the garden and the castle— "to know why she did it. But as it is, I am confused and sad and cannot take the pride I should in my daughter's legacy."

"We all have principles that guide us. Jutta had hers, and I have mine. Yet I wonder if deep inside she was truly that different from me—after all, she designated me as her successor and gave me a free hand to take the convent in whatever direction I chose."

"Tell me about this new direction." She turned to me like a thirsty person hoping for a drink of water.

I thought for a long moment. "There are many who believe—and they will find passages in the Bible to justify it— that God gave us this world to use as we please, but also a set of rules that we must follow to achieve salvation. According to those people, He is a severe judge who observes how well we comply, and at the End of Days, his wrath will come down on those who diverged from the path. This, to me, is inconsistent with the nature of God, which is love.

"I see the world and everything in it—living or inanimate—as connected and dependent on one another. Nature willingly offers its benefits in service to mankind, but we need to be its guardians and protectors. We must respect it like a good general respects his army, not use it like a greedy landlord until it is exhausted and barren. We are not better than the rest of creation—we are all endowed with the same life force. Mortifying the body and denying it food is not the route to redemption. The best way to please God is to constantly look for ways to restore us to harmony with the world. That is what I want the sisters to practice every day."

The countess's eyes were moist again, but this time I saw hope in them. "I cannot think of a better course than that, but . . . is it possible that my daughter was so gravely mistaken?"

"It is not for me to judge." I paused. "But if you want to begin to comprehend what may have inspired her, it is significant that she was an admirer of St. Augustine, whose doctrines can be interpreted in extreme ways by prone minds."

"Augustine." Sophia smiled ruefully. "My own religious education always insisted upon venerating him as a great Church Father, and his doctrine of sin and redemption once had a powerful influence on me. I acquainted my daughter with his writings — was I wrong to do that?"

"I am sure your intentions were good, but it is easy to find justification for one's beliefs by reading biblical interpretations in certain ways. When Augustine warns us that it is not sufficient to simply give up evil, but we must do painful penance and exhibit sorrowing humility, some will heed this as a call for the most severe punishment of the flesh. But," I added, "Augustine also compares prayer's restorative effects on the soul to food's nourishing influence on the body."

Sophia was becoming tired. I led her to a nearby bench from which we looked on the garden, drenched in the golden light of a summer day and full of busy life.

"As a physician," I resumed, "I am concerned with healing the body, but I have often observed that it is the first step toward the healing of the spirit, and that is as it should be because harmony of the flesh and the soul is indispensable to salvation. Yet sometimes the health of the soul can be harder to achieve than that of the body." I could feel her listening avidly, even though her gaze was directed ahead. "I always impress upon my patients the importance of restoring this inner balance through a sensible way of living that includes nutritious food, exercise to revive one's vital force, and the enjoyment of beauty. In those who have the means to do so — and unfortunately there are too many who do not — the results can be astounding."

"This seems so different from the sanctioned doctrines of our Church that put the needs of the soul above everything else." The countess dropped her voice as if afraid that someone might overhear us.

"Do not be afraid," I said. "None of this subverts the Church's teachings. Augustine was a great lover of all creation. Many times he gazed on the blue waters of the sea through the windows of his house at Ostia, and their beauty was a source of spiritual elevation for him. I don't believe the human body was hateful to him, nor did he advocate self-destruction in the process of seeking redemption. He would have considered it against nature."

The air was becoming sultry and still, and we returned to the castle courtyard, empty as the household had retreated into the coolness of the keep's stone interior.

"Your effort to remake the convent is the best way to honor my daughter," Sophia said as we reached the door. "There is something I want to do for you too." She put a hand on my arm. "Your mother wrote to me last year about a young woman named Griselda who wanted a place at St. Disibod but could not afford it. She asked me for a donation toward her dowry, but in truth I was reluctant, for I did not want another girl to go down my daughter's path. But now" — she smiled, though there was still sadness in her eyes — "I would like to pay the whole sum."

"That is kind and generous of you. I don't know what to say."

"Say nothing. I have no doubt that under your guidance, Griselda's service will please God and honor the Church, and that is all we need from a religious vocation."

She turned to enter the keep then stopped, remembering. "There will be a feast in your honor tonight." She arched her eyebrows mysteriously. "And someone will be joining us whom I think you may have met before."

26

Sponheim Castle, June 1128

T HUS MY PATH crossed that of Rudolf von Stade once more. He was the mystery guest, and the meeting would have profound consequences for me. But that night, I did not know that.

Unlike our two previous encounters — at Bermersheim when he was a squire in Count Stephan's entourage, and later at St. Disibod before the town was attacked — this one was anything but accidental. When Rudolf had learned of my visit, he had sent a message to the countess that he would like to introduce his niece Ricardis to me.

The girl's father was the previous Count von Stade, an old ally of Count Stephan's with estates adjoining those of Sponheim. He had recently died, and Rudolf had assumed her wardship. In addition to her uncle, Ricardis came accompanied by a thin, dark-haired young man with a sallow face who wore a clerical robe. His bland features, dominated by a large, slightly crooked nose, were in stark contrast to Rudolf's striking and masculine ones, but his black eyes—a shared family trait, apparently—were penetrating and intense. His name was Hartwig, and he was Ricardis's cousin as well as a priest at Bremen.

"You may remember me from my all too hurried visit to Disibodenberg six years ago, Sister." Rudolf bowed slightly when I arrived at the hall. His full head of black hair had grown grayer around the temples, but his gaze was as lively and honest as before, and the scar on his cheek had faded to a white line barely visible under his beard. He was fuller around the waist but still had the same erect and self-assured carriage of a knight.

"Of course." I nodded as the servants conducted us to our seats. I was given a place between Countess Sophia and her son, and the guests from Stade faced us across the table. "Praise God, we meet under more joyful circumstances today."

"Indeed. It was a trying time, but the town put up a good defense, in which you had a hand."

The countess chimed in eagerly. "On returning from his mission, Herr Rudolf told us about how you had rallied the monks"—her countenance beamed with a maternal pride—"and other accounts reached us of how involved you had been throughout the siege. We all marveled at it, for you were scarcely more than a child." Ever the hostess, she gestured to the servants lined up at the entrance. A moment later the hall filled with the appetizing smells of a roasted pig, capons on a bed of greens, haunches of venison in aromatic sauces, and almond balls dipped in honey. I smiled thinking of how Abbot Kuno would enjoy this table.

"My niece credits your accomplishments with awakening her religious calling." As wine was being poured into our cups, Count Rudolf turned to Ricardis. Her big eyes were trained on me like two shining coals. They were as intense as those of her cousin, but the similarity ended there, for her face had a pleasing symmetry of feature and a flawless complexion fresh as a spring blossom. Her beauty was unlike anything I had ever seen in another human.

"That is why she wants to petition to enter your convent." Rudolf's words reached me, and I snapped out of my admiration to consider the girl more closely. The roundness of her face gave her beauty an innocent aspect, but her figure was that of a woman more than a child, with curves outlined firmly under her dress.

"How old are you, Ricardis?" I asked.

"I have just turned fifteen, Sister," she replied, and the sound was like a tinkling of silver coins. Her mouth, neither small nor large but of perfect proportion to her features, was ready and generous with a smile.

Father Hartwig interjected before I had a chance to reply. "St. Disibod is famous for Sister Jutta's holy life and exemplary sacrifices." He had a surprisingly deep, velvety voice—ideal for a preacher, but there was a fawning note in it. "And I am sure you have many applicants, so Countess Sophia has graciously agreed to give Ricardis her strongest recommendation."

The countess inclined her head, and her son lifted his cup so we could drink a toast with a wine of such quality even my abbot would approve.

"There is much interest, that is true, and we are currently expanding our quarters to accommodate more novices." I turned to Ricardis again. "I am happy to hear about your desire for the consecrated life. However, the sort of excitement we experienced during the siege is a rare occurrence. Mostly, our lives are spent in prayer and work, with a good dose of solitude," I added pointedly.

"I understand that, Sister, but I have heard so much about your convent that it is the only place where I want to fulfill my vocation!" There was a childish eagerness in her face that reminded me of how young she was.

"We do not accept anyone under the age of sixteen." I had decided long before on that rule, and I would never break it. That kind of life was not for a child.

The disappointment written all over Ricardis's lovely face was so great that I felt compelled to add, "But for an age-qualified candidate, there might be a place and a worthy occupation to pursue. For instance, I am always looking for help in the infirmary, which is full of interesting cases, and the work is rewarding." But even as I said it, I could not imagine this girl performing menial or messy tasks. She was too refined for that.

"My niece is well educated," Count Rudolf assured me. "She reads the Bible, sings, plays the psaltery, draws, and embroiders. Anything you want to employ her to, she will learn it quickly."

I took another sip of the wine as I regarded her. She was definitely made for finer pursuits. "Your uncle says you can draw—"

"Yes, with a small brush and colored paints." Ricardis said. "I am most proficient in floral designs, which I can also embroider on linens, pillows, and dresses."

Trying to hide my excitement, I responded formally enough. "Then I will await a letter of application from your uncle upon my return." If Ricardis had a talent for drawing—and images of nature, no less—then I had a job for her. "But you will have to wait until your next birthday."

A satisfied smile spread over Rudolf's face. "I can think of no better house for my niece to enter and no better *magistra* to guide her."

I returned his smile, but when I looked at Hartwig I was surprised to see that he did not seem to share in the family joy. Instead, the glimmer in his eyes was one of triumph. I thought about how odd it was, for, despite our rising stature, the Abbey of St. Disibod was no Fulda or St. Gall. But the fragrant steam rising from my plate quickly distracted me, and I forgot all about it.

We set out for home early in the morning on what promised to be another beautiful day of June, the last of that month. Well provisioned with bread, cheese, and wine, we were on the road as soon as the first rays of the sun, already hot, topped the eastern hills. Gertrude squinted and smiled placidly as the light touched her face, and I recalled the wariness with which I had welcomed her arrival at the convent. But she had since won me over with her love of singing, agreeable personality, and moderate devotion.

"Tell me about your childhood," I said as we entered the wooded tract dappled by shafts of sunshine streaming through the green canopy overhead. Now and then small forest creatures — hares, lizards, or squirrels — crossed our path, eliciting nervous whinnies from the horses. Otherwise, it felt like we were alone in the world, so peaceful was our passage.

Gertrude reached back for the memories. "I was raised in a castle overlooking the Rhine, the fifth child and fourth daughter of my parents." She paused, and I gave her time to master the emotions this may have brought up. "My early life passed mainly in play, but I began to take singing lessons when I was twelve, and my brother's tutor taught me to read. It was a happy time."

"And the monastic life — what brought you to it?" I asked, although I already suspected the reason.

"There wasn't enough land left for me to make a good marriage." A superfluous daughter, then; no surprise. "Before my enclosure I had travelled quite a lot; my father would take me and my brother to Mainz by boat, and I loved it." She gave a small laugh in which there was more amusement than wistfulness. "I used to tell him that if I had been born a boy, I would have become a sailor. I still believe that." She smiled.

"So this life was not something you desired?"

"Not particularly," she replied honestly, "but neither did I dislike the idea. I am used to it now, and I am content. More content still," she added after a pause, "after the changes you made."

Alerted to our approach, a deer family sprang up from behind the tall ferns on one side of the road, froze for the blink of an eye, then fled, swiftly and gracefully, deeper into the safety of the forest. We slowed down to watch them then resumed our progress under the branches of the ancient trees, sunlight filtering through and shrouding the undergrowth in a diaphanous veil.

All at once I was transported to another summer day, when I had sat with Volmar under the big ash downhill from the abbey, telling him about the chant I had composed. *O frondens virga* had since become one of the convent's favorites, preserving the memory of warmth and light during long winters, and celebrating the reawakening of life in the spring and its full glory in the summer. Gertrude was one of the most eager chantresses, and I particularly liked her interpretation, slow and steady at first, then rising to hover on one syllable through several notes.

"Tree branches in the summer have a certain musical quality about them," I said musingly. "They inspire me more than anything else."

"Do they?" My companion was a gifted composer herself, and it piqued her curiosity.

"Perhaps it is the way light and wind play among them. Their movement, this gentle swaying is such a pure manifestation of life's greening force." I closed my eyes. "*O viridisima virga, que in ventoso flabro sciscitationis sanctorum prodisti.*" O greenest branch, you budded in the saint's gentle breezes.

Gertrude began humming softly, and the music matched our step, fluctuating in a pattern similar to the swaying of the wagon and the heaving and falling of the horses' backs.

The images filled my mind. "*Cum venit tempus quod tu floruisti in ramis tuis, quia calor solis in te sudavit sicut odor balsami.*" When the time came, your boughs blossomed, for the sun's warmth seeped into you like balsamic perfume.

And she sang after me, adding her favorite melismatic flourish at the end of each phrase.

"*Nam in te floruit pulcher flos qui odorem dedit omnibus aromatibus que arida errant.*" For in you the beautiful flower filled the air with sweet perfume, awakening all that was dry.

Gertrude let the melody scale upward to expand and fill the space under the trees as if it were the dome of a cathedral. When she finished, Arno tipped his hat without dropping the reigns of his horse, and clapped for good measure, making us giggle like little girls.

Toward midday, dark clouds from the west obscured the sun, and the birdsong ceased as a sudden stillness descended on the forest. Arno, an experienced traveler, suggested we look for shelter. Even before the words died on his lips, a distant rumble rolled across the sky. For an instant, it looked like the storm might catch us right there, but just then a wisp of chimney smoke came into view above the tree line, and we promptly turned in that direction. The rain began slowly, the first heavy drops tapping the leaves rarely, but as we entered the village, the spattering rose to a crescendo. By the time we reached the inn, it was falling in torrents that obscured everything beyond an arm's reach.

Nature's rage lasted all afternoon and included a brief hailstorm, eliciting a lament from the innkeeper's wife that her vegetable garden would be ruined. The wind howled and bent tree boughs, and it was so dark that it seemed like the night had already fallen. By the time the last of the clouds had dissolved, the sun was low and we could not hope to reach St. Disibod before nighttime; I took two rooms, and we retired shortly after the sun went down.

The next day, as we approached the fork where the high road turned toward Disibodenberg, I beckoned Arno to my side. "I have a favor to ask you." I took a silver coin out of my purse. "Take a message from me to the village three leagues from here across the Glan."

"I will be happy to do it, Sister, after I have seen you safely back to the abbey."

I shook my head. "It's very important. We are but a short ride from Disibodenberg, and it's only midday. Once on the high road, we will be within sight."

"I don't want to leave you unprotected." He hesitated but relented when I pressed another coin into his palm.

"There is an inn at the entrance to the village run by a man named Burchard; find his daughter and tell her to come to the abbey after the harvest." I heard a note of uncertainty in my own voice, for, in truth, I had no idea if Griselda had gone back to her parents.

But Arno did not seem to notice. He nodded, and when we came to the crossroad, he spurred his horse on toward the bridge while the two of us continued toward the town.

The sisters had just finished singing the afternoon service when Gertrude and I arrived. Even though we had only been gone a week, the construction had visibly progressed. The courtyard was cluttered with planks, wood shavings, and tools, but, as it was a Sunday, no work was being done. Juliana took me to the new dorter, almost complete and twice the size of the old one, though still bare of furnishings.

"I love the smell of new timber." I inhaled deeply, running my hand over the walls that were yet to be white-washed. "It reminds me of when we rebuilt the infirmary . . . that sense of being on the verge of doing more, reaching farther." I looked around. "What else?"

"The roof replacement on the old dorter is finished, and the workers will move our beds out tomorrow so they can start converting it into the refectory."

"Excellent."

We stepped out into the courtyard again. "Oh, and" — Juliana stopped, suddenly remembering—"we had an unexpected arrival when you were away. Brother Volmar has returned."

27

July 1128

"A RE YOU FEELING unwell?" Juliana eyed me with concern. "You have gone pale."

"I'm fine." I drew the back of my hand across my forehead, the summer heat suddenly intense on my skin. "Just a little tired from the road, that's all."

"Shall I send for some wine?"

I shook my head. "Thank you. I'll manage."

I left her and walked to the chapel to be alone with the confusion that assailed me. I knelt before the altar, but my head swam as joy, anxiety, and so many questions I had stopped asking myself resurfaced all at once, making my thoughts swirl chaotically.

After some moments, the upheaval began to subside. My mind cleared, though a new concern presented itself. Had Juliana noticed anything? The news had come so abruptly I had no time hide its impact, and what had Juliana's stare signified if not a recognition of the truth? Was it condemnation I saw in her eyes? But Juliana, of all people, would have understood.

I was also unsettled by the fact that a mere mention of Volmar's name had caused my pulse to quicken and cheeks to grow pale, only to burn the next moment. I had thought that chapter of my life closed and felt betrayed by my body that refused to follow the dictates of my will.

For two days, every knock on the infirmary door or sound of footsteps on the gravel caused my heart to leap to my throat. I dropped a glass vial when Elfrid entered the workshop to collect some powdered oak bark, and she looked on with surprise and concern as I fell to my knees to pick up the shards, laughing off my clumsiness. That evening I was to sup with the abbot to apprise him of my visit to Sponheim, and I walked to his house on weak knees hoping—or fearing—to see Volmar at any moment, but I did not.

Kuno made no mention of his return, and I began to doubt the truthfulness of the story. Perhaps Juliana had mis-heard, or he had paid a brief visit and was gone again. He might not have remembered me anymore . . . The idea filled me with dismay, but I could not bring myself to ask the ab-bot. I did not trust myself to be able to talk about Volmar as if he were merely an old acquaintance.

The feast of St. Disibod came and went with only a few broken noses and arms to set, and the morning after was rel-atively quiet. I had just administered drafts of lemon balm, lavender, and skullcap to several revelers to soothe the excess heat in their heads from drink, when a woman's scream, pro-longed and anguished, reached us from the abbey courtyard. It ceased as suddenly as it had started but rent the air again a moment later. Although muffled by the infirmary walls, it was still heart-wrenching; the next time it sounded, it turned into a pitiful wail before trailing off. I thrust the flask into the hands of a nearby patient and ran out to find a scene of confusion outside the church.

A young woman—a pilgrim by the look of her, and no more than seventeen or eighteen—was half-kneeling on the ground, her arms held by two men. Held, but just barely, because she was in a fit that seemed to endow her with a strength that was unlikely to habitually reside in her slender frame.

As I approached, she managed to wrest her arms free and fell to her knees, folding her hands and bursting into sobs. The younger of the two men who supported her was white-faced with shock, but the other, perhaps the father, tried to comfort the girl, though his soft words were being drowned by the wailing amidst which I could discern a few phrases, "Lord, save me . . . forgive my sins . . . do not condemn me to the fires of hell . . . I am damned . . . I am lost!"

The commotion began to attract curiosity as monks streamed out of the church, and the stable boys ran from their work to look on.

"What is happening here?" The abbot stepped in front of the group, looking alarmed.

"We came as pilgrims, Father." The older man dropped the girl's writhing arm and bowed deeply. Brother Fabian, who had followed me from the infirmary, took over from him and tried to keep her steady. It required some effort, although he was a big man at least a head taller than everyone else. "Since we arrived she has refused to eat and sleep, and we have been unable to reason with her," the man added, his face a picture of tenderness and concern. "She knelt all of last night in the middle of the room praying, then this morning as we were preparing to take our leave, she suddenly ran outside and started screaming." He twisted his cap in his hands with a puzzled and pained look.

As he spoke, I bent down and put a hand on the girl's head. "What is your name?"

She ceased to struggle and hung her head. "My name is Sin, my name is Damnation."

"Her name is Angmar," the youth spoke for the first time, his voice shaking. "I am her brother, Simon. We came all the way from Brauweiler for the feast and to pray at Holy Jutta's grave." He looked to be a year or two younger, and like his sister, he was dressed neatly but not expensively. A trader family, I guessed.

Angmar began to wail again, softly at first, then in more agonizing tones. "We are all damned if we don't repent! Pray for mercy on your sinful souls before He comes again in terrible judgment!" Tears were streaming down her face, red and contorted in a frightful grimace, and she was panting heavily.

Brother Fabian looked up at me, a silent question in his eyes. The girl was beginning to weaken, her struggle subsiding and her voice falling to a gasping whisper as she continued to mumble her exhortations.

"She needs rest and something to calm her nerves—"

"This woman is possessed!" Helenger interjected authoritatively, materializing out of nowhere. "What she needs is an exorcism!"

"Humors in her brain are out of balance, Brother Prior," I said patiently. "It is an illness like any other—"

Before I had a chance to finish, Angmar burst out of the men's loosened grip and ran toward the church, tearing at her clothes and hair. Two lay brothers intercepted her at the door, and she swayed between them, flecks of white foam appearing in the corners of her mouth. "You are all going to hell if you don't beg God for forgiveness!" Her eyes darted around wildly. "You must do it now! There can be no more delay!"

"Father Abbot, you can see that this is a case a mere draft will not cure." The prior sneered. "She needs more powerful medicine—holy water and the rites!"

I opened my mouth to protest, but Kuno shook his head to forestall further argument. "Man's remedies are insufficient in these situations. This poor girl needs help that is not of this world . . ."

I did not hear the rest, for that was when I saw him, not five paces away in the church's doorway. I felt blood leaving my face as our eyes locked. Those eyes I knew so well, clear and deep, were full of pity for the wretched woman and contempt for the prior, but they softened when they met mine. I looked back down at Angmar, my mind blank as I tried to remember what to do.

". . . you will still be able to make her a calming draft." The abbot's voice finally broke through the fog and brought me back to the matter at hand. "Put her in one of the empty guest cells at the far end of the cloister," he addressed the lay brothers, "so she does not disturb the peace of this place any further. Sister Hildegard will bring her medicine, and we will perform the exorcism after vespers."

I watched as Angmar was taken away, still swaying. Back in control of myself, I was already thinking about the best way to deal with what was clearly an acute case of melancholy. This affliction was sometimes attributable to a bodily illness, sometimes to a loss or a fearful experience, and sometimes it had no discernible cause at all. But I never believed the popular notion that God sent it as punishment, much less that it was the work of the Devil. Still, even though I was skeptical of exorcisms, it would not hurt for Angmar to be prayed over, and as long as I could take care of her, she might yet stand a chance of recovering.

But even as I plotted the treatment, I remained keenly aware of his presence. I did not look in his direction, but I knew he remained by the door after the courtyard had emptied. Every fiber in my body pulled me toward him to tell him of my joy at this meeting I had thought would never happen, yet a sense of pride kept me where I stood.

Why had he not come to find me in the workshop, even though I had been back from Sponheim for nine days? Perhaps he did not want to, and if so, why should I care? After all, he was the one who had left without one word of farewell.

After one more moment of hesitation, I turned on my heel and walked back to the infirmary, feeling—or imagining—his eyes following me. But then, perhaps he was gone already.

Angmar slept all afternoon after I had prevailed upon her to drink a cup of wine infused with valerian and lemon balm mixed with honey. But when I returned shortly before vespers with some bread, she was restless again. She refused to eat and took to whimpering and repeating her exhortations about sin, damnation, and the flames of hell.

In that state she was taken to the church and I followed, curious about the rite I had only seen performed once before. On that occasion, it had been an old monk who had started seeing the Devil in various nooks and crannies of the abbey. Helenger had conducted that exorcism, after which the monk took to his bed and died a few days later. Of course, the prior would once again be the one to perform the rite, which I suspected was one of his favorite.

The monks stood as witnesses as Angmar was brought before the altar. She was supported in a kneeling position by her father and brother, although she kept sliding toward the ground, alternately moaning and sobbing, and appearing faint at times. Helenger, in priestly vestments and accompanied by a novice holding a basin of holy water and a cross, planted himself in front of her. Sensing him, Angmar flinched, her eyes widening with fear.

Oblivious, Helenger put both hands on her head and asked in a sonorous voice, "Demon, who are you, and whence do you come?"

He paused dramatically, but the only voice that could be heard was Angmar reciting her implorations in a frantic half-whisper, "Christ protect me . . . God forgive me . . . do not cast me into the pit!"

The Devil having failed to respond, Helenger cleared his throat and intoned the Benedictine formula for warding off evil spirits, raising his voice above the girl's mumbling.

Crux sacra sit mihi lux, Non draco sit mihi dux
Vade retro satana
Numquam suade mihi vana

And the monks repeated:

Let the Holy Cross be my light,
Let not the dragon be my guide
Step back Satan
Never tempt me with vanities.

As the echo of their voices died down, so Angmar's cries began to diminish, and the prior cast a triumphant glance in the abbot's direction. But Kuno's face remained impassive, and Helenger proceeded to sprinkle holy water on the girl. Then he took the cross from his assistant's hand and made a sign with it, stretching his arm up, down, and to each side as far as it would go as another novice rang a hand bell urgently. The prior paused, waiting for the Devil to resist, but there was no evidence of any demonic activity; in fact, Angmar appeared to have fallen asleep on her knees, and an awkward silence fell on the gathering.

Helenger looked slightly disconcerted and clearly disappointed at not being able to demonstrate his strength against so formidable an enemy. Meanwhile, Angmar's exhaustion and the half-measure of the valerian infusion I had given her just before the ceremony were now causing soft snores to rise from her chest. I worked hard not to laugh, and in the light of the candles around the chancel, I saw the same struggle on the faces of some of the monks.

The prior delivered a hurried final blessing and motioned for Angmar to be taken away, and I followed again to ensure that she was comfortable. Earlier, Simon had told me his sister had always been a good-natured girl, and that the illness had taken everyone by surprise. It may have been unexpected, I thought, but it was not without a cause, and I needed to discover what painful experience had brought a healthy young woman to such a wretched state.

The chirping of crickets outside the window grew louder as the sounds of the summer day began to die down. I was in the surgery, recording my observations of the herbs encountered on the way to Sponheim. I could hear the usual sounds of activity as Elfrid and Fabian went about their work in the ward next door.

A knock on the door caused my hand to jerk sideways and make a horizontal line on the parchment with the stylus.

I knew immediately. Years had passed, but the sound was unmistakable. "Come in." The words came out as a whisper, and I had to clear my throat. "Come in!"

Volmar's face, when he entered, was serious, but I could see a smile flickering behind his eyes. The amber-green depths of those hazel eyes hid so many memories and so much meaning. I dropped my gaze so he would not read my thoughts or see the joy that filled me to overflowing and pushed out the last vestiges of my resentment.

"I did not think I would see you again."

"And yet I am here." His voice had a deeper, warmer timbre than I remembered, and suddenly I was out of breath. "Let's go outside." I motioned to the open door that led to the infirmary garden. "It's a fine evening."

"It is beautiful." His eyes had not left my face.

Outside, a few patients ambled among the flowerbeds. I led the way to a bench at the far end by the hedge as the last rays of the sun spilled over the abbey wall, flooding the middle of the garden with fiery light. I studied Volmar discreetly. He was more mature now, the lean silhouette of youth having given way to the fuller frame of manhood.

"So you are *magistra* now," he said as we settled side by side. His features had lost the mischievousness of childhood and the melancholy of adolescence, and assumed a look of quiet serenity. "I cannot say I'm surprised."

"Prior Helenger was." I grinned, recalling my moment of triumph in a decidedly non-Benedictine fashion. Volmar was still the only person who could bring that kind of smile to my face. "But all that is past, and I am taking the convent down a different path."

"Father Abbot mentioned it, but it was the prior who felt it his duty to fully apprise me of this scandalous development." Volmar shook his head in mock despair. "Some things never change."

Elfrid came out to help a patient on a crutch back inside and cast a curious glance in our direction. We sat quietly for a while, and I relished the eloquence of our silence. We were still friends, accomplices, and, judging by his garb, we had chosen the same way of life after all, a fact that delighted me more than I ever would have expected. Until a few days before, I had imagined him — and it had been a bittersweet image — with a wife and children somewhere in the rolling countryside on the other side of the Rhine.

"I am glad you ruffle their feathers." Volmar laughed quietly when we were alone again, and I savored the gentleness of the sound. "It's not good for them to lead a stuffy existence without fresh ideas or new ways of doing things. You are doing them a favor."

I made a dismissive gesture. "There is not much anyone can do to change the way Helenger sees the world, and that is not my goal. What I want is to make the convent as great as it can be using the authority our charter gives me." I lowered my voice, for I could not be sure that any of my patients did not report to the prior. "Who knows, maybe one day I will find a way to remove us from under their control once and for all." It was the first time I had confided this to anyone, and I was glad I did, even if Volmar was likely to disapprove.

But he did not. Instead, he turned to me with an honest look. "I think you will. Confines are not for you, they make you unhappy —" He broke off as he realized the intrusion of our past. He changed the subject. "Few people I met in France know anything about the Abbey of St. Disibod except that it has an accomplished physician in you, and that its infirmary has the reputation for being the best in the Rhineland."

I blushed. "Surely it cannot be known as far as France!"

"But it is. Abbot Bernard himself questioned me about it when he found out I had been a novice here."

"Abbot Bernard, the Cistercian who is leading the movement for monastic reform?!" I exclaimed, astonished. Bernard's fame had spread throughout Europe like wildfire. He had founded a small reforming house at Clairvaux not long before, and it had already grown to the point where its monks were being sent to establish new foundations in France and beyond. He had gained a devoted following for his strict observance of *Regula Benedicti*, which was rumored to have once brought him to the brink of death after an extended period of extreme fasting. It was also said that his cell at Clairvaux was too low to stand upright in and his bed too short to fully stretch his legs. It was he who had been instrumental in condemning Master Abelard and having his writings on the doctrine of the Holy Trinity burned.

"The same." Volmar nodded. "I met him when he visited Cluny, where I took my vows."

Then he told me the story.

After leaving St. Disibod, Volmar had gone back to his father's estate, thinking to abandon the monastic life. But he soon realized that the world held no interest to him, and before the year was over, he was on his way to Cluny and the grandest Benedictine abbey in the world. It turned out to be all he had hoped for—a place of great learning, with a magnificent library and monks from all over Christendom copying and translating ancient manuscripts, including Mahometan writings. It had the largest church he had ever seen, full of splendid ornaments and rare relics that made the treasures of St. Disibod pale by comparison.

It was among that opulence that he saw Abbot Bernard for the first time, and the famed monk was not happy. He had come to see Abbot Peter—to whom Volmar served as a scribe—about a dispute within the reform movement. They met in the abbot's parlor, a room the size of the entire monks' refectory at St. Disibod. Volmar was sitting at a small desk in a corner, and Bernard did not see him at first. He was just as Volmar had heard him described: small in stature and reedy thin with a careworn air as if the lot of the entire Church rested on his meager shoulders. But when he spoke, the intensity of his conviction made him fill the chamber with his presence.

"It has been almost four years since Abbot Pons was forced out, but I see that the brothers have not lost their taste for choice food," Bernard had said by way of a greeting, and his eyes blazed with pious outrage. "I hear that delicate veal, juicy chickens, and plump pigeons are served regularly at the table."

"I admit that things are still a little lax, for the extravagance was deeply rooted," Peter replied coolly. "Change takes time."

"How much time is necessary to do away with those soft robes? Luxury is a vice that devours the brothers' souls."

A shadow of irritation crossed the abbot of Cluny's face, but his reply was respectful. "Faith and commitment matter more than the robes we wear, and I can vouch for the strength of our reforming spirit."

"What about this vast church with all its glitter and adornments?" Bernard was implacable as he shook his bony arm in the direction of the church. That shrine had numerous chapels and belfries clustered around its apse, and it was so tall that anyone who looked down from the top gallery of one of its octagonal towers could barely distinguish any human shapes below. One had the sensation, Volmar said, of having left the earth and arrived among the airy realms inhabited by the angels. "All this ostentation is mocking God, deflects the attention of those who pray, and hinders their devotion. And the living quarters are furnished with every worldly comfort!" Bernard continued argumentatively.

"We extend hospitality to travelers, as you well know, Father." Peter's patience was beginning to wear thin. "We must provide what they expect, or they will go elsewhere. The income we thus earn supports our holy work."

The Abbot of Clairvaux's face softened, but only slightly. "I love my Cluniac brothers well and hold them in high esteem, and that is why I encourage a renewal of the spirit of modesty, sacrifice, and humility so dear to our Lord."

"I assure you of my great admiration and sincere friendship too." Abbot Peter inclined his head. "Your abbey truly is the City of God upon earth, but I am not sure that your interpretation of The Rule would find quite the same resonance here."

Bernard responded that a lack of fervor was no excuse for not trying harder to reign in the excesses, and Volmar felt sympathy for his abbot because Peter really was intent on reforming the order. He must have shifted in discomfort because his stool screeched on the stone floor, and Abbot Bernard turned in his direction, still shaking with disapproval.

Abbot Peter was visibly glad at the distraction. "This is my assistant, Brother Volmar. He is from the Rhineland and spent time as a novice at St. Disibod."

Bernard's eyes lit up in his gaunt face. "Is that not the place where Jutta von Sponheim founded a holy community of anchoresses?"

"It is."

"She was a saint, a true martyr!"

Volmar was surprised. "What do you mean 'she was', Father?"

"She is gone to God." Bernard's eyes rose heavenward. "And the little abbey is seeing more pilgrims than ever before."

Volmar had no idea Jutta had died. "Do you know who replaced her at the head of the convent?"

"The sister who runs the abbey's infirmary and who is said to be a capable physician," Bernard replied. "Though I know nothing about her mortification practices," he added regretfully.

At that point in the story — fascinating though it was — I looked at Volmar in alarm.

"I did not say anything." He raised his hands in a mock defensive gesture. "I did not want to disappoint him." He laughed and reached for a small packet he had brought with him. "I have something for you."

It was wrapped in soft cloth, and when I pulled back the folds, I saw a small book. The inscription on the title page read *De Gratia et libero arbitrio*, written by Bernard, Abbot of Clairvaux. I was filled with admiration and uncertainty in equal measure. Abbot Bernard's asceticism was alarming, but what was indisputable was his power and sway; after all, he had scolded the abbot of the greatest Benedictine house like a little boy. His other work, *De gradibus humilitatis et superbiae*, was read and debated in abbeys and churches under the jurisdiction of Mainz, and he was known for travelling and preaching widely. There had even been rumors of his involvement in conflicts among Parisian bishops, a highly unusual and audacious move for a monk.

"He had given it to me before he left Cluny, and I think you should have it. He considers grace in ways that hark back to Augustine," Volmar explained, adding with his mischievous grin of old, "and I know your special interest in that particular saint."

I turned the pages. The copy had been made recently, the ink still fresh, but its bare nature was striking. It had none of the colorful images typical of religious works.

"Abbot Bernard is apparently also against illuminations."

"He rejects embellishments on principle. The scriptorium at Cluny is as big as our entire cloister, and the most talented illuminators from around the world work there with the finest paints and brushes, but he was adamant that nothing but basic copying work be done on his manuscripts."

Despite myself, I was impressed with the cleric's spirit and perseverance, and his seemingly inexhaustible energy and industry. The influence and recognition they had brought him had a powerful appeal to me.

"I have no doubt we will hear more about him," Volmar's voice reached me. "His dispute with Abelard is not over yet. They are both equally tenacious, and I suspect we have not seen the last of it."

I studied Volmar again. He had been to a foreign land and lived at a great abbey where reform ideas and other weighty affairs were discussed as a matter of daily routine. "When are you going back?" I asked, unable to fathom any other course.

His gaze met mine. "I am not."

The breath caught in my chest. "But St. Disibod must seem so dull now." I loved the infirmary and the workshop and felt a certain attachment to the abbey, but all the same I was aware of its provincial character. "In a few months, you will change your mind."

"I doubt it." He averted his eyes, but the conviction in his voice was unmistakable. "I need a quiet place for my study, and the constant bustle of Cluny was a distraction." He laughed briefly, and I thought I heard a note of relief in it. "It felt like the archbishop's court at times."

The dusk was deepening, and our sense of intimacy and isolation from everyone was growing. "We should get ready for vespers." I rose as a memory buried in the recesses of my mind pushed its way into my consciousness, enhanced by the scented air of the summer night.

We crossed the garden in silence, but before we parted, Volmar turned to me. "I want you to know that no matter what the prior or any of the monks say about what you do with the convent, I will support you."

I nodded, too moved to respond.

When I was alone again, I pressed the little book to my heart.

He had forgiven me.

Finally, I was at peace.

28

April 1129

T HE WORKSHOP TABLE was littered with half-empty vials of liquids and bowls smudged with dried paste, and the washing bowl was full of used cups. I had been ill for nearly a fortnight, the pain in my head making my eyes hurt at the light and my body fold in on itself. But it was also the season of chills and fevers. The infirmary was overflowing with patients, and though I knew that Elfrid and Fabian were doing the best they could, I heaved a deep sigh. So much work to do, and I was still weak.

"I will clean it." A voice spoke behind me, and I smiled even before turning.

Griselda, wearing a novice's robe, stood in the door of the workshop, a rake and spade in her hands. It was the day before the Sabbath, when I normally did gardening work, but of course I hadn't been able to when I was ill. And she had come, at this critical time of spring planting, to dig out old roots, cut dry stems off the shrubs, and loosen the soil for herbs to start growing again. She had even pruned the rose-bushes. I gave her a grateful look—what would I do without her?

She had arrived at the abbey the previous autumn, barely able to contain her excitement at the chance she had thought would never come. I was excited too, but also nervous; what if someone recognized her, and her former subterfuge came to light? The charter gave me discretion over choosing my novices, but the abbot was my nominal superior and could, if he wanted to, make it difficult for me.

As it turned out, I had no reason to worry. Volmar knew, of course, but none of the others put it together. After Griselda's blessing ceremony, I overheard one brother remarking to another that she looked familiar, but he could not think why. A few days later, an elderly monk came to the infirmary for an application of aconite oil for his sore joints, and swore that Griselda had to be related to a baron whose lands bordered those of his family further up the Glan. Something in her features reminded him of that nobleman, long dead he must be, but perhaps she was a granddaughter? He was so determined to review the family tree for me that it was all I could do to distract him from the subject, and I finally offered him a cup of undiluted elderberry wine. He drank it happily and fell asleep until vespers.

And so Griselda was with me once again, in the convent this time, and I had never seen her so content—I had never seen *anybody* so content there. She was perfectly happy not to have to leave the enclosure, devoting her time to serving our small community, but, as I could see now, she was as reliable outside of it as ever. Her offer of help and her very presence gave me great comfort.

I eyed the messy interior of the workshop. "Are you sure this is not too much for you? Maybe we could do it together."

Griselda shook her head. "You had better check on the infirmary. Sister Elfrid says Brother Fabian has been a little lost."

I sighed again. My monk assistant was the best of the ones who had come through the infirmary over the years, but he was not as passionate a healer as I or Elfrid nor as skillful. I suspected he had chosen this work to avoid the scriptorium duty, for he had even less aptitude for the patient and precise work required of scribes. But I had no choice; amid the dearth of talent, I had to take what was available. "I am going to make medicine for Angmar and go see her first. What she suffers from is much harder to cure than a cough."

"Sister Elfrid has been making her fennel and lemon balm drafts like you did. Says she drinks them but still refuses to speak."

I made a quick calculation. "It has been nine months, but these things take time. What she needs is wholesome food, peace, and fresh air, and what we need is—"

"Patience."

"Indeed." Griselda's ability to catch my meaning and anticipate what I needed without being asked had always amazed me. I took her hand in mine. "I am really glad you are here," I said. "There are few people I trust more than you."

Probably no one.

Save Volmar.

And with Wigbert and Jutta gone, trust was something I needed more than ever.

Angmar's brother had first come from Brauweiler in the early autumn. By then, her frenzy had largely gone away, but there were still occasional attacks. They were followed each time by a round of exorcisms performed by Helenger, who, I suspected, was finally enjoying himself. But most of the time, she either slept or sat gazing at the opposite wall for hours.

The monks had begun to murmur that she should be sent home since there was nothing else one could to do for her. But I was not convinced; I had found signs on her body of whip lashes, which brought back memories I had been trying to forget. But Angmar's scars were superficial, so she did not have the same zeal, or her tolerance for pain was lower. Either was good news. It also gave me an inkling into a possible cause of her breakdown.

Simon was much dispirited when he found his sister sitting with her knees drawn to her chest. She gazed at him fearfully.

"Do you think she will let me take her back home?" he asked me in a low voice.

"She is in no condition to travel."

The young man ran a hand through his hair. "What am I going to do with her, then?"

"She should stay here until she recovers. I still believe it is possible."

Simon shook his head. "My father cannot pay for such a lengthy treatment. What I have brought with me" — he unclasped a small leather purse from his belt — "may not even be enough to cover the costs the abbey has already incurred." He blinked back tears as his gaze drifted toward his sister again.

I rejected the payment with a gesture. "Cost should not stand in the way of helping an anguished soul find joy again." I had started paying a fee for Angmar's upkeep myself, including the guest cell. "Keep it." I pointed to the purse. "And on your way back, give it away to those who need it more."

It was spring now, and Angmar's condition had not changed much, even though I made sure that in addition to the nerve-soothing drafts, she ate a diet of lean poultry, fruits, and uncooked vegetables, whose cold and wet properties might help counteract the overheating of the brain and return the humors to a more favorable balance. The day was sunny and mild, and I decided to take her to the infirmary garden.

At first she balked at the idea and asked to be taken back inside the moment we stepped out of the cloister. But I held her hand firmly and promised to take her to the herb garden, which was quieter and more private, and by degrees she calmed. We crossed the courtyard slowly, and I led her to the bench under the fruit trees, their branches covered with swollen buds on the verge of bursting.

We sat quietly for a while, my patient seemingly lost in her world while I admired Griselda's work. Not a remnant of the previous year's growth was visible anywhere. In another week or two, the garden would be greening, filling with life energy I would then capture and lock into fresh batches of medicines. And just like that, my weariness dissipated, new strength infusing the blood in my veins, and I wondered how I could make Angmar feel the same way.

As if in response, Angmar's voice, soft and dreamy, broke the stillness of the moment. "Is it not strange that such beautiful places exist in this world?"

My heart fluttered, but I knew I had to proceed gently. "Why do you find it so?"

"It is at odds with the terrible fate that awaits us." Her voice lost the dreamy quality then and came out bleak.

"What makes you think that?"

But she did not respond. The moment had passed, and I took her back to her cell.

Several days later, on a rainy afternoon, I came to her with medicine and a Bible in which I had marked several passages. I sat by the window and opened it on St. Paul's first letter to the Thessalonians. Now that Angmar's mind seemed to be returning from the dark place it had inhabited for so long, it was time to try a new approach.

"'Rejoice always and in everything give thanks'." I began to translate the Latin into German. "'Quench not the Spirit, and may the God of peace make you holy and whole, and preserve your spirit, soul, and body unto the coming of our Lord'."

"And this from Jeremiah," I continued, turning to another passage. "'For I know the plans I have for you, says the Lord, plans to prosper you and not to harm you, plans to give you hope and a future'."

Angmar raised her head, and her gaze wandered to the window where low rain clouds tumbled across the sky. It was not exactly an invitation to a conversation, but I felt an interest; she wanted me to go on. "'Rejoice in the Lord always, and again I say, Rejoice! Let your moderation be known to all. The Lord is near. Fret not, but let your requests be made known unto God. And the peace of God, which surpasses all understanding, will keep your hearts and minds'." I paused. "From a letter to the Philippians."

A candle burned placidly on a low shelf next to the bed, and I wondered if things would have turned out differently, all those years before, if I'd had the ability to relieve Jutta's suffering with similar readings? To counter the passages of doom with those of hope? But I had been too young and inexperienced, with nothing to guide me but my instinct, and it had told me that healing the physical pain would soothe the mind. Now I knew that sometimes it had to be the other way around.

"My parents are great admirers of Sister Jutta." Angmar's words shocked me with their correspondence to my thoughts. "Ever since I can remember, hardly any day passed without them mentioning her," she continued as if to herself. "They called her 'the holy lady.' Following her example, we live in fear of the sin in whose shadow we are all born, and of the damnation that awaits all but those who are strong enough to resist the Devil."

I closed the book gently. "Tell me more about it."

She was quiet for a long moment, then resumed. "When I was a child, there was a priest in Brauweiler who liked to quote the Book of Revelation . . . all those prophesies of God's wrath, the plagues, the eternal fire . . ." She rubbed her forehead with a frantic gesture that, for a moment, made me worry that she would relapse. But then she dropped her hand in her lap. Gazing at the small wooden crucifix of the sort commonly carried by pilgrims that she was clutching, she said, "Father would repeat them to us when we misbehaved, and though my brother was not much bothered by those images, they terrified me, especially the prospect of being thrown into hell."

"And why would that happen? You are a good person. You have nothing to fear."

"Am I, Sister? Am I?" She spoke with sudden passion, and her lips quivered as she drew a loud breath. "Devotion, charity to the poor, chastity—that is easy enough. The body can be controlled, but thoughts are more fickle; it is not always possible to master them as we would wish." She looked down again and her cheeks flushed.

"There is a young man, isn't there?" I put my hand on hers.

The flush rose higher. "A neighbor's son. Even though I don't want to, I cannot always stop myself from thinking about him." She wrung her hands.

"God is forgiving, especially with weaknesses of that nature!" I assured her with a zeal that made her look up.

Suddenly my cheeks were burning too, but before I had a chance to be embarrassed, Angmar's look melted back into the familiar despair. "God is vengeful!"

I squeezed her arm in what I hoped was a comforting gesture. "Is that what terrified you when you came here on your pilgrimage?"

"Mother and Father had always wanted us to visit Sister Jutta's grave." Her voice was flat again. "Simon had already made one pilgrimage when he had turned sixteen; this was his second time, and he came to accompany me. Both times he had looked forward to it, but I had grown more and more worried as the day approached. And when I was finally here, I felt as though the prophesy would be fulfilled at any moment—my belly would not tolerate any food, my lungs refused to inhale the air, and the ground seemed to sway under my feet."

"And yet nothing happened."

"I don't know why!" Angmar looked around, bewildered, as if she expected the walls to cave in.

"Nobody knows when He will come again; what we do know is that He is loving and merciful."

"Was Sister Jutta wrong, then?"

She was a clever girl. Sensitive and clever. The former made her more prone to a breakdown like the kind she had suffered; the latter gave me hope that she might yet be helped. "Sister Jutta had a selective way of interpreting God's word," I said. "There are apocalyptic passages in the Holy Scriptures, but there are even more joyful ones. I have given you some of them so you may feel fortified in the promise of salvation."

Angmar watched the rain silently for some time. "So the sin we are born with does not condemn us?"

"Some in our Church are greatly concerned with it, but we must not forget that baptism washes it away." I said. "Then we are left only with the gifts bestowed on us at birth—the capacity to love, to know justice, and to feel compassion—and we must decide what to do with these blessings."

A flicker of light animated Angmar's eyes. "Blessings," she repeated wonderingly. "They are original, just like the sin."

I still remember the satisfaction that leading Angmar—leading both of us, really—to that realization gave me. "Yes, let us call them original blessings," I said. "And instead of looking back at what you have been freed from, direct your gaze to the future, and nurture these seeds so they may reach their fullest expression in the time you have." I reached for the cup with the fennel draft, which she accepted with what came as close to a smile as I had yet seen on her face. "Now drink this and rest. This has been a lot for you."

She looked toward the window again. "The night is falling early with this storm, but tomorrow the sky will be clear again."

And those words, more than anything else, showed me that she was back.

I stayed with Angmar until her breath softened and steadied, listening to the rain lashing against the stone of the cloister. I tucked the blanket around her shoulders like I would do to a child I would now have if I had chosen a different life. But that was a sacrifice I'd had to make, and moments like this made it worthwhile.

I left the cell quietly, not knowing that I was about to come close to losing everything for which I had worked so hard.

29

April 1129

W E WERE AWAKENED in the middle of the night by a loud banging on the gate. Gertrude ran to see what was happening and returned saying that the abbot had been taken violently ill.

Within moments I was dressed and rushing to his house. The rain had stopped, but water was still dripping from the roofs and eaves, their soggy splashes amidst the predawn silence providing an eerie background to my rapid steps. I was frantically trying to imagine what could be ailing Kuno. He had always been a healthy man, still robust and full of vitality at the age of fifty-four. But I was a healer—my duty to deliver the best care to my patient—and for that I needed to be clearheaded and banish all other thoughts, especially those crowding at the edges of my consciousness telling me what my future would be if the abbot died that night.

Kuno's private chamber was crowded, but the monks withdrew when I entered, leaving only a bleary-eyed Brother Fabian and Prior Helenger, looking focused and alert as if he had never slept—or needed sleep, for that matter. The abbot was in the throes of a spasm that made him clutch his stomach as it heaved. A lay brother crouched by his bed with a basin into which the abbot emptied the contents of his stomach, their pungent, acidic odor filling the room even though the shutters had been thrown open. He was pale, beads of sweat stood on his forehead, and his skin was cool and clammy to touch. Those manifestations, their suddenness and violence, told me that the illness had originated from the food he had eaten.

I turned to Fabian. "Did he eat with the rest of you in the refectory last night?" I already suspected the answer as nobody else seemed to be similarly afflicted.

"No." My assistant shook his head but clearly could not provide more information.

"Herr Emmerich sent a pair of rabbits yesterday, and the cook made a pie. Father Abbot dined on it alone in his parlor," Helenger informed me.

Emmerich von Bernstein was a nearby landowner and a benefactor of the abbey, though his patronage was limited mainly to sending venison and smaller game to the kitchen every week, for he was an avid hunter. "He had invited me to join him, but I decided to go to the refectory because I don't like rabbit," the prior added, glancing with relief and faint repugnance as the abbot vomited into the basin again.

"Some of the meat was still pink, but it was well seasoned . . ." Kuno managed through clenched teeth when the lay brother wiped his mouth with a cloth.

That must have been the cause of the illness. The abbey rarely received rabbits—it had been years since Volmar had gone hunting and delivered them surreptitiously to the kitchen—and the current cook, with us for just over a year, probably had not enough experience to prepare them properly. A rabbit required thorough cooking before it was served.

"How long since the spasms started?"

"He first fell ill when we returned from matins," Helenger answered as the abbot groaned again.

I took Kuno's pulse. It was still strong, but as it was almost time for lauds, it meant that he had lost a lot of water from his body, and the vomiting had to be stopped.

I went to the workshop and returned with a draft of mint leaves and chamomile. I gave it to him to drink throughout the day, but he could not keep anything down. In the evening, I cut up my remaining piece of ginger root and sent Fabian down to Renfred's shop for more. The ginger tonic seemed to calm Kuno's stomach for a little while—he even fell asleep after compline—but by matins, he was awake and sick again, visibly weakening.

What I had thought was a simple indigestion was clearly more serious. Although not frequent, cases of death caused by excessive vomiting were not unheard of. It was important to make sure the patient drank, so I kept a jug of spring water at hand in addition to the medicine, and forced a few spoonfuls down his throat after each purging.

Toward noon on the second day, the abbot had fallen into a slumber, though his breath was labored and his skin waxen. Helenger entered the bedchamber with an ominous look. I felt my own stomach clenching.

"I convened a Chapter meeting this morning to keep the brothers abreast of Father Abbot's condition," he began without asking how Kuno was faring or even so much as glancing in his direction. "They all agreed that I should take over his responsibilities to ensure that the abbey is run without any interruption, and the transition—if such becomes necessary—takes place smoothly."

I stared at him. "The abbot is not dead yet, and you are already thinking about the transition?" I managed finally, keeping my voice low both for Kuno's sake and because I could not trust myself.

"He is not, but seeing how your treatment is going, he may soon be." He dropped his voice too, finally casting a brief glance at his superior in which there was not a shadow of sympathy. "My duty is to this abbey first and foremost."

The abbot groaned and clutched his stomach, and I was just in time to grab the basin and thrust it under his chin before he was sick again. After it was over, he lay back without opening his eyes. My hands shook as I wiped his mouth.

Helenger waited as I finished, then said, his voice still low but cutting like steel, "My first decision as acting abbot is to remove you from your post in the infirmary. You will return to the convent and not leave unless you have my permission. The same will apply to Sister Elfrid."

I whirled around. "You cannot do that!"

"Yes, I can."

"Who is going to look after the infirmary?"

"Brother Fabian."

"The abbot needs care. Brother Fabian cannot be in two places at the same time." I tried to keep contempt from my voice, but I fear I failed.

"I will have monks take turns at the abbot's side, and Brother Fabian will check on him from time to time," Helenger replied dismissively. "What Father Abbot needs is not your potions, but prayer, and that we can provide day and night." He smirked, clearly enjoying my distress.

As I stood there helplessly, he turned and opened the door, beckoning to someone waiting outside. Brother Fabian entered, looking miserable. I felt sorry for him, but also for myself and for my women.

"You can go now," Helenger said to me, stepping aside and pushing poor Fabian out of his way.

I walked to the door with as much dignity as I could muster but stopped before crossing the threshold. "Boil fennel seeds and add them to the tonic I have been making," I urged Fabian. I had just been thinking that fennel, a herb of wide-ranging curative properties, was worth trying. "Give it to him three times a day — "

"Go!" Helenger hissed behind me.

I ignored him. "Make sure there is always fresh water in the jug, and he is given to drink regularly—"

"Sister Hildegard, you will listen to me!"

"And do not bleed him under any circumstances! He has already lost a lot of vital humor," I added, knowing that Helenger would not physically push me out. He would never touch a woman.

Fabian nodded, though he could not help glancing fearfully at Helenger. It occurred to me that the moment I was gone, the prior might forbid my assistant from carrying out my dispositions. But I was powerless to do anything about it.

As I stepped out of the abbot's house—perhaps for the last time in my life—I knew that my fate truly was in God's hands.

For ten days, I had no news. We were shut off completely from the world. Even the servants who brought our food were forbidden to speak to us and only looked down when I pressed them for information about the abbot's health. Those were the days of despair like I had never known.

On the tenth day, I was summoned to the abbot's house. As I crossed the courtyard, my legs were so weak I was afraid I would not make it, even though the May morning was fresh and sunny. My mind had gone blank, or rather there was only one thought in it, and that was that I had no idea who the current occupant of that house was. If it was Helenger, everything was over.

I stopped before the door and for a long moment could not gather the courage to open it. The fact that it was completely quiet inside made it even more difficult. All at once I pictured Helenger sitting at the desk, eyes trained on the door, a rapacious grin distorting his lips. The image made me so dizzy I had to lean my forehead on the door and close my eyes to stop the world from spinning.

I pushed the door and stepped inside. For the space of a few breaths, I could not see anything as my eyes adjusted to the dim interior from the bright day outside. Then the occupant's silhouette became more distinct and my heart sank — the man was tall and lean, so not Kuno.

He stood with his back to the door, gazing out the arched window over the graveyard and the vineyards, greening now with new leaves, something which had always thrilled me but now I barely even noticed. He turned slowly, and as he faced me, my eyes widened.

"Sister." He inclined his head.

"Brother Peter." My head swam in a chaos of relief, surprise, and puzzlement at seeing the treasurer in front of me. Did that mean Kuno had died and he had been elected in his place? That would have been a development I had not expected. "Or should I say Abbot Peter?"

He smiled briefly, a pleasant and modest smile, before his features became serious again. "Oh no, I am only acting on Abbot Kuno's orders."

Relief washed over me again, fully this time. He was alive! "I take it the crisis is over?"

"It is, but he is still very weak." Peter pointed with his chin toward the door leading to the bedchamber. "He sleeps most of the day."

"I see."

"I wanted to speak with you to let you know that last night he reversed Prior Helenger's decision regarding your removal from the infirmary. You may resume your duties."

I inclined my head in grateful acknowledgement. I wanted to know what Kuno had thought about Helenger usurping his power in eager anticipation of his demise, and if he was going to keep him as prior or replace him with someone worthier, like Peter, but I thought it prudent not to ask any of this. I would find out in time. "This is a happy development indeed, Brother," I said. "I look forward to returning to serve my patients."

"Your patients have been asking for you, and they will be glad to see you back, but . . . you should know that the prior has sent Angmar home."

I gasped. "He did not!" She was not ready yet; she still needed care.

"I'm afraid he did, without even bothering to summon her brother." A muscle in his jaw twitched. "He hired two men from the town to escort her to Brauweiler."

I gazed around in disbelief as if there were someone else there who could dispute what I had just heard. But it was true, of course. It was entirely in line with Helenger's character.

"Thank you for letting me know." I took a steadying breath. "I am only glad I heard this from you and not from him."

"Welcome back, Sister."

Thus I had narrowly avoided a catastrophe, but the precariousness of my position and of the convent's future had become clearer to me than ever before. I could not remain at St. Disibod because here, under the monks' control, I would always be at risk of losing everything and of being relegated to oblivion.

Still, it was one thing to want independence and quite another to have the means and the support to achieve it. In order to relocate the convent, I would need significant resources which I did not have, and the abbot's permission — and how likely was Kuno to give it?

But it did not matter. From that day onward, I knew I would do anything to save myself and the sisters, even if it meant breaking *Regula Benedicti*. Even if it meant establishing my own order, like Bernard of Clairvaux had done.

30

December 1129

"I HAVE A proposition for you, Father Abbot," I said as we settled down to our monthly supper a few days before Christmas. Before us was laid out another excellent meal of roasted partridge seasoned with garlic and thyme, in a sauce of honey, mustard, and ale, and the smell tickled my nose pleasantly. I had come with an idea to significantly increase the convent's income, and the only thing that dampened my excitement was the unexpected presence at the table of Prior Helenger, a fact that always carried a risk of derailing my plans.

The abbot gave me an inquiring glance as he helped himself to a generous portion of the meat. He had almost fully recovered from his violent illness five months earlier and his appetite was back to normal, though there were still dark circles under his eyes, and he was thinner than before.

I cleared my throat. "It recently occurred to me that if I could have copies of my medical writings made, I could sell them to Benedictine houses throughout the Rhineland, perhaps even beyond—"

Kuno raised an eyebrow as he bit into the bird's leg, sauce dripping down his chin. He promptly wiped it with the linen napkin the servant had laid on the side of the table.

I continued, "I have received inquiries from the infirmarians at Lorsch and the new abbey at Schönau, and also from Fulda"—I knew that the latter would make a particular impression, Fulda being an ancient, imperial foundation—"who are interested in acquiring volumes. I would share the proceeds with the abbey, of course."

"That is preposterous!" Helenger had been chewing a piece of the fowl the way someone else might gnaw on a moldy potato skin. When he heard my words, he swallowed it with effort before offering his opinion. "It is unnatural for a woman to write about anything, but especially about herbs, the favorite tool of witches and sorcerers through which they seek to confound the faithful. The Church frowns upon the use of herbs for healing." He looked at Kuno expectantly, the unspoked accusation hanging in the air.

The abbot closed his eyes with a sigh.

"Benedictine monasteries have kept collections of herbals for centuries," I countered. "Hippocrates and Dioscorides wrote about plants extensively, in addition to surgery, bloodletting, and leech treatments. We have copies of both at St. Disibod."

The abbot nodded once. By now I knew that when he refused to speak, it was a sign for the prior to drop the subject, which, to his credit, Helenger always did, though not without letting his dissatisfaction become apparent through headshakes, exasperated murmurs, or scowls.

"How do you propose to do that, Sister?" Kuno asked, taking a sip of the spiced wine.

I saw that my offer had piqued his interest and took heart from that. "With your permission, Brother Volmar could do the copying. It would take him about two months to complete one."

"What price would a copy like that fetch?"

"I estimate eight silver marks." I was ready with the answer. "With six copies done in a year, it would bring us about fifty marks." A small fortune.

I studied his reaction as I took my first bite of the savory partridge. His bushy eyebrows went up, and underneath them his eyes showed me that he was already thinking about how such income could be spent — to the glory of God, of course. "We have four scribes now," he said. "I think we could spare Brother Volmar?" The latter question was directed toward Helenger, but the prior pretended not to understand the abbot's intention.

I smiled. It was time to get to the crux of my plan. "Eight marks is no small sum, but if we had each copy illuminated, it could sell for much more than that."

"How much more?" The greed was now plain on the abbot's face. Even Helenger's eyes flickered with a faint interest.

"At least ten, maybe even as high as twelve marks, depending on the workmanship."

The abbot scratched his chin. "We only have one illuminator," he said unhappily.

"How about" — I threw my head back as if the thought had just occurred to me — "we train one of the sisters? Young Ricardis has a talent for drawing and painting; we could apprentice her to Brother Einhard."

Ricardis had been with us since the summer, having turned sixteen in May, and had already captured our hearts with the bright and happy way she had about her. Already, we could not imagine the convent without her cheerful presence, perpetual smile, the confidence she exuded in her own charm, and the sense of occupying her rightful place.

She had become our pet of sorts, as we admired her glossy black hair and rosy, supple skin, caressing her cheeks after she read a passage or sung a chant, even though her voice was not nearly as beautiful as Gertrude's. I delighted in Ricardis, finding her exquisite form a reflection of God's basic principles for the universe — those of harmony and balance that tend toward perfection. She was eager to please me in devotions and study, and whenever I praised her, which was often, the pink of her cheeks grew deeper with pleasure.

"Absolutely not!" Helenger wiped his mouth with one vigorous stroke and threw the napkin aside.

Kuno raised his hand to silence him. "It is a difficult art to master; are you sure she is capable?"

"I have seen her work. It is exceptional." It was true. Ricardis had a sure hand but a delicate touch. We had no dyes in the convent, but from what she had told me about her work at home, she had a good eye for colors. And her favorite designs were animals and flowers — perfect illustrations for my guidebook. "Sometimes she draws for us in wax. Her gift is a rough gem that needs a little polishing under an experienced eye."

The servant brought in candied cherries and apricots which the abbot and I sampled eagerly under the prior's disapproving gaze. Kuno sat back, thinking as he munched on the sweets, and I sought to give him more assurance. "I have faith in Ricardis's talent, and I trust her completely."

Those words had a strange effect on Helenger. His scowl morphed into an ironic lift of his thin eyebrows, giving him a calculating look as if he were trying to decide if I were telling the truth.

"It is an interesting idea," the abbot said at length, casting an almost imploring glance at the prior.

Helenger turned to me, and just as I was expecting another outburst, he said stiffly, "I think it is a reasonable proposal." We must both have stared at him, for he added, "Sister Hildegard's reputation is undeniable" — he said that with a grimace one might make after biting into something bitter—"and if it can benefit us—benefit both of our houses, that is—then we should work together." The statement had about as much enthusiasm as consenting to having one's limb amputated.

The relief in the abbot's face was all too plain. "It is decided, then." He raised his cup and the tree of us toasted, though only the abbot and I drank our wine. "Have Ricardis come to the scriptorium tomorrow morning, and I will arrange for Brother Einhard to start training her."

I smiled broadly, hoping, for the sake of Benedictine modesty, that my smile was not too triumphant. "By the time Brother Volmar finishes the first copy, she will be ready to start her work. And you won't regret it, Father."

The next morning it was Sister Juliana's turn to read from the Bible, and her monotonous voice provided a steady background to the sound of spoons scraping against the wooden bowls of porridge. Once in a while, she would lift her eyes from the holy book to cast a somber, almost disapproving glance across the table, where the contrast of mood could not be greater; that was where Ricardis was seated between Elfrid and Gertrude, radiating beauty and enthusiasm even in the quiet act of breaking her fast.

As we rose from the table, I pulled Ricardis aside. Griselda was clearing the bowls, depositing them on a tray she would take to the gate for collection. "You will go to the library to start an apprenticeship with the abbey's illuminator." I paused to take in the mix of surprise and joy that lit up her features. "It will develop your talent and put it to use on embellishing copies of my medical book."

Ricardis pressed both hands to her heart. "I am humbled." Her face beamed with such light that it was hard to imagine anything less apt to be described as 'humble.' "You will not be disappointed. I will make you proud of me."

As I watched her walk briskly to the gate, sidestepping the tray with our breakfast bowls, I hoped that she was right. For, in truth, I could not imagine feeling any other way about Ricardis.

I gathered all six of us in the refectory that night.

"An idea has been growing in my mind for a long time, a hope I dared not speak." I started as five pairs of eyes stared at me unblinkingly. "But the time for silence is over, and we must work together to make it come true."

I could feel the tension rising in the small chamber. "You may remember back in the spring, when the abbot was so gravely ill, Prior Helenger sent my patient Angmar away, even though she had not yet fully recovered." Heads nodded somberly. "That showed me that in order to be able to implement cures as we see fit and work unfettered for the benefit of our patients, we must leave this abbey and establish ourselves elsewhere, where we will be free from the interference of those who know nothing about healing and who want us locked away."

The women seemed frozen except for Elfrid, who absorbed my intention immediately, and, judging from her vigorous nods and a broad smile, already agreed with it. I knew I could count on her.

Burgundia was the first to recover. "When are we moving, Sister?" she asked practically.

I was comforted by her confidence. To her, it was an issue of "when," not "if." But there was a naïveté to her question that made me smile. "Not yet. It will require funds — significant funds. And we don't have them." I had to be honest. "Since Sister Jutta's passing, we have acquired endowments that are entirely under our control and are bringing us income." I acknowledged both Burgundia and Ricardis to whose dowries I was alluding. The income included rents from a swath of oak forest, three houses in Rüdesheim, a vineyard near Bergen, and two mills on the Nahe. "I have also obtained the abbot's permission to sell copies of my medical writings that will bring us twenty to thirty marks a year."

The women looked at one another, surprised and excited. To manage their expectations, I added, "But it will be a long time before we have enough set aside to acquire land and set up temporary accommodations as we build a new foundation. I cannot tell you how long—three years or five? Maybe more. I don't know. But it *will* happen," I stressed, seeing the deflated looks on their faces, "and it will be worth the wait."

"What about the rule of *stabilitas loci*?" Juliana asked. It was rare for her to speak without being addressed, and it was all the more valuable to me when she did. Being the best educated among us, she brought up an issue I had preferred to ignore but one which would have to be dealt with sooner or later.

I considered my answer carefully. "The principle that monastics do not move away from their abbey is an important one, and it has been largely observed since our founder's time. But"—I raised my finger—"there are certainly precedents for *monks* leaving their mother houses to establish new foundations elsewhere. So there is an argument to be made in our favor, and I intend to make it if necessary when the time comes."

A faint smile flickered on Juliana's lips, another rare sight. I knew how much she detested St. Disibod, and it occurred to me that that alone would be a sufficient reason to move.

"Would it be Sister Jutta's wish too?" Griselda's quiet voice floated up.

I had thought about that, and although I could not have absolute certainty, something told me she would approve. "I believe that for all the choices she made for herself, she would want us to be respected. And that is not possible for as long as we remain a part of this abbey."

"But Abbot Kuno is good to us." Gertrude offered timidly. She was the only one who seemed worried about the plan. "And who is to say with certainty that Prior Helenger will replace him?"

"There is never any certainty about anything in life," I replied, perhaps a little too harshly, "but he is the most senior of the obedientiaries, and that alone puts him in the direct line of succession. But even if that does not come to pass — if, for example, he dies before Kuno — what I have just told you will still stand. None of the other monks will grant us the freedom we need." A woman's role was not to speak but to listen, to nurture, and stand behind. There was no abbey in the land where my work would be fully acceptable. I would always have to fight for the right to practice medicine and to share my knowledge. I would never be certain of having access to a library or a scriptorium. I would always be at the mercy of someone else's goodwill, whim, or greed.

I could only count on myself.

Ricardis was the only one who had not spoken up but only gazed at me, smiling and radiant as ever. I had no reason to doubt her support.

I had the sisters behind me.

There was only one other I needed to tell.

31

January 1130

I STOOD AT Jutta's grave on a frosty afternoon. Her tomb was the largest in the abbey cemetery and made of stone, in contrast to the tiny mounds with wooden crosses that marked the monks' resting places. It had not started out that way; it was the humblest grave of all on the day she was reburied, but with so many pilgrims flocking to it, the abbot had ordered a sturdy stone cross carved and placed over it. On its arms, visitors had been leaving rosaries and wooden crucifixes on leather thongs in such quantities that they had to be removed from time to time.

As I watched them fluttering in the icy wind, I could not help but think that Jutta would be unhappy at such prominence. But it also made me proud because she deserved it, although for reasons different from those that attracted the pilgrims. For me, Jutta was my *magistra*, a teacher alongside

Wigbert who had planted a seed in my mind that had blossomed into a belief that my pursuits were just as worthy of consideration as those of any man.

I came on this little private pilgrimage to tell her that I had been made abbey physician. A few days after our last month's supper, Kuno had summoned me to let me know of his decision, Helenger hovering over his shoulder. I was surprised and pleased, yet something bothered me about the announcement, and it was not just the unusual fact that the prior had remained silent.

On my way back from the abbot's house, I had met Ricardis as she came out of the side door of the cloister that we, as women, had to use to enter the scriptorium to avoid walking through the monks' quarters.

"Is everything all right?" The glow on her face dimmed somewhat when she saw the frown creasing my forehead.

I smiled in an effort to soften my face. "I was just offered the position of abbey physician."

Ricardis's big eyes rounded into two lovely pools of liquid dark. "That is wonderful!" She joined her hands together the way she did when finding something very exciting.

We started toward the convent, and I wondered if I should mention my misgivings to her. But Ricardis was a sweet and innocent creature whom I trusted almost as much as I did Volmar. "It is practically unheard of for women to hold such positions" — I thought back on Trota of Salerno — "which makes me wonder why the abbot would do it. I know it was not at the prior's request." I could not help the sarcasm.

"But there is nobody here with the skill and experience that match yours."

That was true enough; still, doubts gnawed at me. "But why so suddenly? Why now? We could have gone on like this indefinitely, with me fulfilling the role of physician without being officially called so."

"Patients ask for you and leave generous gifts to the abbey." She walked slightly ahead of me as we approached the enclosure. When Griselda opened the gate, Ricardis slid between her and the door and held it for me. "It makes perfect sense for Abbot Kuno to elevate you like this," she added with assurance as we continued to the chapel, for it was almost vesper time.

I grimaced. The reduction of my relationship with the monks to a transaction guided by a calculation of cost and benefit had never sat well with me, even though I had taken advantage of it more than once.

"I must accept it and be glad," I said as the other sisters arrived and we filed into the chapel. "It is un-Christian not to show gratitude for a gesture of goodwill, especially when it is so unexpected."

In the pew, I opened my Book of Hours just as the first notes of the chant floated from the church and the sisters intoned, *"Deus, in adiutorium meum intende. Domine, ad adiuvandum me festina."* O God, come to my assistance. O Lord, make haste to help me.

I looked over my shoulder at Ricardis, her head bowed and eyes closed, and was charmed by her humbleness as much as I had been by her exuberance.

Now at the grave, I reached into the pocket of my robe and took out the little box with the heart-shaped lump of salt my mother had given me. My mother had been so strong and protective of me and had not hesitated to confront the monks to ensure my right to make my own decision. Through this gift, the memory of her wisdom had guided me through the years, reminding me where I had come from and of the work I had been called to do.

I turned the piece over in my fingers, as pure and white as it had been on the day I first laid my eyes on it, then closed the lid again. "I promise I will spare no effort to shield our community from attacks, save it from neglect, and give it independence so we can control our present and determine our future," I said, my words caught by the wind and carried away into the universe.

As I walked back to the convent, I wondered whether I had made that pledge to Jutta or to my mother, or perhaps to both.

What I did not know was that on that same day Abbot Kuno wrote a letter to Abbot Heinrich of Fulda, a monk learned in canon law, and an authority on *Regula Benedicti*.

You see, my plans had already reached the abbot's ears. He was quite certain that as my nominal superior he would have to consent to my relocation, and if I defied him he could escalate the matter to Mainz. There, the archbishop would be unlikely to side with me, especially as the monks had a new ally at his court — Helenger's nephew Walter who, although only twenty-three, had just been made a junior canon and was poised for a brilliant career. Kuno's letter to Fulda was just a way of reassuring himself.

But I would not learn about any of it for years. For a long time, I would not be aware that just as I was vowing to save the convent and free the sisters, the monks were preparing to ensure that everything remained as it was and that the order of things was preserved.

Thank you for reading *The Greenest Branch*. I hope you enjoyed it. Would you kindly take a few minutes to support independent publishing by leaving a review on Amazon and/or Goodreads? I will greatly appreciate it!

If you would like to learn more about Hildegard or about my future writing projects, feel free to get in touch via my website's Contact Me form at www.pkadams-author.com. You can also follow me on Twitter @pk_adams

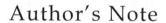

Author's Note

THERE IS A lively debate within the historical fiction community as to whether, as authors, we must strive for maximum accuracy, or whether we are allowed artistic license in the service of a good story. I fall into the latter camp — within reasonable bounds. If the story is based on a real person's life, that life should be recognizable. However, novels are judged on their pacing and flow, both of which can be affected if, for example, the historical timeline calls for a large gap in the narrative. Therefore, I believe we are justified in modifying certain facts or dates to fit the story we are telling. That said, the reader deserves to know if we do that.

I wanted to make *The Greenest Branch* as historically accurate as possible. However, reliable record of what Hildegard did from the time of her enclosure to about the age of forty is scant (for her later life, which is the subject of the second book in the series, we have more solid historical evidence). Scholars can't even agree on how old she was when she was first sent to St. Disibod: some claim as young as eight, others as old as thirteen. Most seem to accept that she spent around thirty years in a small convent with a handful of other women in an environment of great privations, according to the rules governing anchorite monasticism.

I have always been skeptical of that. I cannot imagine that a young child separated from her family and subjected to decades of what can only be described (at least based on our modern sensibilities) as psychological abuse could re-merge, in her middle years, as an accomplished physician, writer, musician, theologian, and a correspondent of bishops, popes, and even a Holy Roman Emperor. Clearly, something happened during those years that allowed her intellect and creativity to develop. A dull existence in an isolated enclosure would have been too mentally devastating.

The result of my skepticism is *The Greenest Branch*, in which I imagine what Hildegard's life may have been like after her arrival at St. Disibod. To do that, I permitted myself a few timeline liberties. Firstly, I made Hildegard slightly younger — in the book she is born in 1104 rather than the more commonly accepted year of 1098. It helps the narrative flow more smoothly. For the same reason, I had Jutta von Sponheim die in the year 1124 rather than 1136, and I kept Archbishop Adalbert of Mainz in prison until 1117, although in reality he was released in 1115.

That said, the main cast — Kuno, Helenger, Jutta, Volmar, and Ricardis — were real people (even if some of the events involving them are fictionalized). Brother Wigbert's name is fictional, but the character is based on a real infirmarian at St. Disibod. Of the major characters, only Griselda is entirely fictional.

Some people may be forgiven for wondering about the relevance of Hildegard's story to the modern reader. Her experience may, on the surface, appear distant from ours; but I would argue that although women's condition has improved significantly since the 12th century, many must still make the kinds of choices that men are not expected to make. This is especially the case when it comes to choosing between family and a career (while the romantic storyline involving Volmar and Hildegard is an invention, chronicles suggest that he was her life-long friend, confidante, and secretary. In turn, she wrote about him as "the man whom I had sought and found." This makes my take on their relationship less than far-fetched).

Moreover, in the workplace many women still feel that they have to prove themselves over and over and to justify their participation. Often (especially at St. Disibod) Hildegard was the smartest person in the room, but it was only by diminishing herself and her abilities that she was able to gain—and maintain—a seat at the table. I had not set out to write *The Greenest Branch* to underscore these points, but as the story unfolded I became increasingly convinced of these remarkable parallels.

Throughout her life, Hildegard struggled with migraines, which in the Middle Ages were not recognized as a medical condition. It is well documented how physically debilitating those episodes were, and that has made me wonder about the nature of her religious visions. Her descriptions are uncannily similar to the auditory and visual hallucinations that accompany strong migraines (I am not a migraine sufferer myself, but I have spoken with people who are, and some described experiencing bursts of bright or shimmering light and even echoes or whisper-like sounds during episodes).

While my book focuses on Hildegard's achievements as a physician, it is worth remembering that it was her visions and the theological commentaries she wrote in later life that earned her widespread recognition and acknowledgement. I chart a delicate course in the book with respect to whether these visions were real or a ploy to allow her to speak out (and write). After all, aside from royal wives and daughters the only medieval women whose stories or writings were recorded were those who claimed to have visionary experiences. It makes for an interesting, if counterfactual, debate, and I will leave it to the reader to decide for herself or himself what to think.

Finally, a note on the title. Hildegard's creative spirit is perhaps most visible in the dozens of chants she composed, many of which contain at least some reference to nature, which she deeply loved and championed. "The Greenest Branch" is the title of one of her better-known chants (*O Viridissima virga*). It conjures an image of something new, fresh, and prolific . . . much like Hildegard herself.

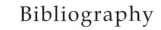 Bibliography

In researching this book, I found following sources particularly helpful:

The Letters of Hildegard of Bingen ed. by Joseph Baird and Radd Ehrman

The Creative Spirit. Harmonious Living with Hildegard of Bingen by June Boyce-Tillman

Heretics and Scholars in the High Middle Ages by Heinrich Fichtenau

Original Blessing. A Primer in Creation Spirituality by Matthew Fox

Planets, Stars, and Orbs. The Medieval Cosmos 1200-1687 by Edward Grant

The Holy Roman Empire by Friedrich Heer

The Ways of the Lord by Hildegard of Bingen (ed. Emilie Griffin)

Scivias by Hildegard of Bingen (ed. Elizabeth Ruth Obbart)

Hildegardis causae et curae ed. by Paulus Keiser

Cambridge Illustrated History of Germany by Martin Kitchen

Medieval Thought: St. Augustine to Ockham by Gordon Leff

A History of the Church in the Middle Ages by F. Donald Logan

Hildegard of Bingen. The Woman of Her Age by Fiona Maddocks

Daily Life in the Middle Ages by Paul B. Newman

Frederick Barbarossa by Marcel Pacaut

Natural History by Pliny the Elder (Book XXVI)

Life in Medieval Times by Marjorie Rowling

The Gracious God: Gratia in Augustine and the Twelfth Century by Aage Rydstrom-Poulsen.

The World of Hildegard of Bingen. Her Life, Times, and Visions by Heinrich Schipperges

"Hildegard of Bingen and the Greening of Medieval Medicine." *Bulletin of the History of Medicine*, 1999, 73:381–403 by Victoria Sweet

"Text and context in Hildegard of Bingen's *Ordo Virtutum*." by Patricia Kazarow im *Maps of Flesh and Light. The Religious Experience of Medieval Women Mystics* ed. by Ulrike Wiethaus

Lyrics to Hildegard's chants in Latin and English can be found at http://www.hildegard-society.org

For biblical quotations I used the New International Version translation.

# Acknowledgements

I WOULD LIKE to express my gratitude to the Boston Public Library for finding – through the interlibrary loan program - the more academic texts they did not have in their system (particularly the three volumes of the Baird and Ehrmann translations). Public libraries are an invaluable resource for readers and writers alike, and well worth our support.

Many people contributed to helping me make this book the best it can be. They include my beta readers Elaine Buckley, Viksit Gaur, Bill Laforme, and John Shea to whom I owe a debt of gratitude for their insightful feedback. Enormous thank you to my editor Jessica Cale and cover designer Jenny Quinlan from Historical Editorial. Any errors that remain are mine.

I also want to give a shoutout to the ladies from the Fearless Female Writers group—Anne Marie Carmody, Deborah Coffey, Kim Jaso, Quenby Solberg, and Elise Tanimoto—who listened patiently; and to the small but tenacious group from the Boston chapter of the National Writers Union. The monthly dinners at *Christopher's* help me unwind and keep things in perspective.

Finally, thank you to my family for cheering me on. Liam, you are a ray of sunshine.

About the Author

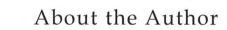

P.K. ADAMS IS the pen name of Patrycja Podrazik. She is a historical fiction author based in Boston, Massachusetts. A lifelong lover of history and all things medieval, she is also a blogger and historical fiction reviewer at www.pkadams-author.com. She graduated from Columbia University where she first met Hildegard in a music history class. *The Greenest Branch* is her debut novel and the first in a two-book series about one of the medieval era's most fascinating women.

Made in the USA
Las Vegas, NV
19 August 2022